LAKE of SHADOWS

LAKE of SHADOWS

Martha Harris

iUniverse

LAKE OF SHADOWS

iUniverse books may be ordered through booksellers or by contacting:

iUniverse
1663 Liberty Drive
Bloomington, IN 47403
www.iuniverse.com
1-800-Authors (1-800-288-4677)

Because of the dynamic nature of the Internet, any web addresses or links contained in this book may have changed since publication and may no longer be valid. The views expressed in this work are solely those of the author and do not necessarily reflect the views of the publisher, and the publisher hereby disclaims any responsibility for them.

Any people depicted in stock imagery provided by Thinkstock are models, and such images are being used for illustrative purposes only.
Certain stock imagery © Thinkstock.

ISBN: 978-1-4917-0134-8 (sc)
ISBN: 978-1-4917-0135-5 (e)

Library of Congress Control Number: 2013913629

Print information available on the last page.

iUniverse rev. date: 12/08/2015

Chapter One

Like her mother, Meg, the eldest daughter of Bobbi and Lance Wolfe, was not only psychic but also needed water to calm herself, her body and her mind. She could mentally regroup and think better. However, unlike her mother (also known as Bobbi Wheeler-Wolfe), who found peace at the ocean, Meg found a lake did the job for her. A quiet, tranquil body of water. She could sit for hours staring at the glass-smooth surface or floating on it—usually in a canoe—though she preferred simply wading out, laying back and floating with her eyes closed, drifting peacefully, calmly, as she was doing now.

She had nearly drown as a child doing just that. It was the first time shadows had appeared to her. She had been floating, near sleep, when she felt a breeze, then another and another, each crossing over her from different directions. Somewhere in her mind that had seemed odd but she didn't dwell on it. Then the sun was blocked, a cloud, she presumed, until she remembered it was a perfect cloudless day. She opened her eyes to see the shadow of a woman hovering over her with barely discernible features. Barely discernible features except her eyes . . . they glowed white.

Meg tried to sit up as though she had been laying on something solid. She sank, trying to scream. Her arms flailed. Her legs kicked. She took in water in gulps. Hands grabbed her. She fought them off. They grabbed her harder. Sure those hands were pulling her under, she fought harder, trying to surface. A male voice, that of her father, was telling her she was okay, he had her and to stop fighting him.

"What happened?" Her father asked. "You moved . . . jack-knifed and it looked like someone was either pulling or pushing you under."

"I . . ." Did someone . . . something . . . No. "Don't know what happened."

She wasn't being dishonest. She really didn't know exactly what had happened. Looking out over the lake she saw nothing except the cloudless blue sky reflecting off the surface. She must have imagined something else. Maybe she had fallen asleep and had been dreaming. As hard as she tried, she couldn't quite convince herself of that.

"Are you cold? Let me get you a blanket."

"No." She looked out over the lake again. Shadows were flying criss-cross everywhere. "Can we just go home now, please?"

The ride home was quiet. When asked if she was okay, she simply nodded. Once home, she remained quiet and stayed to herself. Hours later, as her mother was getting supper, Meg went into the kitchen.

"Mom?"

"It's about time!" Though her daughter had been quiet since leaving the lake, she had appeared normal but Bobbi knew something was bothering her daughter.

"What's . . . ? Oh, yeah, you already know." She was used to her mother's psychic powers, of knowing what she was thinking and feeling.

"I only know something is bothering you." Though her mother could have touched her and gotten all the information she needed, she had made a practice of turning her power off unless absolutely necessary.

"You see and dream about people after touching them, but has it ever happened just out of the blue?"

"I don't believe so, though I don't need to touch them to hear their thoughts."

"Are you hearing mine?"

"No, and I won't unless I have to. Do I?"

"No mom. Have you ever seen spirits?"

"Yes, you know I have."

"What about . . . shadows . . . with bright white eyes?"

"Is that what happened at the lake?"

Meg told her mother about the shadows. Together they decided the spirits or shadows meant her no harm and they were simply part of her psychic abilities. Since then, she had talked to them and they had talked to her.

At the lake, a man's voice, a stranger, called to her from shore.

"Hey, lady."

She sucked in air, opened her eyes. She stiffened, started to sink, then moved to tread water.

"You're not dead are you?"

"I don't think so." She swam to shore.

"I saw you floating out there and, quite honestly, I thought you were dead." She stood in front of him, studying his face. He felt awkward and somewhat foolish now. "My name is Zeus, by the way.

"Meg." She answered, still looking at him.

"You do know you aren't suppose to go swimming alone, don't you?"

"I wasn't swimming."

"Okay, you shouldn't imitate a floating dead body alone either." He smiled at her.

"And what were you going to do here?" She finally looked away.

"I was sent here to save you!" Her head snapped around to look at him only to see his smile deepen. Odd choice of words she thought. The fact that she didn't need saving she kept to herself.

"Really? Who sent you?" He shrugged.

"Powers that Be, I suppose."

"Oh, them." It was very likely he was right and didn't even know it. Often last minute decisions were the prompting of "powers that be" whether it's a Spirit Guide, or a loved one who had crossed over. Most believe it was luck or a coincidence.

"Yeah, them. I go wherever they send me."

"So, you save damsels in distress often, even when they're not in distress?"

"It's a knack." He shrugged.

She wanted to question him further to find out if he really believed in such things, if he was serious. His grin belied that he did, but . . . Trying to decide she glanced out over the lake again. What she saw made her breath catch in her throat. Shadows floated and flew in all directions weaving around and through each other. Many with those white glowing eyes.

"I suppose I should get going." She smiled up at him. "Thank you, and the powers that be, for the thought of saving me."

"Anytime. I may have, at the least, saved you from floating out to sea." She started to walk away, then turned back to him.

"Why did you come to the lake?"

"I don't know. I hadn't planned on it. As I approached I suddenly got the urge to stop." From what she knew, he would play some role in the near future. What role that would be, she didn't know. "This is a fairly secluded lake . . . not much traffic. Does it have a name?"

"I believe it's called Crystal Lake." She had referred to it as Lake of Shadows for so long she'd almost forgotten it's real name.

"How long have you been coming here?"

"Since I was eight. There aren't many people who know about it so it's usually fairly quiet here."

"I gather you come here to relax and be alone. I won't tell anyone about it."

"It's public property."

"If they don't know about it by now," he shrugged, "they don't need to."

They left it at that. She got into her car, waved, and drove away leaving him standing there watching her. Until she took a bend in the road, she kept checking the rear view mirror to see if he had also left. He hadn't, so she hoped he enjoyed a peaceful time at the lake.

After that moment at the lake, Meg thought about Zeus for a few days, then more or less forgot about him. A week later she ran into him at a grocery store. They walked around together shopping and talking. Then, they went to the parking lot. They were parked four cars apart. Stopping at midpoint, they shook hands.

A scene flashed through her mind. A murder . . . two adults . . . lots of blood and Zeus reaching for a small child . . . a girl, who was obviously terrified. It took everything she had to not yank her hand away or otherwise show any signs of shock or fear as she slid her hand out of his grasp. Her hands were shaking so much she had to stuff them in her pants pockets.

"Maybe I'll see you later." He smiled at her.

"Yeah, maybe." The slight quiver in her voice made him look at her oddly.

"Are you okay?"

"I might be coming down with something. I'd better finish my shopping and head home." His brows furrowed. Her mistake. She'd just done shopping with him. She hooked her thumb over her shoulder toward a few other stores. "I need . . . other stuff."

She couldn't remember what other stores there were besides the grocery store. He glanced over her shoulder, then back at her.

"Car parts or pizza?" She tilted her chin in defiance unwilling to have him get the best of her.

"Both." His eyebrows raised.

5

"You so carefully got healthy food . . . organic produce and grass fed meats, then you buy pizza?"

"It's for my parents and before you ask, I'm not getting car parts. I'm getting oil, a squeegee, WD-40 . . ." She trailed off.

"You change your own oil?" He asked with humor.

"Is this the Spanish Inquisition?" Irritation edged her voice.

"Are you Spanish?" He almost chuckled, irritating her further.

"Are you an interrogator?"

"Not quite. Sometimes, when I have to be, I guess." She heaved a silent sigh letting her irritation go.

"Unless you want to be responsible for my parents starving to death, I'd better get going."

"No, I wouldn't want to be responsible for them dying like that!" The image of two bloody dead people and one horrified little girl flashed through her mind.

"I guess not." She swallowed hard. "Bye." She hurried away.

A few days later while getting ready for work, she had the TV on, and as usual, was listening to the news. A follow-up on a story caught her attention. They were still looking for the person or persons responsible for the grisly deaths of two people . . . the parents of a little girl. This little girl was perhaps the only witness to the murders.

Meg ran to the living room, toothbrush in her mouth, to see a photo of the man and woman. The same couple she had seen when she shook Zeus' hand in the store parking lot. She swallowed, forgetting she still had a mouth full of toothpaste. Hurrying back to the bathroom she rinsed out her mouth. Still tuned into the TV, she heard the announcer say that they didn't "have a suspect or motive and if anyone knew or saw anything to please call . . ."

She stopped listening as her mind raced. The double murder was recent. Very recent. And Zeus was definitely involved, she had seen that much when she had touched him! As she dressed she wondered if he had killed them the day they met at the store, or soon after that. Shuddering at the thought, she left her apartment for work.

As soon as she was inside her office, she called Barry Kerbs, a police officer and long time family friend. He didn't answer so she left a message. Throughout the day she tried to get hold of him and each time had to leave a message. Leaving for the day, she headed for the police station hoping to catch him as he left work. Having to turn her phone off at work, and even though she'd done so frequently already, she checked for a message from Barry.

"Meg." She looked up to see him coming down the steps. "I hope it's a pleasure to see you but the look on your face tells me it isn't."

"Where have you been? I've called and left messages all day."

"You called the station?"

"No, your cell."

"I don't use my personal cell at work. It's been in my car all day. What's wrong Meg? Are your parents okay?"

"Yes, they're fine." She hesitated, looking down at her hands, then back up at him. "Barry, do you know of someone called Zeus?"

"Zeus Garrett, yes." He answered warily. He knew of the psychic abilities that ran in her family. "Why?"

"What do you know about him?"

"I wouldn't say we're friends but I have spoken with him a couple of times. He's a first rate detective and seems to be a nice enough guy. Again, why?"

"Do you know what he's working on right now?"

"A double homicide."

"Is he the one who found the little girl?" Barry looked surprised. "She was hiding in a closet or somewhere dark."

"We haven't released that information. What did you see . . . and when?"

"A week or so ago, I was at . . . Crystal Lake." She'd almost called it 'The Lake of Shadows.' "He stopped, we talked, I left. A few days ago I ran into him while shopping. I shook his hand in parting and saw the dead couple and his hands reaching for the little girl. The little girl was terrified; she was pressed in the corner of a dark closet or something and looking at Zeus."

"So you are thinking he is the murderer." It was a statement, not a question. "He found her like that. She was so scared she couldn't even cry. It took him a long time to get her to trust him and come out. She hasn't spoken, or cried, at all yet."

"Can she speak?"

"She's not mute. The home they placed her in . . . the woman there . . . she says she had nightmares and screams out words at night . . . every night."

"She's what . . . four?" He nodded. "Poor child. Who's working with her?"

"Departmental, right now. Would you like the case?"

"I don't want to step on anyone's toes . . ."

"You won't be. Your name has already come up."

"You've . . . ?"

"No." He shook his head. "It wasn't me. Like Zeus, your reputation precedes you. You both can crack cases no one else can." Barry knew she wouldn't refuse. "Come by tomorrow to get everything started."

Chapter Two

With no clients first thing in the morning, Meg went to the police station. On her way out she saw Zeus. Trying to decide whether to acknowledge him or slip out unseen, the decision was taken out of her hands when he looked up and met her eyes.

"Meg!" He smiled at her as though they were old friends. "Not in trouble are you?" He teased. Usually fairly even-tempered, Meg's temper flared. He seemed to have that effect on her.

"No more than usual." She snapped back and headed for the exit, annoyed when he followed her. Outside he stopped her.

"Is something wrong?" She looked at him evenly. "Was it something I said?"

In the few seconds that passed before she spoke, she realized she was angry with herself. She had no reason to be angry with him. She was also relieved he wasn't the murderer she had thought he was. For whatever reason, that relief made her angry.

"It's what you didn't say!"

He looked confused.

"Why didn't you tell me you were a detective?" She cut herself off from adding that she thought he was a murderer.

He smiled at her, then replied. "I'm sorry. Was I supposed to have mentioned that the first or second time we met?" She shook her head and descended the steps. "I'm not psychic you know. What about you?"

She stopped in her tracks, looking up at him, wondering if he knew. He descended the steps also, stopping in front of her.

"What about you?" He repeated. "What work do you do?" She visibly relaxed.

"Counselor."

"Legal?"

"Psychiatry. I work with children."

"Hey . . ."

"I'm already on it." His expression was less confusion and more curiosity.

"On what?"

"I'm working with the little girl you found. I just got assigned to the case." A split second went by. "A family friend of mine said I was being considered so I came down to . . . sign up." She finished lamely. He was back to looking at her with total confusion. She couldn't blame him. She'd been hearing his thoughts and answering questions he hadn't asked yet.

"I'd better get to work." Before she could move away, he touched her arm.

"Wait." She closed her eyes for a moment feeling his emotions run through her-confusion, disbelief, curiosity, and then an attempt at logic. "Shouldn't we get together to discuss this case?"

"I can't right now. I'm already late for work."

"Lunch?" She shook her head. "Dinner?"

"Please Zeus, I really have to go." She walked away.

"Coffee after work?" He called after her. "I'll wait right here."

She didn't respond. She got into her car as quickly as she could and drove away.

All day she pictured him standing where she left him, waiting for her. They may discuss the case, but she knew he had other questions for her—questions she didn't want to answer. Besides, anything about the case could be gotten by reading the file and talking to the departmental psychologist. She didn't need to meet with Zeus for any of it. As she left work, driving out of the parking lot, instead of turning left to go home, she found herself turning right and heading toward the police station, against her better judgment.

She told herself he wouldn't be there and she'd simply turn around and go home. She told herself she needed to avoid him. She told herself she had to watch herself for showing signs of being psychic. She shouldn't have been answering questions before they were asked. She told herself there was no logical reason, personal or professional, to meet with Zeus. She pulled over to the curb when she saw him standing right where she'd seen him standing all day in her mind.

"I knew you'd show up." Irritation flared. Deep down she'd known it also. She exited her car.

"I'd really like to get home so if we could make this quick . . ."

"Just coffee then?" He nodded toward a diner a few blocks away. She nodded and fell into step beside him. Neither spoke until they were seated and ordered coffee. She braced herself for the question.

"Have you had a chance to get a feel for the case?"

"A feel?" Was he referring to a psychic feel?

"You've been told something about it, haven't you?"

"Just the basics. I haven't had time to read the file, but I will as soon as I get home."

"Point taken-you want to get out of here."

Their coffee arrived. As soon as the waitress walked away, he started telling her about the murder scene from his viewpoint. She asked a few questions, but mainly listened. The smell of food was getting to her. She had skipped breakfast and lunch to catch up on paperwork. Her stomach growled. Her eyes strayed to the waitress. Realizing what she was doing, she quickly glanced at Zeus. Damn, she was doing it to him, too. Too late. It was already done. She'd imprinted thoughts on them both.

"Let's eat." Zeus looked surprised when the waitress brought them each a menu at the same time that he spoke. "I know you want to get home and go over the file, but you have to eat, right?"

"I am starving. I worked through lunch to make up for being late this morning."

They ordered their food, chit-chatting while they waited for it to arrive.

"Okay, I'm dying here. How did you know what I was going to say this morning?"

Mentally she heaved a sigh. She knew better than to hope it wouldn't come up. She shrugged.

"Standard questions considering our conversation. I told you I work with children, you thought I should work with the girl. I told you I was going to and naturally you wanted to know how that came about, so I told you about Barry Kerbs . . . the family friend. Now you're wondering why me. I, like you, seem to be able to solve hard cases."

"Wow!"

"Not really. I'm sure you do the same thing in your line of work. See things others miss or see them differently than others and that makes you better at your job. My ability makes me read between the lines, hear what someone really means, even if their words say otherwise. We're more in tune, I guess." He nodded.

"I guess that's why we do what we do." She smiled at him.

Their food arrived. They ate in silence for the first half of the meal. As their hunger abated they started talking about the case until one knew as much about it as the other did. Finally, after a break in conversation, he grinned at her.

"I knew you'd show up."

"Did you? What made you so sure?"

"You came out of guilt. You knew I'd be standing there waiting."

"How long were you standing there?" He shrugged.

"An hour or so."

"And it never occurred to you in that hour that I might not show?"

"It crossed my mind, but I knew guilt would make you show up." Meg didn't know if she felt more irritation or amusement at his audacity.

"Curiosity is what brought me here. I had given you no indication I'd be here so if you chose to wait all night that wouldn't have been my problem. I was curious to see if you were actually dumb enough to stand there all night and more curious to hear what you might be able to tell me about the case that isn't in the report."

"Did you purposely make me wait?"

"I worked late to make up for this morning. I would have worked later if I hadn't wanted to get to this case. Besides, I have no idea when your day ends so I might have been the one waiting . . . if I cared to." He digested this then flashed her a grin.

"It was guilt." He teased.

"You think a lot of yourself, don't you? Or are you delusional? I hate to burst your bubble but . . . you don't have the power to make me feel guilty. I'm the only one with the power to allow myself to feel guilty or not." He laughed. His eyes sparkled. She realized he was trying to irritate her. Once aware of his goal, she refused to rise to the bait.

"Would you like dessert?" The waitress had returned, clearing the dishes.

"Yes." Zeus spoke up. "A banana split for two please."

"You must have a wicked sweet tooth detective." Meg placed her share of the check on the table as she stood. "Enjoy. Thank you for the information. Good night."

She felt his eyes following her as she left the diner, crossed the street, and got into her car. He even watched her drive away. Apparently, she amused him.

Meg didn't go home. Instead she went to her parent's house. When she walked in her father, Lance, and her brother, Michael, both looked up. No one spoke in those first few seconds, then Michael grinned at his sister.

"What?"

No words were spoken between brother and sister, yet their thoughts came across loud and clear.

"Meg's in love."

"I am not!" She glared at her brother.

"Michael," Lance spoke out loud, "leave your sister alone."

Her mother came out of the kitchen as though she had been called, stopped in the threshold, then looked from her son to her daughter.

"Meg," her mom held an arm out to her daughter, "come in the kitchen with me."

"Coming, Mom." She kissed her father's cheek and headed toward the kitchen.

Sitting on a stool by the counter, Meg watched for a few minutes as her mother cleared up after supper.

"Mom, did daddy irritate you when you first met him . . . purposely irritate you?"

"No, not at all. Is there truth to Michael's thoughts?"

"No, of course not! Michael just picked up on my highly emotional state of mind."

"Would you care to tell me about it?"

Meg told her mother about her meeting with Zeus, how she thought he was the killer, how he went out of his way to irritate her. During the pause after she had finished, her youngest sister, Carmen, flew through the kitchen door. She stopped dead in her tracks, staring at Meg.

"You're in love with a Greek God! You go from one end of the spectrum to the other, don't you? Tony certainly was at the other end!" Meg looked evenly at her sister.

"Daddy wants to talk to you . . . something about the scratch on the car."

"Geez," Carmen rolled her eyes, "it's barely noticeable." She left the kitchen, temporarily forgetting about Meg.

"That's two." Her mother observed aloud.

"Michael probably told her." Whether it was through telepathy or cell phone she could only guess. "I'll finish up here mom, go join daddy."

"Thank you, Meg." She smiled as she passed her daughter. "Take some leftovers home with you. I know you don't eat right."

Alone in the kitchen, Meg put leftovers away and started the dishes. She worked automatically as her mind went over and over the absurdity of feeling anything but irritation for Zeus Garrett.

The next day Meg met with the department psychologist, Dr. Rose. Meg noticed that he was rather young and wondered, absently, if this was his first job out of college. They entered a debriefing room together. Sitting with her back to the door, she glanced over the file on the little girl.

"No one knows her name?"

"Everyone we spoke to said they didn't."

"She didn't speak to you at all?"

"She wouldn't even look at me. She just had that stare people get when they're in shock . . . void of expression."

"Absolutely nothing?"

"She did glance at me once, briefly."

"What was going on at that time?"

"I was talking to her."

"About what?"

"General stuff . . . did she want to play with some toys or draw a picture." He glanced at the door.

"What specifically were you saying when she looked at you?"

"I told her she had a pretty dress." He glanced at the door again. "When she reacted, I had just told her the buttons were especially pretty."

"Did you just say buttons or did you describe them specifically when she made eye contact?" He looked toward the door again. This time she turned, too. Zeus Garrett stood just outside looking in as if waiting. She turned back to Dr. Rose.

"Is he waiting for you, Miss Wolfe?"

"I was just about to ask you the same thing. Forget about him. Can you remember exactly what you were saying about the buttons?"

Dr. Rose contemplated the question. Meg had all she could do to keep from reaching over and touching his hand. It would have been much quicker and easier to get the information she needed. She refrained, only using that method when there was no other way and it was a matter of serious information needed as fast as possible. His voice brought her attention back to him.

"I told her how the sparkly flower-shaped buttons were extra special . . . no, made the dress extra special."

"It's the word buttons that got her attention?" He nodded. "You're sure?"

"Yes. She looked at me when I said it and away as soon as the word was out of my mouth. Actually, she looked through me, not away."

"Like she was remembering something?"

"Perhaps, yes."

"Thank you, Dr. Rose." Meg stood reaching out to shake his hand. Unintentionally, she felt his emotions and heard his thoughts. He was just coming off from being scared, sliding into relief, and he hoped, as it was only his third case, he hadn't messed up. "You have been a great help." She concluded.

"I certainly hope so. That poor little girl . . ." He was flooded with relief now. She released his hand. "When will you see her?"

"I'm headed there right now."

"Please keep me informed of any progress."

Meg agreed she would and headed for the door. Pulling it open, Zeus Garrett didn't move. She stepped out anyway, prepared to bull her way past him, if necessary. What she wanted to do was give a mental shove and smile as he fell backward. A corner of her mouth twitched at the thought but she refrained.

"Excuse me, Detective Garrett." He stepped aside just enough to let her pass. It was either that or she would have at least tried to push past him.

"Were you ever going to tell me your real name?" She stopped, looking briefly at him.

"Why does it matter?" A slight move and he was towering over her. A stance, she was sure, he used in his line of work. "Intimidation doesn't work with me."

His features darkened, then cleared, as he stepped back. His voice softened.

"I can understand giving a different name when we first met. For all you knew, I was a serial killer." He saw something in her eyes change, but only for a second. "Since then, Kerbs has told you who I am, we've met more or less professionally, and you still let me call you Meg."

"Does that mean you still can't be a serial killer?" Not waiting for an answer, she went on. "Anyway, have you also heard Barry call me Meg? Is it possible that that's my name?" His face registered confusion.

"But the psychiatrist at . . ."

"You've been checking me out?"

"I wanted to call you about . . ."

"That's a little like stalking, isn't it?"

"Look . . ."

"No, you look. I gave you all of the information you need, then and now."

"Do you even work at The Commons?" She looked at him evenly, not about to tell him anything more.

"Investigate me." She walked away. "Interrogation doesn't work with me either." She shot over her shoulder.

It took her the entire thirty-minute drive to the foster home, where the little girl was staying, to calm down. She needed to be calm, inside and out, before engaging with the child, any child. Children are very aware of adults' emotions. Being upset could definitely put a damper on, not just their first encounter, but also the following meetings.

Sitting outside in her car, Meg phoned Mary, the foster mother.

"I'm outside, but before I come in, I need to caution you to call me Meg. That will make me more of a friend, the name Wolfe can be scary to a child."

"I understand."

"I'll be right in."

Chapter Three

"Hello, my name is Meg." She said as soon as she sat down. "What's you're name?" Silence and no eye contact met her question.

"Would the two of you like some cookies and milk?" Mary asked from the kitchen doorway. Meg looked at the little girl questioningly. After a reasonable amount of time had passed without a response from her, Meg answered.

"Yes Mary, I'd love some cookies and milk, thank you." As Mary turned away, Meg turned to the little girl again.

"You have a beautiful dress on today." Meg had asked Mary to have the girl wear the same dress she had been wearing when Dr. Rose saw the girl. "I like all the bright colors." Nothing.

Mary brought a plate of sandwich cookies and two glasses of milk, then left the room.

"Mary is a nice lady, isn't she?" No response.

"These cookies kind of look like the buttons on your dress. Don't you think so?" Silence. "Except your buttons are flowers, aren't they?" For a split second there was eye contact. Meg's mind raced for a connection.

"Are they roses?" The girl stared off at nothing. "No, they'd have to be very special flowers." The girl's eyes darted to Meg, then away. "I know . . . Jasmine." The girl's eyes met and locked with hers.

"I'm pleased to meet you Jasmine." She picked up the plate offering her a cookie. Meekly Jasmine took one, but let her hand rest in her lap with it.

"I like dunking my cookies in my milk. Do you?" Jasmine didn't say anything but she watched Meg dunk her cookie and eat it.

"Well," she said, when she'd finished, "I have to get back to work Jasmine. If you tell me what your favorite cookie is, I'll bring some next time." Jasmine just looked at her.

"That's okay. I'll figure it out. Maybe I'll bring Newtons." A slight reaction. "Should I bring fig, strawberry, blueberry . . ." Jasmine's eyes became marginally larger. Meg smiled. "Blueberry it is then! I'll be back with them in two days." She held up two fingers.

On her way out, Meg told Mary of the progress she'd made, as well as the girl's name. Saying she'd be back in two days. She left with an extra spring in her step. She made a major break through with Jasmine and she also thought she'd earned a little trust, on her own. Not once had she had to use gifts to do any of it. This always pleased her at least as much as making headway with a client.

Two days later, Meg met with Jasmine again, bringing the blueberry Newtons as promised. She found the little girl appearing to be happier, though no more verbal. Meg had planned to stay her usual thirty minutes with Jasmine, not wanting to tax her too much. At the end of that time, she got the feeling Jasmine didn't want her to leave. Her stay was extended another half hour.

Jasmine didn't speak, though she did get a smile from her when Jasmine took a cookie from the plate when she thought Meg wasn't looking. Meg's reaction to the missing cookie, her look of surprise and pretending to look for it, brought a smile to Jasmine's face.

As usual, Meg told Mary of the progress. Meg found Jasmine had seemed happier since her last visit. Jasmine had even looked interested in playing with the younger children in the foster home. She hadn't acted on it, but she had looked like she had wanted to.

Two weeks and four visits later Jasmine giggled. On the fifth visit, she laughed out loud. During the last visit of the third week, she spoke. Meg was up to one-and-a-half hours when she announced it was time for her to leave and she stood. Jasmine blurted out, "Don't go!" Meg stayed a full two hours during this meeting. Jasmine didn't speak again, but she did reach out tracing her small index finger along Meg's cheek while looking at her with a mixture of uncertainty and curiosity. Upon leaving, Mary told her she had been playing with the other kids in the foster home.

Very pleased with the progress being made, especially the verbal aspect, Meg headed for the police station to meet with Dr. Rose, if he was available, or she would leave a detailed written account for him. She was in luck, he was available and very interested to hear everything.

Leaving her meeting with Dr. Rose, Meg called The Commons to see if there was anything urgent or unexpected on her agenda at the office. There wasn't. So she decided to go home for some much needed cleaning, then relaxation. She left the room in which she had met Dr. Rose, feeling pleased with her meeting with Jasmine and happy with her unexpected free time. Crossing the lobby, returning greetings from officers she'd known for years, she stopped to pat Oz, one of the dogs from the K-9 Unit; he was just coming in with Officer Brady. She patted Oz on top of his head and scratched him under his chin.

"Do all officers get the same treatment?" She turned to see Detective Garrett.

"I might consider it if they're as well behaved and trained as Oz is." She saw an almost masked sadness behind his eyes.

"I went through training at the Academy." He offered.

"Ah, but are you as well-behaved as Oz?"

"I won't lick your face or jump on you." The last part made her smile.

"Do you bite?"

"Only on request." He teased. She let out a sigh of regret.

"Unfortunately, you are a detective now." He opened his mouth to argue the point, then shut it. Technically she was right. Instead, he grinned at her.

"So, what's going on with our little witness? Any progress?"

"Actually, yes, but nothing you'd be interested in." He looked at her oddly and raised a questioning eyebrow. "She's coming out of her shell a little. I've managed to guess her name, gotten her to giggle and laugh, speak some and interact with the other kids. She's not totally there, yet, but these are vast improvements!"

"And that wouldn't interest me, why?"

"I'm sure you're glad she's starting to recover but she's not at the point where there's any information for you to work with."

"I appear that cold hearted to you? Knowing she's recovering, after what she's been through, means nothing to me unless she can help me get whoever killed her parents? Maybe I want to hurry things along to get to that point regardless of the damage it might do to her."

"I'm sorry, I didn't mean it to sound that cold."

"I'm just a little cold then?" He was playing with her.

"I said I was sorry. I'll keep you posted on Jasmine's progress. What more do you want?"

"I'll consider it an apology if you'll have dinner with me." He must have realized she was about to refuse. His hand touched her arm making her look up at him. She felt sadness and knew someone close to him was seriously ill.

"Will you accept my apology if I agree to dinner?"

He smiled.

"Consider it already accepted."

"Hey, Meg!" Barry spied her from the hall. "How's the little girl?"

"She has a long way to go but she's doing much better."

"That's great!" He said as he approached them. "Any idea how long it'll take?"

"There's no way to predict that Barry. It all depends on her."

"Do you think you'll need to . . ."

"I hope not." Meg cut him off knowing he was about to ask if she'd have to use her psychic gift. She was aware of Detective Garrett listening with interest, especially when Barry glanced at him, then back to her.

"Right, right. Well, keep me posted, Meg. How you shrinks work always fascinates me." He squeezed her shoulder. "Tell everyone I said hello."

"I will Barry."

"Interesting." Meg turned back to Detective Garrett. "What was he about to say before you cut him off?"

"Can't put anything past you, can I?"

"I have a mind like a steel trap . . . rusted shut and illegal in forty-one states . . . maybe more." She laughed out loud.

"I'm sure you're right!"

"So," she felt his sudden change of mind to not pursue the previous question, "shall we meet back here or do you trust me enough to pick you up at your place?"

"Trust you . . . interesting choice of words, Detective. Does that imply I shouldn't trust you?"

"I'm being shrunk by the shrink?"

"I don't think that would be possible . . . with your rusted shut, steel trap mind."

"Then I'm impenetrable?"

"To most perhaps, but I'm very good at my job."

"We're getting off the subject." His tone and outward appearance was smooth and unruffled-the opposite of his inward emotions.

"My place will be fine, Detective." She wrote down her address on a piece of scrap paper and handed it to him. He glanced at it before putting it in his shirt pocket.

"Can you do me a favor, at least for tonight? Please call me Zeus."

"I suppose I could do that."

Hours later she was showered and changed. When he knocked on her door, she opened it and let him in. She noticed that he glanced around as he stepped inside.

"Nice place."

"Thanks. I'll be just a second." She took a light jacket from the coat closet, turning sharply when she heard a book hit the floor. Zeus stood several feet away with a look of surprise and innocence on his face.

"I didn't do it." He half joked.

"Ghosts." Meg replied, making light of it and scowling in the direction of the book.

"Wow, a beautiful apartment complete with its own ghosts. Does that cost extra?"

"They aren't on the lease, so don't tell anyone." Placing the jacket over her arm she glanced at the book, then at Zeus. "Ready?"

All in all they had a pleasant evening. The food was exceptional, the atmosphere and conversation were relaxing. Meg's tension from her resident ghost's antics had disappeared, though not forgotten. Zeus, on the other hand, though appearing relaxed, was concerned about his ill friend or family member. It was her nature to help.

"What's going on in your life Zeus?" She opened the door on the subject. He looked at her with mild surprise.

"Are you asking about a case I may be working on?"

"No, I'm asking about the sadness behind your eyes. I hadn't seen it there before." He contemplated her answer.

"You are good at your job." He was avoiding her question.

"You don't have to tell me. I'm just curious. He smiled then.

"And you have a need to help people. I suspect that's why you chose your particular profession." She nodded her agreement and accepted another cup of coffee the waitress was offering.

"I've always been leery of shrinks. It seems they are always psychoanalyzing everyone."

"And yet you asked me out." She smiled at him. "I'm trying very hard not to analyze that!"

"Is it just the way your mind works and you can't help yourself?"

"Do you mean that singularly or collectively?"

"Collectively."

"Ah, perhaps. Is it any different than yours . . . collectively? Are you not conducting an investigation right now?" He laughed.

"Touche!"

"I hate to defeat my own victory, but my question was out of concern, not analysis."

"I'll answer your question if you'll answer one of mine."

"Seems fair." She agreed.

"My sister has recently been diagnosed with cancer. It literally came out of the blue. She'd felt fine until she got the flu and couldn't get over it. She went to the doctor's office and after some tests, they discovered she was riddled with cancer and should have shown some signs a long time ago."

"Zeus, I'm so sorry!" He sat back.

"Tammy has always been as healthy as a horse. She's never smoked, always eats extremely healthy . . . all organic, like you. She exercised and was in terrific shape, even did marathons. In fact, she had just finished one before she got the flu. And she rarely even got a cold, even when everyone around her had one. The last time she had the sniffles . . . and that's usually all she ever got . . . was ten years ago. Tammy always had her check-ups and always got a clean bill of health. I just don't understand it. She's so full of cancer there isn't much they can do for her. In the span of a month, she's gone from a healthy marathon runner to death's door. She's been at Mercy Hospital for nine days, now, and gets worse every day. They say she won't last a month."

"Mercy has one of the best cancer treatment centers in the country. I'm sure they're doing everything possible for her."

"They are, it just isn't having an effect on the cancer."

Meg wanted to hold him, to absorb his sadness away from him.

"Is she your only sister or sibling?"

"She's my only sister and my twin."

His intense pain showed deep in his eyes, in his sagging head and shoulders. She reached across the table placing her hand on his forearm. He started to pull away then stopped as she held his gaze, penetrating to his very soul. He was close to mesmerized as he looked into her eyes. After a couple of minutes, she removed her hand. For a millisecond, he kept looking at her, confused and, with something akin to fear, at what he had just experienced. Then, as if it was totally forgotten, he gave her a weak smile.

"I'm sorry, I must have needed to talk to someone about that. I didn't mean to go on and on."

"Any time you need, or want, to talk, I'm here Zeus . . . as a friend." He nodded his acknowledgment.

"My turn. Why don't you exist?" She sat back, clearly confused. "I can't find you anywhere."

"Where have you been looking?"

"Everywhere. I can't find a shrink named Meg anywhere within a hundred miles in all directions." She sighed.

"All that detective work and you still came up empty? Why didn't you just ask me? I know Barry must have given you my last name." He shook his head. "It's Wolfe. Let me know what you find."

She smiled at him, knowing he wouldn't find anything under Meg Wolfe. Her legal name was Abby."

"Wolfe? That sounds familiar."

"Wolves have been around a very long time." He grinned at her play on words.

"I bet they have!"

Chapter Four

Meg had really enjoyed herself. It had been fun sparring with Zeus, though sad hearing about his twin sister and seeing the pain in his eyes. She wondered if there was anything she could do for him . . . or if she should. There was a reason she had learned about Zeus' sister. Perhaps it was for nothing other than to alleviate any fears his sister might have about crossing over and to ease her into the Other Side. She'd visit her, one way or another, soon.

Right now, however, she needed to confront Clansey. Though she had always been surrounded by spirits and ghosts for as long as she could remember, most moved on, and crossed over. Clansey hung around. He seemed particularly attached to her, though he wasn't always with her. What he did at those times she didn't know. He had told her there were things he had to do before he crossed over, but he had no clue what these things were and wouldn't until the time was right. In the meantime, he occasionally hung out at her place.

"Clansey," she called to him upon entering her apartment. She always smelled pipe smoke when he was nearby. He couldn't actually smoke, but it was his way of letting her know he was there. "I know you're here and we need to talk!"

"How was your date?" He appeared, leaning against a wall.

"None of your business! What was all that with the book?" He shrugged. "Don't give me that! Why did you shove that book off the table? Were you trying to scare Zeus?"

"Just wanted to get his attention."

"Why?" He shrugged again. "Clansey . . ." Her tone was a warning.

"I don't like him."

"Too bad, I do and I won't have you interfering in my personal life. Do I make myself clear?" He looked around unconcerned, almost bored. "Clansey!"

"Okay, okay, I heard you! Geez, I'd think you'd be happy I didn't follow you!"

Without saying as much, she was grateful for that. Heaving a sigh, Meg went to the kitchen and made a cup of tea. If people could be trying, ghosts could hit a level beyond that. After settling into an overstuffed chair and having a few sips of her tea, she was relaxed and calm enough to talk to him.

"Why don't you like him?"

"There's something dark aound him."

"Of course there is—his twin sister is dieing."

"I'm aware of the sad helplessness, but that's not the darkness."

"What kind of darkness?"

"I'm not sure yet, but it's bad."

"A spirit?"

"Perhaps, though it's more like a cloud. It could be him or something he's into. He could be bad."

Meg hadn't picked up on anything like that. She had only sensed his sadness. Just because he was a cop, a detective, didn't mean he couldn't have a dark soul. She finished her tea and stood.

"I'm going to bed now. Good night, Clansey. Behave."

"I don't have a choice." He grinned at her. "I'm not allowed in your bedroom or the bathroom, unless you've changed your mind." His expression became hopeful.

"Good night, Clansey. Behave." She repeated with a tone of finality, but with a tiny smile at his playfulness.

"Yes, ma'am." His grin broadened just before he disappeared.

In the months that followed, Jasmine blossomed like the sweet, delicate flower she was named after. Under Mary's care, she played with the other children. She engaged in verbal communication with Mary and other adults. For that matter, she talked quite a bit, bordering on being a chatter-box. She just never spoke of that fatal night with her parents. It was time for Meg to give her a little push. In the end, she didn't have to.

Meg was trying to decide how she would broach the subject while she and Jasmine each colored a page in a coloring book. As usual, they chatted about Jasmine's week. It was while they were otherwise engaged, as opposed to full-frontal confrontation, when she thought it'd be best to slowly bring it up.

"Have you had any dreams lately, Jasmine?" She shook her head, concentrating on coloring, with the tip of her tongue poking out of the corner of her mouth. "Really?" she sounded surprised. "Not even about horses, or puppies, or ice cream?" Again Jasmine shook her head.

"How 'bout you?"

"I don't dream very often." They colored in silence for several minutes.

"I saw him you know." It was such an unexpected comment. Meg almost asked who she was referring to.

"Really?" Jasmine nodded. "Would you like to talk about it?" Jasmine shook her head.

"Is it true?"

"Is what true?"

"If I tell you everything, you'll go away and never come back?"

"Is that what you want?" Meg's feelings were a little hurt. She had thought the child enjoyed their time together.

"No." She switched crayons and continued coloring.

"I'm glad to hear that Jasmine. I really like our time together."

"You're like my mom."

"How so? Is it my hair color or my eyes?" She shook her head.

"You're . . . comfy." Meg let out a soft laugh.

"Comfy?" She nodded.

"You make me feel warm . . ." Jasmine placed her hand over her chest. "Here."

"You make me feel like that, too." Meg studied the child's bent head. "Could you tell me what he looked like?" She nodded. "Can I call someone who can draw exactly what you say?"

Jasmine's crayon stopped. Her body stayed motionless. She inhaled and held it, then slowly released it, nodding at the same time.

There was an increase in activity. The last thing Meg wanted was to make Jasmine anxious or nervous. A forensic sketcher arrived within an hour. Jasmine wanted Meg to sit next to her and hold her hand as she described the person who had killed her parents. Though very detailed, the composite sketch wasn't much help as apparently the attacker wore all dark clothing, gloves, and a full-face mask. What stuck out in her mind was how green his eyes were and, even with the mask, he either had an extremely large head or very thick hair as the top of his head, according to Jasmine, was rounded and huge.

Meg was glad she had been holding Jasmine's hand, not only to comfort her through the ordeal, but also to feel what she was thinking and feeling. She could also see what Jasmine saw and what she described was fairly accurate. The attacker was of medium height, slight of build with vivid green eyes.

The sketch was quickly put in the system with no hits. Whoever he was, he either hadn't done anything illegal or had managed to stay below radar. Meg encouraged Jasmine to tell her if she thought of or remembered anything else.

Meanwhile, Meg met with Zeus to compare notes. He had gotten a copy of the composite drawing and of all the people he had interviewed or thus heard about, but no one fit that description. The only people he hadn't spoken with yet were the elderly couple who lived in the apartment building; they were away on vacation.

"Anything new with Jasmine?"

"Nothing pertaining to the case, though she is coming out of her shell more and more."

"That's good. With your help, and a lot of love, perhaps she'll be able to live a normal life."

"That's what we're hoping for."

"Are you free for dinner tonight?"

"No, I have a ton of paperwork to catch up on . . . mostly reviews and new client profiles to go over . . . thrilling stuff like that. Unfortunately, I had to bring it home with me to get it done by tomorrow."

"Spreading yourself thin?"

"Always." She stood. "Speaking of which, I'd better get back to the office, meet with a client, grab my files, and get busy."

A few more words and they parted company.

"Meg?"

"Yes, Dear?" Meg had made an unexpected stop to see Jasmine before going home.

"What's—extra murial affirs?"

"What's . . ." Meg's mind raced to put meaning to a child's words repeated as she had perceived them. "Where did you hear that?"

"Mommy said Daddy had it. Was he sick?"

"No, he wasn't sick." She watched her building with Legos. "Did your mommy and daddy fight or yell at one another often?" She shrugged.

"A couple times." A month? A week? A day? Meg didn't want to push her.

"Did they hit each other or throw things?" She received a negative shake of the head.

"Does C-H-I-L-D spell my name?"

"No, why?"

"They used to say that a lot."

"Can you tell me what they said?"

"Not in front of the C-H-I-L-D. And what about the other C-H-I-L-D?"

That was fairly straight forward. Her parents didn't want to argue in front of Jasmine and it sounded as though the husband had fathered a child during an extra marital affair. She called Zeus as she drove home.

"Are you busy?"

"Not any more . . . Abby." She said nothing. "It seems you followed in your mother's footsteps. She's a psychiatrist, too . . . a famous one who solved a case with a serial killer. As for your father . . ."

"I know who my father is!" She was getting irritated by his smug tone. He had fallen silent as she continued. "Don't you have anything better to do than research me?"

Clearly she had forgotten she had challenged him to find her with just the last name Wolfe.

"I have a feeling you're going to give me something better to do."

His earlier silence and now subdued tone clicked in her brain but she shoved it aside.

"Yes I am. I went to see Jasmine. Actually, I just left. Do you know anything about an extra marital affair and a possible child resulting from that?" A relatively long stretch of silence followed. "Zeus?"

"Yes." For a second, Meg got the feeling Zeus wasn't talking about Jasmine's parents. Again she pushed that aside following his next words. "I'm here. No, no one ever mentioned anything like that. Everyone said they had a picture-perfect marriage."

"Well, today she broad-sided me by asking if her mother said her father had an extra marital affair if it meant he was sick. Then she wanted to know if C-H-I-L-D was how her name was spelled . . . as in "Not in front of" and "What about the other.""

"I guess I'll have to dig a little deeper. Neighbors, friends, and co-workers never mentioned an affair or even that he had a wandering eye."

"You never know. Some men carry on for years and even have second wives and families and no one knows."

"Thank you for the info. I'll get on it right away. Bye." He was so abrupt Meg had said goodbye to dead air.

She found his behavior interesting, passing it off as perhaps just the lead he was looking for or, at a stand still, and he wanted to see where the lead went. In either case, she had Jasmine to think about, monthly case files to do reports on, and a new client's file to review.

Reading the file on her new client did nothing to prepare Meg for meeting Daniel Newman. She nearly audibly inhaled when she saw him. He was average height and could have been considered slight of build. Typical for a teenager. More than that, however, were his eyes. Though she couldn't have said they were vivid, they were definitely noticeably green. The only thing she could think, besides how much he matched Jasmine's description, was what were the odds of her parent's murderer showing up in her office for counsel?

She spoke with him for thirty minutes in which time he danced around what was really bothering him. At the end of the session, all she knew was that he was torn between opening up and running. Upon shaking his hand, he was leaning toward running, as in never coming back and seeing her. After he left, a thought came to her while making notes in his file. Could he know about Jasmine? If he did, it might be safe to presume he thought she'd be an eyewitness. If that were the case, did he know she was in foster care and where? If he knew that, did he know she was seeing her? Could that be why he had requested to see her? She shook her head to clear such thoughts away. She was jumping to the conclusion that he was the murderer when in fact he might just be unfortunate enough to resemble Jasmine's description. He resembled it, not matched it inconclusively.

She called Zeus that evening. There was still that something in his voice. She couldn't decide if it was something extra or something lacking. She tried to weed it out.

"How's your sister?"

"No change, which for now, is a good thing."

"Is everything else okay?"

"I suppose. How about you?" His tone indicated he didn't really want to talk . . . maybe to her or just anybody in general. Suddenly, he surprised her, speaking with a little anger in his voice. "Have you been researching me?"

"No, Mr. Garrett," Her temper flared. He had researched her but she couldn't research him? "I have better things to do with my time." He bristled.

"Obviously, this isn't a social call. Was there something you wanted?"

"You're right, I didn't call just to irritate you. I thought you might be interested in a new client of mine . . . medium height, slight of build, green eyes . . ."

"What did he tell you?"

"You know I can't tell you that. That aside, he didn't say much of anything. I got the feeling he might not come back. I was also wondering if he knew about Jasmine and that I was seeing her."

"That's quite possible. He might have been feeling you out to see if you were a threat . . . or just so he'd know what you look like."

"Stop thinking out loud." In truth, Zeus hadn't spoken the last part but she had heard it anyway.

"I'm . . . I'm sorry. I didn't realize . . ." He was sure he hadn't done more than think those words.

"Don't worry about it. I've already thought about that myself."

"Isn't there some form or something he had to fill out that gives his address, employer, school, and all that?"

"Yes, but here's the thing. He resembles the composite, that doesn't make him the killer . . . perhaps just unlucky. If he really does have a problem and needs my help, I don't want him scared away . . ."

"I'll be discreet, Meg. For now I'll just watch him, unless he does see you again and admits everything."

Whether Daniel Newman came back or not, at least she was able to provide some information toward the investigation. It might not amount to anything but it might lead to something that would.

Chapter Five

A little more than a week later, Meg ran into Zeus as she headed into the police station and he was headed out. They stopped, with her one step above him.

"Hey, Zeus." She greeted him. "Did anything come of the information I gave you?"

"No." He shook his head. "We watched him for a while, checked his school attendance record and his part time work record, and asked about him . . . he's clean as far as we can tell."

"Poor guy. He was just lucky enough to fit the description. At least he's unaware, for a little while, he was a suspect." Zeus nodded his agreement, then changed the subject.

"Did you go to see my sister . . . talk to her doctors?" The question took her by surprise. She had to choose her words carefully.

"I haven't driven over there in a while. Why?"

"I went to see her yesterday. She was talking about an angel who came to see her one night and spoke to Al, whoever that is. The angel she described sounded a lot like you. Exactly like you, actually."

"I'm certainly not an angel!"

"What are you then?" She bristled.

"I'm not sure what you're implying Detective, but I don't have time for it." Meg trotted up the steps.

"Meg . . ." He caught up with her at the top. "I didn't mean anything . . . I just . . . Tammy described you so clearly . . . even your clothes . . . clothes I've seen you wear before. I don't mind that you went to see her, but why . . . not tell me?"

He thought she was lying to him. In a way she was. The situation was quickly becoming difficult. She had to tell him something, but what? How would he react? Why did she care?

"Zeus . . ." She closed her eyes, centering herself. "We can talk about this, but not now."

"Over dinner?" She nodded. "Where?"

"I know a place with decent food."

"Shall I pick you up?"

"Sure, come over."

"What time? Five-six?"

"Make it around seven." He nodded. "I've really got to go. See you then."

She proceeded into the building and he proceeded to the street. Inside, she signed in then headed toward Barry's office. She wondered exactly what she would, or should, tell Zeus later. Barry wasn't a lot of help. Knowing her family and their psychic abilities for years and being used to it, he didn't see a problem with telling Zeus everything. Meg was not so sure; she figured he'd probably run in fear . . . fear of her psychic abilities or fear of her mental state. He'd accept it, right, no problem. Right!

Zeus arrived that evening at 6:50. As he entered he got a whiff of the best aromatic smell he had inhaled in a long time. He saw the table set for two and smiled his appreciation.

"Does this place have decent prices?"

"Enough, so I eat here often."

"Is there anything I can do to help?" She had already entered the kitchen, returning with salad, pork chops, mixed vegetables, and rice on a tray.

"Dishes afterward." She grinned.

During the meal they made small talk, steering away from work topics. Then after dinner, though she tried to steer him away from it, insisting she had been joking, he insisted on helping with the dishes. When they settled in the living room, Clansey appeared, leaning in the doorway, grinning at her. She brought her attention back to Zeus only to see Clansey running a finger up Zeus' neck—causing him to shiver and rub his neck. Horrified she watched as Clansey moved to ruffle Zeus' hair.

"Clansey!"

"What? Who?" Zeus looked around.

"Nothing. Never mind."

"Who were you talking to? Who's Clansey? Is he the ghost?"

"Either that or my cat." She tried to joke it away.

"Do you have a cat?"

"No."

"I didn't think so. If you did, I'd know it. I'm seriously allergic to cats. So, it must have been a ghost."

She heaved a mental sigh. The time was at hand. No matter how many different ways she had imagined how the conversation would start, none of them felt right now. Her silence prompted him to start speaking.

"Let's start with something simply. Why Meg and not Abby?"

"My grandmother always called me Meg and it stuck."

"Is Meg your middle name or part of it?"

"No, she just said I looked like a Meg to her."

"Didn't your grandmother die before you were born?"

"Yes."

"So she was a spirit when she named you?" He was asking a question, but clarifying for himself. "Is Clansey a deceased relative?"

"Not that I'm aware of. He has unfinished business here and won't or can't cross over until it's finished."

"What is it . . . the unfinished business?"

"He has no idea."

"Why does he stay around you?" She shrugged.

"I guess because I can see and hear him. He's been here for a while and even though he finds it fun to be a prankster, I suppose it's also nice to talk to someone once in a while."

"How long have you . . ."

"Since I was quite small."

"You just see and hear ghosts?"

"No," she heaved an uneasy sigh, "there's a little more."

She did not want to get into it. On the other hand, now was as good a time as any and she may as well get it over with. She inhaled deeply and started.

"I can also feel emotions from others, hear their thoughts, see auras, project thoughts, astral travel, and heal, mentally, anyway. I can ease people's anguish, pain . . ." She drifted off.

He sat wordlessly, staring at her. No emotions showed on his face, but she felt his inner turmoil as he tried to absorb what he had heard. Everything she had said went around and around in his mind. As of yet, nothing positive or negative had attached itself to any of it. He was simply trying to grasp and comprehend it. As she looked at him she supposed it was a good sign he hadn't jumped up screaming that she was crazy or run screaming out of the apartment. Instantly, she knew what stuck out in his mind, as she thought it would.

"You're a healer? Can you . . ."

"No, Zeus, I can't heal your sister. It isn't what she wants. It isn't what she chose."

"What she chose?"

She placed her hand on his hand and slowly began to explain.

"Before we incarnate, we chart out what our lives here on earth will be like. No detail, no matter how miniscule, is left out. We choose our families, what country, state, region, our ethnic and social backgrounds, every bump and scrape along the way, every relationship, every pain and joy. We're well aware of how grueling these challenges on earth will be. That's why we build in five exit points or possible escape routes to declare ourselves finished here and head Home. These are five choices, ours to make of when and how to go Home."

"She's just chosen to give up?"

"Not exactly. She has learned all she can from this life on earth. She will cross over to the Other Side . . . what a lot call heaven . . . regroup and go from there."

"Go where from there?"

"She may choose to incarnate or she may want to stay."

"Tammy chose all her pain and suffering?" She nodded. "Why? Why would anyone choose something like that?"

"With pain and difficulty comes knowledge and growth here, on Earth, and on the Other Side. Besides, if everyone chose to be perfect, rich and healthy, we'd all be bored senseless."

"So, I chose her as my sister and the pain and agony of watching her suffer and losing her?" He inquired, angrily.

"I'm afraid so."

"And I chose . . ." He looked at her. Knowing what he wanted she moved her hand from his hand to his forearm and said his thoughts.

"You chose to be illegitimate and be plagued with issues of abandonment." She looked at him—first quizzically, then with understanding. "No, I didn't know that until right now." Meg assured Zeus. "However, it does make sense from a conversation that we had the other day."

"That's kind of creepy knowing you can read my mind and know things about me I may not want anyone to know."

"It's shut off most of the time. I don't invade people's privacy unless I have to."

"Okay," he inhaled, "so, back to my sister. You can't heal her because she chose to die now and like this?" She nodded. "Did you lie when you said you hadn't been to see her, and who is Al?"

"I told you I hadn't driven over there in a while and I haven't. I used astral travel, also called projection. Actually, I just intended to see if I could take some of her pain from her. I never intended for her to see me. Most people can't. Your sister is sensitive; whether she's always been or she became so because of the situation, I don't know. Honestly, as soon as I realized she saw me, I almost left."

"So, who is Al?"

"He's her Spirit Guide. Oh yeah, I'm suppose to tell you she's not in as much pain as you think. She spends a lot of time on the Other Side."

"You don't have to die to . . . go there?"

"No, you can go whenever you want but you can't read the charts in the Hall of Records . . . at least, not your own. By design, you forget what you charted for yourself and you can't read it until you're Home for good, or between incarnations." Zeus shook his head.

"I'm trying very hard to wrap my mind around this."

"Tammy said you'd be okay. I thought she meant with her crossing over, but she must have meant with this."

"I'm trying to be." He ran a hand through his hair. "Please explain about Spirit Guides."

"Okay. We have an animal Spirit Guide that we bring with us from the Other Side. The Animal Spirit Guide joins our Spirit Guide and our Angels in watching over us throughout our time on earth. This is referred to as our Totem.

As for our Spirit Guides, we all have one. It's someone we literally trusted with our soul on the Other Side, who agreed to be our constant, vigilant companion and helpmate when we made the choice to experience another lifetime on earth. They are with us from birth to death. They can't make us do anything. As their name suggests, they can only guide us. Whether we accept that guidance is up to us. They're that little voice telling us to take a different route to work or to do something we wouldn't normally do. What we shrug off as just instinct, or your conscience, or "something told me" is more than likely your Spirit Guide."

"And Tammy's is Al and she sees him and you see him. Where's mine?"

"Right behind you and to the left. Her name is Sheila. Mine is more beside me to the right. I call him Shim, short for Shimaniwa."

"How do you do it? How do you deal with seeing ghosts, spirits, Guides, and feeling and hearing things without going nuts?"

"I've been doing, seeing, and hearing since I was quite small. It's as natural to me as you walking down the street hearing people's voices, cars, planes . . . smelling all of the different smells, seeing all of the colors around you and yet you don't really see, hear, or smell any of it. Sometimes I forget myself and speak to them in front of other people . . . like with Clansey, tonight."

"Do you help them . . . cross over?"

"Sometimes."

"What about that thought projection thing? It's rather scary that someone can mess with your mind like that."

"I don't mess with people's minds. I rarely use it actually. But when I do, it's out of necessity and I can't make anyone do anything they don't want to or wouldn't do on their own." Without saying a word, she suggested he get a drink of water.

"I need a glass of water."

He headed toward the kitchen, passing Clansey, who was grinning at him. She then suggested that he put salt in the water. He started to reach for the shaker, then stopped. He then turned toward her, his eyes slightly larger than usual.

"Did you . . . ?" He shook his head.

"What?"

"I just had a thought. It was something very dumb."

"What was it?"

"Salting my water." His eyes grew large. "Did you . . . ?"

"I did, and see, if it's something you don't want to do, I can't make you."

"Please stop doing . . . that."

"I was just showing you. Unless it's an emergency, I won't do it again."

Zeus' Spirit Guide leaned down speaking quietly in his ear. Zeus looked at his watch, then at Meg.

"It's very late . . . almost one in the morning. I feel the need to see Tammy. Would you like to come?"

They left for the hospital. His Spirit Guide spoke to him and he parked in the emergency parking lot. They entered, passed through ER, took an elevator to the fifth floor, exited and walked into Tammy's room. She was awake and smiled weakly at—all of them.

"I knew they'd bring you, Zu. Hello again, Meg." Obviously, she had been told who Meg was as Meg hadn't introduced herself when she had been there before through astral travel.

"Hello, Tammy." Meg took her hand while Zeus bent down, kissing her temple.

"Zu, don't worry about me. I'll be leaving shortly." She stopped to catch her breath.

"Of course you will, Tam, and once you get your strength back . . ." She shook her head.

"No, Zeus, I don't mean that. I'll be leaving this body and going to a much better place. Al and Meg have eased my fears. I look forward to it now." Tears filled Zeus' eyes. "Please don't be sad Zu. I'll be pain free, healthy, happy, and I'll come around to check on you. I promise." She looked beyond them and smiled, then returned her gaze to Zeus.

"I love you." Closing her eyes she slipped away, the smile still on her lips.

Meg saw her enter the bright light. As Zeus held his sister's hand and openly cried. Meg left the room. At the nurse's station, Meg told them Tammy had passed away.

Chapter Six

The ride back to her apartment was fairly quiet. He seemed always on the verge of saying something but perhaps he was too busy blinking away tears. Meg wished he'd open up. The macho thing about men not showing emotions was ridiculous and she had all she could do to not read his thoughts or suggest he just let it all out so she sat facing forward, giving him sideways glances and kept her peace. When he did finally speak, she jumped.

"Who-who told me I had to go to the hospital?"

"Sheila, your Spirit Guide." He nodded. They fell into silence for several minutes.

"I'm glad. That's the only way I would have been able to say goodbye before she . . . left. Is she happy-there?"

"Yes, of course, everyone is. She's with friends and family . . . even pets that have crossed over. She's very happy and content."

"Good." He paused. "I want to know everything about the Other Side." He stopped at her apartment building. "When can we get together for that?"

"Now is as good a time as any." He looked at the clock on the dashboard.

"It's five in the morning."

"We can both sleep in tomorrow, can't we?" She knew he wouldn't sleep or even rest, at least until he knew about the Other Side.

"Are you sure?" She nodded smiling at him.

They talked for hours . . . while sitting in the living room, while making breakfast together, eating, doing dishes, and back sitting in the living room again. There Zeus leaned his head back on the couch trying to absorb everything.

"It's a lot, I know. If it interests you enough we can always go over it again another time. Maybe in smaller chunks." His head came up.

"If I'm interested?"

"You may decide it's all hogwash, I'm crazy, and the further and faster you get away from me, the better."

"I'm happy knowing Tammy isn't dead; end of story. She's happy on the Other Side." He rested his head back against the couch.

"Her body did die. Her soul, her spirit, her essence has crossed over." She clarified. With no response, she looked over to find Zeus' eyes closed. She eased him down, covering him with the couch blanket. He smiled faintly.

"I think you're crazy, but so cute!" She smiled at him, resisting the urge to pat his head.

"Thanks-I think."

As she climbed into bed, she wondered if he really thought she was seriously crazy. He wouldn't be the first, or the last.

"Good morning." Clansey sat on the counter, smiling at her as she entered the kitchen.

"Good morning, Clansey." Meg mumbled as she made coffee. She hadn't slept.

"I see your boyfriend spent the night." He teased.

"I'm not in the mood, Clansey."

"Mortals!" That had always made her smile. Now was no exception. "He's angry."

"About last night?" She asked in surprise.

"No, he is more confused about that. He's angry about his father. He's been angry for a long time."

"Is that the darkness you see around him?"

"Partially. There's still something else though. Can't put my finger on it yet."

"Evil dark?"

"Appears to be." He inhaled deeply. "Man, that stuff smells good."

Meg poured two cups of coffee placing one on the counter beside him. He couldn't drink it but he could enjoy the aroma. Taking her cup, she leaned against the counter sipping the hot aromatic brew.

"I don't feel that." Her brows knit together.

"Maybe it's his name." Clansey offered.

"Zeus was the Greek God of Gods, not of War, like many think."

With mussed hair, not yet fully awake, Zeus entered the kitchen.

"I'm not Greek, I don't think. As for being a god . . . Your Eminence will do."

Clansey chuckled. She rolled her eyes at both Clansey and Zeus. A tiny smile played on her lips.

"Not a chance!" He shrugged, helping himself to a cup of coffee. He nodded toward the full cup on the counter.

"Clansey?" She nodded. "Can he . . ."

"No, but he enjoys the smell." From the counter Clansey greeted Zeus. "He says good morning."

Zeus looked around. Meg pointed to where Clansey sat grinning, clearly amused.

"Good morning, Clansey." It almost sounded natural.

"Why were you named Zeus?" He shrugged.

"Just one more thing for me to deal with, I guess."

"At least you're not some scrawny guy with that name."

"No, but I had to fight just as hard because of it."

"Did Tammy feel abandoned by your father?"

"No, she didn't care who her father was. She said she was here and that's all that mattered."

"She's right about that. Is it a guy thing . . . is that why it bothers you?"

"A guy thing." He repeated. "Perhaps from your head shrinking point of view." The words held no malice. Clansey laughed, clapping his hands. Meg shot him a look.

"Why didn't she feel abandoned?"

"Probably because she was treated differently. I wasn't exactly what was ordered, being a male.

Maybe she looked, acted, sounded less like him."

"Do you know anything about your father at all?"

"Not a thing. My mother refuses to talk about him. I've often wondered if I look like him."

"Was your mother not affectionate?"

"Let's say she wasn't as affectionate with me, though she wasn't cold and indifferent."

"Just lacking." He nodded sadly. Again she wanted to hold him and absorb his pain. Again she refrained.

"Were you a difficult child?"

"I suppose." He shrugged. "I got into a lot of fights from a young age either about my name or the fact I didn't have a father like the other boys." He looked up, then at her. "Why don't you just . . . find out about this on your own?"

"Because you need to work through it yourself."

"Wonderful. I try not to think about it."

"But you do, anyway." Clansey appeared beside her.

"I'm outta here." He stood beside Zeus, patting him on the shoulder. Zeus shivered. "Your Eminence." Meg smiled.

"Clansey is leaving. He patted your shoulder and called you Your Eminence."

"Bye, Clansey. See you later . . . or not." Zeus chuckled. With a wave of his hand, Clansey disappeared. As soon as his eyes met hers again, she asked a question.

"Are you in any kind of a relationship?" He held her gaze, his mind flipping through possible answers. Suddenly, he broke into a grin.

"Are you asking if I'm attached?! Are you trying to find out because you're interested? Do you want to apply for the job?" He teased. Her gaze never wavered.

"Are you?"

"I am not attached to anyone in any way." That spoke volumes.

"Why?"

"Good question, especially since I'm such a good catch." Still looking into his eyes, she waited . . .

"I don't know."

"Yes, you do."

"None of them . . . we didn't . . ."

"What?" He shrugged.

"They weren't what I was looking for."

"Why?"

"I don't know."

"Yes, you do. What are you looking for?" He was irritated.

"Look . . . why don't you just . . . get the answers your way?"

"Because you have to work through this. Why didn't any of them work out?"

"Because . . ." He left the rest hanging, looking away.

"Because?" She prompted.

"I'm afraid of commitment okay? Are you happy now?"

"Nice try, though partially true. Why would you be afraid . . ."

"I'm afraid I'll get stuck with someone like my mother!"

"Now we're getting somewhere! And?" His irritation flared.

"Is this how you do it-you badger your patients until they tell you everything?" She wouldn't take the bait.

"And?" His irritation deflated as suddenly as it had risen.

"I'm afraid I'll abandon them like my father did us." He briefly rested his forehead in his palms. Without raising his head, he continued. "Maybe he couldn't take my mother's cool affection. Maybe she was just a one night stand. Maybe he was just passing through. Maybe he couldn't take the responsibility. Maybe he doesn't even know about Tammy and me." He raised his head. "Maybe he did and didn't care." She gently asked the next question.

"Why does it bother you that he wasn't around?"

"I was the only kid on the block without a father. In school there were others, but their fathers had the decency to die, not run off. Why wasn't I good enough to love?"

And there it was. He was emotionally abandoned by his mother and physically abandoned by his father. To a child it was somehow his fault. In Zeus' case, he wasn't deserving of their love. That had carried over into his adult life. Regardless of the relationship level, he didn't feel worthy of anyone's love, eventually they'd also realize that and leave him. So, he had left them—ended the relationship before that happened.

"Zeus," she gently placed her hand on his, absorbing some of the pain he felt, "it wasn't you. He abandoned your mother. And whether he knew it or not, he left her to give birth to twins and raise two children on her own. I'm sure her dreams of a family were dashed. In the best of circumstances, that isn't easy to handle." She let that sink in for a minute. "I'm a firm believer that nothing happens for nothing. If your father had stuck around, you may have learned some unsavory things from him that would have made you less of a man. Kids learn what they live. The abused child swears they'll never treat their kids like they were treated but a stressor can bring it out. That's the only way they know how to deal with it . . . by example."

"So, chances are, I'll abandon my family or not be warm and loving towards them because that's what I've learned?"

"There is that chance. However, you're aware of it. Not all abused children grow up to abuse their children. The cycle can be broken Zeus."

"But I won't know until I get to that point; and, if I don't make the grade, I'm just continuing the cycle through my children. That's one hell of a risk!"

"Life is one hell of a risk! With all of the pain, uncertainty, joy, and happiness, I wouldn't miss a second of it!"

"What doesn't kill you makes you stronger?"

"Learning and growing from all those experiences makes you stronger. If you get to that point and realize you're about to continue the cycle, you can stop yourself and change directions, seek counseling, any number of things."

"If I can stop myself." He wasn't going to crack easily. Up to this point, he had trained himself too well.

"You can. I have faith in you, Zeus." His expression clearly showed he thought her faith was misplaced.

Meg met with Jasmine again, later in the week. They had been sitting in the living room talking about her dolls, dreams, and playing with the other children when, as usually happens, she opened up a little more, taking Meg by surprise.

"I was with my daddy when he met with another woman. She didn't pay any attention to me or Zeus at all."

"There was someone else there? A man? What did he look like?"

"No man . . . a dog . . . his name was Zeus."

"What kind of dog was it?"

"Big. Ugly."

"What did the woman look like?"

"Tall. Pretty. Skinny. Big nose. Blue eyes. She smelled nice, too. Daddy liked her a lot."

"What made you think that?"

"He held her hand the whole time and he kissed her when she left."

"Did they talk about anything? Do you know her name?"

"They talked about money, her husband, and her kid. She didn't sound nice when she talked to daddy. He called her Honey. I don't think she liked him as much. I think she was mad at him."

"Why would she be angry with him? Were they fighting?"

"She didn't sound happy. Most of the time her teeth were closed. She wanted daddy to leave something but he wouldn't. She's not a nice lady."

"Maybe she was just upset." Meg offered. Jasmine shook her head.

"She said she'd kill him and let Zeus have him for dinner." Meg and Zeus looked at each other.

Chapter Seven

Meg didn't think much of that. After all, lots of people said similar things when they were angry. However, usually the person they said it to didn't get murdered.

"Know what?" Jasmine's voice brought her back from her thoughts. "The man . . . at my house . . . kinda sounded like her."

He sounded like a woman?

"He spoke?" She hadn't mentioned that before. "What did he say?"

"Die!"

In a highly emotional state a man's voice could rise a couple of octaves. Meg watched Jasmine start to emotionally withdraw. She spoke comfortingly to her which eased some of the turmoil inside the child, enough so she climbed on her lap. Laid her head against her chest and softly cried. It was the first real emotion Jasmine had shown.

Over the next week they spoke a fair amount of her parents-peaceful, loving memories she should hold dear. Meg knew she needed some type of closure and felt her way through how Jasmine would handle going to the funeral.

She concluded she'd be okay and started asking about relatives. Jasmine had no memory of grandparents, aunts, uncles, or cousins. Child Protective Services couldn't find any either. She hated to see her stay in the system for the next several years.

"Where have you been? I haven't heard from you all week!" Zeus didn't sound happy.

"I've been busy working, otherwise fine."

"Great! Anything more on Jasmine?" She bristled. He hadn't called her to see if she was okay. He had called angry that she hadn't reported to him.

"I wasn't aware I *had* to report to you! Show me where that's written and I'll gladly submit a weekly report to your in-box! That aside, I have given you the professional courtesy of passing along information that's pertinent. There hasn't been anything. I haven't called."

"Meg . . ."

"I'm rather busy right now. When I have something I'll call you." She hung up before he could say more.

"What happens when people die?" Meg asked Jasmine.

"They go to heaven, if they're good."

"What if they aren't good?"

"They go . . . you know . . . to live with the devil." She studied Meg for a minute with eyes full of wisdom well beyond her years. "Mommy and Daddy were good so they will go to heaven. When are we going?"

"Where?" She thought she was asking when the two of them would go to heaven.

"To bury Mommy and Daddy so they can go to heaven."

Jasmine had a knack of knowing what she was thinking. Meg found this curious and wondered about it. It may just be that Mary, or one of the other children, had been talking to her about people dieing and being buried. Still, she wanted to check it out at some point.

"Have you ever been to a funeral . . . where they bury people?" Jasmine shook her head. "Next week . . ."

"Will you come with me?"

"Of course! I'll be right there beside you."

Days later, as they drove to the cemetery, Meg wondered how Jasmine would handle it. Parking the car they started walking across the lawn toward two freshly dug graves with two caskets waiting beside each one. A few people were there-neighbors who had known Jasmine's parents-perhaps ten people plus the minister.

She stood beside Jasmine firmly holding her little hand in hers waiting to absorb whatever she needed to that would help her get through the ordeal. Meg felt emotions pass through Jasmine—sadness . . . curiosity . . . recognition. Recognition! Was the killer here? . . . She looked at Jasmine. On the other side of Jasmine stood Zeus. Jasmine was looking up at him, a faint smile on her lips as she reached up and took his hand, then solemnly faced forward as the ceremony started.

Meg saw things most people couldn't. A glance at Jasmine showed apparently she didn't either. Her parents were there as well as one of her Angels, wings wrapped protectively around her. At the end she heard Jasmine ever so quietly say "Goodbye." Again she wondered if she had seen her parents spirits, or felt the Angel's wings.

In silence the three of them walked back to where the cars were parked. Jasmine didn't let go of their hands. If anything, she held on firmer as memories of her parents flooded her mind. They stood by Meg's car, each still with a small hand in theirs. Meg was letting Jasmine's memories pass through her and Zeus waited for Jasmine to release his hand when she was ready to.

In the meantime, they looked at each other until Zeus finally looked away and asked, "Are you ready to go, Honey?" Jasmine released their hands to hug Zeus around his leg.

"Yes." She released him, taking Meg's hand again.

Zeus went to his car, and Meg went to her car, putting Jasmine in the car seat. Before withdrawing from the car, Meg kissed Jasmine on her temple then got behind the wheel.

"Ready?"

Without expecting an answer she started the car, pulled away from the curb, circling around heading for the exit. She drove watching the road and checking on Jasmine through the rear view mirror, who sat looking out the window at nothing in particular. Her cell phone ringing interrupted her.

"How is she?"

"Fine."

"She seemed to take it quite well. Is she aware of what was going on?"

"Yes, she had a fair grip on the whole thing. I absorbed some of the sadness for her."

"Why didn't you take it all?"

"It's a part of healing. I left some for her own healing."

"I wish I could do that."

"Be careful what you ask for Zeus."

"Meg?" Jasmine's small voice came from the back seat.

"Yes, Dear?"

"Are you and that man married?"

"What man?"

"The one that was with us."

"Zeus?" Jasmine giggled.

"That's a dog's name. He's big but he isn't ugly." She heard Zeus chuckle through the phone.

"You can call him Detective or Mister Garrett if you want to and no, we're not married." She spoke to Zeus.

"You liked that did you?"

"I've been called worse!"

"Is he your boyfriend?" Zeus chuckled in her ear again.

"No, he isn't. We're friends."

"Do you live together?"

"No, we don't."

"I'll let you go so the two of you can talk."

"Okay, Zeus. I'll talk with you later." She closed the phone and glanced back at Jasmine through the mirror.

"Too bad."

"Why?"

"I'd like to live with you and him."

"You're not happy with Mary?"

"Yeah, but I'd rather live with you and Mr. Garrett."

What could she say? There was nothing to say. Obviously Jasmine had attached herself to the two people that had been the first ones to make her feel safe. Zeus had rescued her from the closet she had hidden in while her parents were being murdered. And, she had made Jasmine feel safe by reaching out to her letting her know she could trust her. It was only natural that Jasmine would want to stay with them.

As Meg dropped Jasmine off, staying with her a few minutes, Jasmine asked if she could stay longer. She couldn't but promised she'd be back in a couple days.

For whatever reason, Jasmine's words stuck with her. She had even imagined a situation where she and Zeus arranged to be roommates just for her. Meg had to shake herself hard mentally to rid herself of such thoughts. They kept slipping back into her head the next day when she met Zeus.

"Was she okay afterward?"

"Aside from normal sadness she seems to be dealing well with her parents going to heaven and being happy there."

"Is there any other news?"

"She reaffirmed her father had a girlfriend. She was with him once when he met with the girlfriend . . . and her dog, Zeus."

"A big, ugly dog!" He chuckled as she nodded.

"She didn't hear a name but said she was tall, pretty, skinny, had a big nose and blue eyes, and she smelled good. Other than that she wasn't happy about something-her dad not leaving something. They talked about money, her husband, and her kid. She talked with clenched teeth, offered to kill him and feed him to the dog."

"Every man's dream girlfriend!"

"Jasmine also mentioned that the girlfriend sounded like the man who killed her parents. Most people, in a highly emotional state, have raised pitches to their voice. He only said, "Die!"

"True. Do you suppose it could have been her husband?"

"That thought crossed my mind. Why kill the wife, too? Wouldn't it make more sense to catch the husband alone rather than kill them both?"

"If he knew about the wife. He may have assumed the guy his wife was fooling around with was single."

"Obviously he didn't stake him out once he found out where he lived or he would have seen him with his wife and child at some point."

"A rage killing. Normally he'd have killed the man, then the woman if he had to. I don't know what he would have done if he had seen Jasmine."

"Is there a way to know who was shot first?"

"It appears she was first, the husband woke and was sitting up when he was shot and fell back at an angle."

"Why her first?"

"Probably woke up hearing the killer's footsteps or something."

"Poor Jasmine saw the whole thing." Meg sympathized.

"Yes, from her parent's closet. Why wasn't she in her own room?"

"What if we're looking at this wrong? What if the target was the mother? Or a robbery gone wrong and their deaths have nothing to do with anything except they woke up? The robber killed them, feared someone heard and ran off before stealing anything and didn't know either of them."

"Have you always secretly wanted to be a detective?" He gave her a half smile.

"If I had, apparently I would not have been good at it as obviously you've already thought of those things." The half smile became whole. "I suppose that's why you're the detective and I'm the shrink."

"Well, let me go back and ask co-workers and neighbors if they recognize the description of the woman . . . and her dog. Maybe I'll get lucky."

The next day Meg decided she'd see Jasmine at the end of the day. That way if she stayed longer she wasn't keeping another client waiting. Her last client at the office was Daniel Newman. He spoke of little things-his childhood in a vague way, his half sister, his parents in passing. She was sure, just under the surface, was his real reason for seeing her. As she shook his hand before he left, his thoughts were of wondering if he should say anything . . . about what, wasn't clear. Looking into his eyes as she told him she'd see him the following week, she saw his green eyes get greener and for a split second his facial features changed. For that fraction of time, she knew she was looking at the killer. With that thought, Daniel's face reappeared. With no way to prove it, she was positive he knew the killer.

"You know, Daniel, if you need to talk with me before next week, you can always make another appointment." He only nodded and left the room.

Meg made notes, filed them in his folder, made sure her office was in order and stepped into the reception area. She made a point of letting Luce, the secretary, know if Mr. Newman wanted to make an earlier appointment she was to shift appointments around and get him in ASAP.

What she had experienced swirled around her mind as she drove out to see Jasmine. It wasn't any wonder she didn't make much progress with Daniel. He knew something horrible, he wanted to tell someone, but he was scared. Whether it was of the killer, or what could happen to him for not reporting it sooner, she didn't know.

What she was sure of was that she had seen the killer as real as if he had been standing right there in front of her. Somehow Daniel was associated with the killer. It could be someone he knew well or just in passing . . . a friend of a friend type of thing. Either way, she had to try and make sure he came back to see her. She feared, however, he was too scared, might change his mind, and be lost to her.

Chapter Eight

Jasmine ran to Meg as soon as she stepped into the house. She wrapped her arms around her waist looking up at her, beaming as though she knew something Meg didn't.

"My goodness, you're certainly excited about something! What's going on?" Jasmine shrugged, still smiling up at her.

"She's been like that all day." Mary said. "It's like she's been waiting for something only she knew was going to happen."

"Well, my little friend," Meg smoothed her hair, "how would you like to go swimming?" Jasmine squealed with excitement.

"She doesn't have a suit." Mary told her.

"That's okay, I'll get her one."

Within minutes Meg and Jasmine were headed to town. Jasmine chatted excitedly, stopping briefly as they passed the apartment building she had lived in with her parents. After a few minutes of silence she seemed to have come to terms with her emotions and started chatting again.

She was a whirlwind of excitement as they shopped for a bathing suit, flotation devices, and beach toys. Finally on their way, Jasmine wanted to know where they were going. Meg told her they were going to Crystal Lake, a place she'd been going to since she was a little girl.

"Will there be a lot of people there?"

"I don't think so. There aren't many people who know about it as far as I know."

"Why not?"

"Probably because it's too far for most people to drive."

That seemed to satisfy her. Her eyes got big when Meg pulled off the road driving through tall grass. Without a lot of traffic there wasn't a path but Meg knew exactly where to go. Just before the sand started and well out of sight of the road she stopped the car. For a few seconds she looked out over the lake. No matter how many times she'd been there the beauty always amazed her.

They climbed out of the car and Meg helped Jasmine into her bathing suit and flotation device; she grabbed the toys, towels, a blanket, and the picnic basket with fruit and drinks. Together they walked the few yards to the beach.

They spent a long time splashing around in the water, building sand castles, making designs in the sand with sticks and chasing each other around. All the while Meg was aware of the shadows, spirits, and ghosts around them but she paid no more attention to them than she did the grass or trees.

Meg and Jasmine finally settled on the blanket and began eating grapes and apple slices, and drinking juice. Meg felt it before she heard a vehicle. Even Jasmine glanced back the way they had driven in and smiled just before a car pulled in following the path Meg's car had made. Both watched, unsurprised, as Zeus exited his car, a broad smile on his face. Jasmine ran to him wrapping her arms around his waist.

"Mr. Garrett!" She squealed.

"I'm not interrupting, am I?"

"No, come join us." He didn't have a choice as Jasmine was pulling him by his hand in Meg's direction. "You must really need to relax if you drove all the way out here."

"It never hurts to relax but I just had an urge to come. Somehow I knew you'd be here."

"Have you always secretly wanted to be psychic?" She grinned at him, eliciting one in return.

"If I have, I apparently would not be very good at it or I would have . . ." He looked at Jasmine. ". . . solved this case already."

"All in good time." Meg handed him some fruit and juice. "When exactly did you get the urge to come here?"

"A couple hours ago or so. Why?"

"I saw Daniel Newman today and as soon as I brought Jasmine back I was going to call you. That was a couple hours ago."

"Did you summon me here?"

"No," She chose her words carefully. "I wouldn't discuss one client . . ." She glanced at Jasmine and back to him. ". . . in front of another client."

"Mr. Garrett, look at the castle we made!" Zeus stood offering to help Meg cleanup.

"Go ahead, I'll put the food away and join you in a minute."

Meg had almost finished when Clansey appeared. At first he didn't say anything as he watched Zeus and Jasmine playing. A sad smile formed on his lips.

"Did you have children?"

"I had a little girl. She died twenty years ago."

"I'm sorry."

"She was eighty-four."

"Oh!"

"She was still my little girl. I think she knew when I was around but she never saw or heard me. Hell, she may not have even remembered me. She was five when I died. I thought that was why I was hanging around." He shrugged. "Guess not."

"Did she have any children?"

"A whole brood . . . nine . . . five boys . . . four girls."

"Wow!"

"Yeah . . . wow!" A mischievous grin spread across his face. "Duck!" Instead of ducking she followed his gaze just as water splashed her. "Go play."

"Come on!" Zeus called to her with a giggling Jasmine beside him.

A water splashing war ensued with a lot of laughter, chasing, and squeals. Finally, they collapsed on the blanket exhausted and laughing. Jasmine sat between them with a look of contentment. Zeus looked slightly melancholy and Meg was just happy everyone was enjoying themselves.

"I'm hungry." Jasmine announced.

"Well," Zeus ruffled her hair, "we'll just have to find a place to eat, won't we?"

"Let me check with Mary." Meg already had her phone out and was dialing. A few minutes later she snapped it shut. "We're all set."

They gathered their things. Then Meg and Jasmine went behind some bushes so Meg could help Jasmine change back into regular clothes. Then they met Zeus by the cars.

"I'm going to buy Jasmine some clothes first. We can meet you somewhere to eat."

"I may as well go home and change. I can call you in an hour to see if you're ready and we can decide where we want to eat then."

"Sounds good. I'll talk with you in an hour."

They got into their vehicles, and with Zeus following Meg and Jasmine, they headed for town. Jasmine happily chatted for a few minutes then fell silent. Meg checked on her through the rear view mirror and found she had fallen asleep. Her romping around in and out of the water had worn her out.

When they stopped at a store, Jasmine woke up and was ready to shop with renewed energy after her power nap. Meg had only intended to get her an outfit. She ended up getting four outfits, underwear, socks, and two pairs of shoes along with some barrettes, rubber bands, and head bands. She couldn't resist as there were so many cute things for little girls. They were just leaving the store when Zeus called.

"Sorry I'm late." Meg looked at her watch. It had been an hour and a half. "Have you been waiting long?"

"Actually, we're just leaving the store. I bought her more than I intended but I couldn't help it . . . everything is so cute!"

"Women and shopping!" He heaved an exaggerated sigh. "Any ideas where you ladies want to eat?"

"Let me see if the little lady has any ideas." She looked into the rear view. "Jasmine, where would you like to eat?"

"Denny's!" She shouted with enthusiasm.

"That was loud and clear!" Zeus commented.

"A little surprising, too. I expected she'd rattle off one of the popular hamburger joints. We'll head to my place to change and head out to meet you as soon as possible."

"Or I could meet you at your place and we can all ride together."

"We're probably going to be a little while. Are you sure you want to wait around for us?"

"No problem . . . I'll just chat with Clansey while I wait."

"As you wish, Sir. See you at my place in a few then."

By the time Meg and Jasmine pulled into the parking lot Zeus was already there. As soon as Jasmine was set on the ground she ran to hug him. Sliding her hand in his she held her free hand out toward Meg, expectantly. Meg shifted the bags with Jasmine's clothes to her other hand so she could take Jasmine's hand. Together the three of them walked into the apartment building. Mrs. Northrop was just leaving; she stopped to look at them and smiled.

"You have a beautiful family, Meg. I didn't know . . ."

"Thank you!" Zeus replied. Meg reddened slightly.

They by-passed each other and the conversation was over.

"I'm going to have some explaining to do at some point!"

"If Mr. Garrett and I stay they'll think we really are a family."

Meg looked from Jasmine to Zeus, who was looking at her with an expression that said "Now what?!"

"Let's get ready to go before I'm a grandmother!"

Meg ran Jasmine through a quick bath to get any remaining sand out of her hair and off her body. She dressed her in her new clothes and was about to brush her hair when Zeus offered to do that while Meg got ready. By the time she entered the living room, Jasmine's hair had been brushed, put into two ponytails with a barrette on either side. There wasn't a hair out of place.

"Great job! You're so beautiful Jasmine!" The child beamed at her. "You're a natural Zeus. You may even be able to give up your day job."

"I'll take that under consideration. Now let's go . . . we're starving!"

They left the building as they had entered. Jasmine walked between them, each of her hands holding one of theirs, a happy expression on her face.

Seated at Denny's, their waitress brought them each a menu, commented on how pretty Jasmine looked, then took both Meg and Zeus in simultaneously.

"You have a beautiful family."

"Thank you!" Jasmine piped up, giving the waitress a dazzling smile. Meg smiled feeling as though she were being over ridden in the matter.

Together they brought Jasmine back to Mary's. She wanted to stay with them and her unhappiness showed in her pouting lower lip. Meg contemplated getting her for the weekend but she was already getting more involved with the little girl than was professionally acceptable. She had to restrain herself even though she had fallen in love with her by their second visit.

"You look almost as sad as she did." Zeus observed as Meg got back in the car.

"I think I am. She's such a wonderful child. I hate leaving her even after our sessions."

"You love her." It was a statement, not a question.

"Yes, I'm afraid I do. By all rights, knowing that, I should back away, let someone else take over. Jasmine wouldn't understand that. It would confuse her and quite possibly she'd shut down again. I hate to think how she'd turn out in the years to come if she bottled all that turmoil up forever. It would manifest in one way or another. The scars she'll always have will be bad enough."

"How do you deal with the kids you work with? They must pull at your heart."

"They do, but most have loving families. Sometimes it's their parents and sometimes it's relatives. Jasmine had neither . . . just a house full of strangers . . . all wonderful, but not hers."

"Does she like it there?"

"She's never really said otherwise."

"Which means she has said something?"

"Well, yes." Meg was starting to feel uncomfortable.

"Which was?"

"She has asked if . . . she could live with me . . . and you, again."

"How does she think that will work?"

"She wants us to . . . live together so she can live with both of us."

"Interesting." Zeus mused. "Nothing about being married?"

"She's asked if we were, or at least dating. Finding out we weren't doing either, she settled for us living together, I guess."

"What a focused little mind!" Meg heard the humor in his voice.

"You don't have to enjoy the dilemma so much!"

"I'm sorry." He cleared his throat but a glance at him showed his smile. "I've just never been proposed to by a four year old."

"But you *have* been proposed to?" She knew that would change the subject. He shifted uncomfortably, clearing his throat again.

"How about we go out to eat tomorrow night?"

"How about an answer?"

"That's what I'm trying for." Avoidance. Uncomfortable. Too personal.

"I'd love to Zeus."

"Do you have a place you like?" He was clearly glad the subject had been changed.

"Not really, I don't go out much."

"How about Applebee's or Claim Jumper? Have you been to either of those?"

"No, but I hear they're both very good."

"We'll start with Applebee's, then." A thought occurred to her.

"Zeus, is this a date?"

"It does fall under that category, yes."

"Yes, yes it does."

"Does that bother you? It doesn't mean we're exclusive or anything. It doesn't commit us or anything."

"It doesn't bother me in the least." Apparently, it suddenly bothered him. "Do we dress up, or jeans and a t-shirt?"

"Either would be appropriate for Applebee's. However, let's dress up a little. I don't think either one of us gets to do that very often."

"That sounds like fun! A little dressy it is then!"

From the moment he arrived to pick her up he seemed on edge. Something was clearly bothering him. Perhaps, she thought, he was bothered more by calling this a date than she was. For half of the evening he talked around what was really bothering him. Finally, with the meal finished, lingering over dessert and coffee, she questioned him.

"What's bothering you, Zeus?"

"Nothing. Why?" He answered quickly. Too quickly.

Meg just looked at him, watching him physically fidget and feeling him mentally squirm.

"I may be able to help." She offered.

His eyes locked on hers for a long minute as he tried to decide if he should tell her. He looked down at his half-eaten cherry pie, briefly pushing a cherry around the plate with his fork, then speared it and ate it. Meg sipped her coffee, waiting.

Chapter Nine

She felt him bolstering himself from his feet up. He inhaled deeply, quietly to carry it up to his chest and exhaled slowly as it spread to his head. Clearly he didn't confide in someone often, if at all.

"It's . . . um . . . there's . . ." He stopped, looking up at the ceiling, then back down, but not at her, speaking in a rush. "There's someone I'm interested in."

He finally let his eyes slide to meet hers. She was surprised to see he was looking for a reaction from her. How was she suppose to react?

"That's good, isn't it?" He didn't answer. "How long have you been interested in her?"

"A couple of months." He shrugged, still watching her.

"Have you said anything to her? She knows, right?"

"No and no."

"Why not?" He shrugged. "Taking it slow is good. Have you asked her out . . . casually?" He nodded.

"Mainly work-related lunches . . . a couple after-hour meals."

"You work together! That's great, isn't it? She likes you, right? You get along?"

"We butt heads but lately we seem to be getting along better."

Still he watched her, waiting for some kind of reaction. Puzzled, Meg took in his entire face, one section at a time . . . . eyes, mouth, chin, and skin coloring. Was he expecting her to be jealous? The thought shocked her. There was no reason in this world, or another world, for her to be jealous.

"Well," she reached over patting his hand, "keep working on it. Maybe step up to dinner and a movie, or a concert. Let her see you off duty."

"Yeah," he nodded. "I'll do that."

"Does she show any signs of liking you back?"

"Beyond work? Beyond casually? Not really."

"Does she have a boyfriend? I trust you'd know if she was married."

"She isn't married and I'm quite sure there's no boyfriend."

"You really like her, don't you?" He covered her hand with his, looking intently at her, again searching for a reaction.

"Yes and that scares me." He removed his hand rubbing it over his chin and along his jaw.

That was it. It had to be. He was watching for her to pick up on his fear of getting into a relationship, then ruining it when it became too serious as he had done twice before.

"Zeus, follow this wherever it leads and remember I'm always here to help you if you need or want it."

He leaned back, exhaling. She picked up on relief and irritation, which confused her slightly. His tone was about the same.

"Thank you, Meg. I appreciate it."

Over a last cup of coffee they talked of different things. He looked at his watch, drained his cup, and looked at Meg with half a smile.

"It's early, yet . . . how about a movie or something?"

They did go to see a movie. The new vampire movie that was all the rage at the time. The "something" was something else.

"Hey," Zeus nudged her, "wanna bite me?"

"I'm a . . . witch, not a vampire!" He shrugged as if he couldn't see the difference.

"So, wanna bite me?" He stretched his neck toward her. "Come on, bite me." Meg giggled.

"Shhh!" The collective sound from the audience made her giggle harder.

"Yeah, shhh." She managed. Zeus settled down for a few minutes, then he leaned over again, whispering.

"Are there such things . . . vampires, I mean?"

"No . . . , well yes, but not like this." She nodded toward the screen. "There are people who need regular blood transfusions . . ."

"Yeah, I've heard about that."

In silence, they finished the movie. As the music played and the credits rolled, they remained seated, waiting for the theater to empty a little.

"How about aliens?"

"That's playing across the hall."

"Are there really aliens?"

"Please don't tell me you think we're the only planet or galaxy to have intelligent life."

"So there are?" She stood to join the line leaving the theater. He followed.

"Of course."

"Seriously? Are they among us?"

"Definitely. They always have been." She nodded toward the back where people waited to merge with the line of people leaving. "Some are even here."

Zeus scanned those people then everyone else there. He squinted his eyes as though that would help him see them better. She smiled hearing his thoughts.

"Amazing how they look just like us, huh?"

"You're serious?" He asked as they made their way into the lobby.

"Very."

Once outside he scanned people as they walked down the sidewalk toward the car. She wasn't sure who stopped first, her or him. All she knew for sure was she saw a spirit across the street staring at her. And there was no one or anything around Meg. She glanced around and saw to her right a man and woman, and even though they were talking, the woman was also staring across the street towards the spirit. Following her gaze, Meg realized the woman also saw the spirit. It was obvious she wasn't used to seeing them because from what Meg could see of the woman from her three-quarter profile, she was quite surprised. Then again, it may have been because the woman wasn't used to seeing spirits with such darkness and foreboding surrounding them. Slowly, Meg let her eyes go back across the street. The spirit was definitely there to speak to Meg as the spirit was concentrating her stare at Meg and nowhere else.

"Oh, great!"

Zeus' preoccupation with the people milling around stopped abruptly and his eyes turned to her. His eyes followed her gaze but all he saw was the tree, some bushes, and flowers.

"What? Is Clansey over there?"

"No, it isn't Clansey." Her eyes never left the spirit.

"Who is it?" He tried to see it but couldn't.

"I don't know . . . we haven't been formerly introduced."

"Is it an alien?"

"Definitely not."

"Does it need your help?"

"No, she wants something."

"Like what?"

"I don't know yet. She hasn't told me. But she's not here on a mission of mercy."

"Does she want to hurt you?"

"I don't think so. I think she's a warning."

Meg glanced back at the woman to her right. Though trying to appear normal, she kept looking across the street.

She blinked several times then stopped looking. Meg glanced across the street. The spirit was gone.

"Let's get out of here." She hooked her arm in his and started walking toward the car.

"Is she gone?"

"Yes, for now. I'm sure I'll see her again though."

In the car, just after buckling in, Meg suddenly pressed her body against the backrest, inhaling sharply. The head and upper torso of the woman spirit from across the street was suddenly in front of her. After the initial surprise, she relaxed.

"What do you want?'

"What?" Zeus asked in surprise.

"Him." The spirit answered.

"Him who?" She asked.

"Him who, what?" Zeus asked, noticing she was staring straight ahead but not looking at anything outside of the car. "We're not alone, are we?" She shook her head. "Is it . . . her?"

"Yes." Zeus turned in his seat slightly and leaned toward her a fraction. The spirit leaned toward her more than a fraction. Meg didn't move away.

"Get out of my face." She spoke firmly.

Zeus moved back quickly, eyes slightly wider. The spirit smiled, hesitated and moved back. From her deadlock stare straight ahead of her, he realized she hadn't been speaking to him.

"I'm not your first." The spirit stated.

"No, you're not my first and you won't be my last. Now, him who and what do you want with him?" She feared she knew who she was referring to. She watched her glance at Zeus, then back to her. She'd been right.

"What do you want with him?" The spirit smiled slightly and faded away.

"What was that all about? What did she want?"

She looked at Zeus for a long minute. She was angry for no apparent reason. She had to sort things out. Noting her irritated and angry expression, he asked another question.

"What's going on Meg?"

"Just take me home, please."

It wasn't a long ride, yet with the silence and her unexplained anger, it seemed to take forever. Zeus thankfully had the sense to remain quiet as she sorted through her sudden mood swing. By the time he parked outside her apartment building she had beaten it down inside her but knew it wouldn't take much for it to surface again.

"Would you like to come up?" Her tone was just this side of irritated. Knowing he was about to refuse she tried to soften it. "Please?"

"Are you sure?" Her anger flared.

"I . . ." Her voice was quite sharp. She tempered it. "Yes, I'm sure."

He agreed, cautiously. She couldn't blame him. Irritation and anger weren't emotions she normally experienced, especially for no reason. Something else was going on and she thought she knew what it was. Also, she needed to talk to him about something that occurred to her in the car but her emotional roller coaster prevented her from being able to bring it up and have a civil conversation. She still wasn't sure if it was possible.

In silence, they entered the building, crossed the lobby, got in the elevator, and exited on her floor. She heard his questions and felt his curiosity though he hadn't uttered a sound. She did her best to quell the anger this caused. Now she wasn't sure how much was explained anger and how much was irritation from feeling the anger and not knowing why she was feeling it. She was quite sure she knew where it was coming from, however.

Entering her apartment she saw Clansey. His usual smile faded as he nodded behind her.

"You shouldn't bring strays home, Meg."

For a split second her anger flared thinking he was referring to Zeus. Then she realized he had nodded toward her left and Zeus was standing on her right.

"Silence! You're sad and pathetic. Silence or I will . . ." The spirit had followed her home and was trying to subdue Clansey. Clansey wasn't having it.

"Or you'll what? Kill me? You're a century or so too late!" He laughed.

"Quiet, both of you!" Meg demanded. The spirit faded in, materializing beside her.

Clansey's silence was from shock at seeing her angry, something he hadn't seen in all the years he'd been with her. The spirit, however, became quiet and angry at being spoken to in such a manner. She became vaguely aware of Zeus' presence and turned toward him. His expression was of surprise but not shock. He figured the spirit had followed them there, and though he couldn't hear what was going on, he presumed she was speaking to it, and another one. Anger welled up inside her.

"How can you be so calm? Why are you accepting this so readily?" She held up a hand to stop whatever he was about to say. "Hold that thought. I've got something to do first."

Meg closed her eyes briefly, calming and centering herself. She inhaled slowly and deeply calling on the bright white light of love and divine protection to enter her from the head down through the rest of her body. In doing so, it would push out the darkness camping there that had caused irritation and anger—the irritation and anger the spirit had put there. Exhaling the darkness within her left side. She opened her eyes and looked at the spirit.

"Be gone!" It stepped closer, its stare intensified. "You won't control me again. I won't allow it! You have no power here. Be gone!" She quickly turned to Zeus.

"Zeus, I surround you with the bright white light of love and divine protection."

Immediately a bright white light appeared above his head and entered him. He felt it and inhaled sharply. It spread throughout his body in the flash of a second. He glowed from it as the light emanated off his body by several inches.

"Good show!" Clansey shouted. Meg turned to him. He held up his hands, palms toward her. "I'm good. There's nothing worse than a glowing ghost!" Meg smiled at him. "Besides, I'm immune. I've chosen a different path."

Meg glanced around, then took stock of her emotions. The spirit was gone. She looked at Clansey.

"That was the darkness you saw around him?" Referring to Zeus.

"That would be it."

"Him *who*, for crying out loud?!"

"You." Meg and Clansey said together, though he could only hear her.

"Me?!" What just happened anyway?"

"What just happened was that a spirit has been around for a while but wasn't letting us see her. Clansey felt her presence around you and noted the darkness I couldn't detect. She changed our moods, or at least mine. I've been angry and off center and didn't know why. Things that shouldn't have gotten to me, did. Sometimes, not knowing why, it made me angrier."

"She said she wanted you, though I don't have the foggiest idea why. She was doing her best to keep us from being together . . . which leads me to believe there's something about this case we're both working on that it doesn't want us to find out."

Chapter Ten

"Does that mean we're getting close?"

"I don't really know but we must at least be on the right track. We were kept . . . I was kept . . . emotionally distracted . . . off balance. Irritated mostly." Zeus grinned.

"I do seem to have that effect on you . . . sometimes on purpose."

"I'm sure." She grinned back.

"Now, I have a question to answer. First, I was far from calm. Stunned. Shocked. But not calm. You were yelling at something I couldn't see, but presumed it was the spirit from the car and I'm a little freaked that I can't see or hear them. Next, I have a question to ask: Why have I accepted . . . what you do . . . so readily? That spooks me, too. No pun intended, Clansey." Clansey nodded slightly toward him. "But it's," he shrugged, "I don't know . . . natural somehow . . . I guess."

"Have you seen it before?"

"Actually, I believe I have. When I was a kid there was this old lady . . . Crazy Mrs. Casey. Most of the time she was as normal as could be, but there were times when she didn't think anyone was around and she'd talk to herself. More precisely, like she was talking *to* someone only she could see and hear. I remember watching her and trying to see or hear who it was. She'd carry on a conversation . . . one-sided as far as we could hear, but I always wondered. It sounded so . . . natural . . . in an odd way. And then there's my sister, when she was in the hospital that night . . ."

"Mm." Meg nodded; she got it, but her mind was already working on something else.

"Okay, now it's my turn again to ask a question, or two. Between the car and here I've gathered that spirit has been around me for a while and wants something from me. Should I be worried? Can she hurt me?"

"No, not in the traditional sense. She can mess with your mind, apparently, so you've got to stay on your toes."

"Mess with my mind how?"

"Well, so far, all I know, and it's from personal experience, is that she can give you wild mood swings-anger mostly."

"And you think it has something to do with this case . . . Jasmine and her parents?"

"Maybe. Or it could be she's been with you a lot longer and no one knew until I came into the picture. Hopefully, I've banished her for good."

"Do you think so?"

Clansey perched on the arm of the couch, facing Zeus.

"Well, no." Meg and Clansey said together.

"That's comforting. What can I . . . we . . . expect?"

"Irritation, anger, perhaps confusion, second guessing yourself, your decisions, and your self-worth."

"Great!"

"If something seems not quite right, second thoughts about a decision or idea, think it through. Remember why you thought that way to begin with. If you suddenly find yourself getting irritated or angry, try to step back and see if there's a good reason for it. If not, push it down until you can disperse it into the universe."

"Disperse . . . ?"

"I'll show you how and how to protect yourself from attacks."

"And this stuff goes on all the time . . . with people everywhere?"

"Yes, but it's not always the reason people do bad things. Some people are . . . just that way . . . dark souls."

"I suppose I should be glad I know about this stuff and will learn to deal with it, but right now it seems life was easier when I didn't know."

"Ignorance is bliss?"

He nodded, running his hand through his hair.

"Really?"

"Probably not." He admitted. "At least now if I want to punch some guy in the face and there really isn't a good reason for it, I'll know why I have that urge."

Meg looked at Zeus' well-developed arm and imagined the hand curled into a fist and flying toward someone's face.

"Get urges like that often do you?"

"Not so much . . . anymore."

She let it go, remembering he had said he was a bit of a difficult child and fought often.

"Tell me again, how will I know if this . . . thing . . . comes back?" He effectively changed the subject. She allowed it.

"Watch for mood swings and second guessing yourself."

"I've been second guessing myself for years."

"In relationships, not at work." He stared at nothing for several seconds before looking at her.

"Must come in handy."

"What?"

"You can "read" any guy you want to date to see if he's worth your time and effort."

"That sounds romantic! Even though that's true, I don't. If there's something seriously wrong with them, I sense it, usually right away. However, like most people, I tend to ignore it. I'm afraid I take my chances like everybody else."

"Do you sense anything with me?"

"No, nothing we haven't already talked about."

"Meaning my problem with relationships?"

"That's what I mean, though you're not unique in that respect. Perhaps the new interest you have will help you through that."

"That's what I'm hoping for."

To Meg, it looked like he gave her a knowing look. Unless he thought she could see that in his future, which she didn't, she was clueless as to its meaning.

"Now that we're on the subject, how's it going with your lady of interest? Anything new?"

"Not really. Work throws us together now and again, but . . ." He shrugged. "How about you? Any interests on the horizon?

"Me? No, no interests. I don't really have the time or inclination."

"Hm, last one must have been a bad one for you to give up when you're so young and beautiful. Come, lay on my couch and tell me all about it. I won't even charge you for the session."

Meg laughed out loud, shaking her head when he offered her his hand.

"Again, I neither have the time nor inclination." With his quizzical look, she added, "It's a long story."

"One day?"

"Perhaps, yes, one day I'll tell you all about it. Just not today or any day soon."

"What about your family? Are they all like you? How many siblings, if any? Parents?"

"Parents. Let's see, I have one of each. Siblings. One brother, two sisters. I'm the oldest. Are they like me? In a very broad, general sense, yes . . . we're human."

Meg smiled at him as an idea came to her. She cocked her head slightly to one side, wondering how he'd react.

"How would you like to meet my family tomorrow after work?" She stopped briefly, looking at her fingertips, then back to him. "We could go for supper, unless you have other plans, it being Friday."

"No, no plans. Meeting your family, huh? That's a big step."

She caught his meaning after feeling the slight rush of panic run through him, then dissipate.

"A very big step." She agreed. "We can stop before or after. Which would you prefer?"

"Stop? For what?"

"To get married, of course. Doesn't that come with meeting the parents?"

"You're . . . feeding off me . . . off my . . ."

"Yes." She interrupted. "I am, but only because it jumped out at me. Don't worry, we all bring friends home for supper. Sometimes there's quite a houseful. So, what do you say, wanna go?"

"It sounds like fun." For the most part, he meant it.

Meg was glad he had accepted and that he did not ask any question about her family being psychic. She'd answer that after he met her family—if she still needed to. Until then, she figured he'd feel more at ease meeting normal people.

"Let's leave at 5 PM," she concluded.

The next day didn't go fast enough for Meg. On the other hand, it went too fast. She was worried, off and on, about Zeus' reaction to her family. She was worried he'd freak out if he learns that her whole family is psychic, and yet alternately reasoned with herself that he had basically accepted her as she was and would accept her family. Still, she cautioned her parents, her brother, and her sisters, to be on their best behavior . . . no overtly psychic shenanigans. Of course her brother had to make a big deal of her request, making a bigger deal of her relationship with Zeus than there was.

Finally, too soon, the end of her work day arrived. Meg went home to shower and change clothes. Realizing they hadn't made any arrangements about who would drive, she called Zeus.

"Hey, I was just thinking I'd pick you up at your place and we'd go to my parent's in my car."

"Good idea that you drive. However, you can't pick me up."

"Why not?" The doorbell rang.

"I'm already here."

Opening the door, she saw him standing there with a large bouquet of flowers in one hand and a single flower in the other. He handed her the single flower.

"This one is for you. The rest are for your mother." She moved to let him enter.

"Thank you." She closed the door. "What did you bring for my father?"

He turned to look at her. A flicker of panic ran through his eyes.

"What do you get a guy? Beer? Whiskey?"

"Daddy doesn't drink. Don't worry about it." She laughed. "I was teasing."

"That's just mean!"

"Couldn't help myself. I'm sorry."

"Not yet, you're not." She eyed him and giggled.

"Ready?"

They found plenty of things to talk about on the drive to her parents' house, though Meg made sure they stayed away from talking about her family. She had been right in thinking Zeus was nervous. She was even more sure that his nervousness would quadruple if he knew he'd be walking into a house where psychics abound and their gifts were as varied as the people were.

Meg was relieved when she finally pulled into the driveway and had successfully avoided the topic of her family's talents. To her, it seemed to have been a natural question for someone to ask . . . if she was psychic, what about the rest? She patted Zeus' hand as they each started to open their car door.

"Here we go!"

Her father heard them pull in and met them in the foyer as Meg, followed by Zeus, entered the house. She hugged her father, kissing his cheek, as he looked straight at Zeus.

"Hi, Daddy." She stepped back. "This is Zeus Garrett. Zeus, this is my father, Lance Wolfe."

They shook hands and she was aware they greeted each other but her mind was on her brother, Michael, who stood just behind their father. Zeus noticed Meg and her brother's eyes were locked as if sending messages to one another. Lance nudged Michael, speaking quietly.

"They're "talking" to each other," Zeus thought to himself.

Zeus looked at Lance to see if he was joking, then back to Meg, who by now had diverted her attention back to him.

"Zeus, this is my little brother, Michael."

"The "little" brother who has six or seven inches on her." Michael grinned as they shook hands. "So, Zeus, what are your intentions where my sister is concerned?"

"Michael!" Meg was mortified. She turned to her father. "Daddy!"

"I . . ." Zeus started.

"Never mind, son." Lance patted his shoulder. "Michael isn't serious and he *will* behave himself. Besides, that's my question."

"Daddy!" Meg grabbed Zeus' arm. "Time to meet my mom. Forget about these Neanderthals."

She hurried him past the living room, through the dining room, and into the kitchen. Meg's mother looked up with a smile on her face.

"I see by your expressions that Michael is at it again."

"Daddy, too . . . they both need to eat on the porch!" Meg's mother laughed and handed them each a glass of juice, then patted the block table. Dutifully, both Meg and Zeus sat on the high stools at the table. Zeus handed Meg's mother the bouquet of flowers.

"For you, Mrs. Wolfe."

"Thank you, but please call me Bobbi."

"Mom, this is Zeus. Zeus-my mom." Meg sipped her juice, then added, "She's the only sane one here."

"How sane can I be living with your father and Michael all these years? Then, add your sisters, and well . . ."

"Speaking of them, where are they?"

"Carmen and Julie will be here soon. This is one meal they wouldn't miss for anything." Meg caught her mother's meaning and quickly veered away from it.

"Are either of them bringing anyone?"

"Not that I've heard, but with an open door policy, you never know."

"So, I'm the evening attraction?"

Zeus brought up what Meg had tried to avoid. Mother and daughter looked at one another. Bobbi looked at Zeus, an apologetic smile on her lips.

"I'm afraid so, especially considering Meg hasn't invited anyone . . . a man, here in years."

"Oh?" He turned to Meg.

She had been trying to be invisible. Now in the spotlight she squared her shoulders as she sat up straight, glanced at her mother, then squarely at Zeus.

"I told you, I don't have time for a lot of men friends . . . or female ones, for that matter. For whatever reason, they want to make a big deal out of you being a male. Mainly, I suspect, to embarrass me. I apologize ahead of time, if that embarrassment reaches you."

He gave her an odd grin as she heard him say, "Thanks." She may have wondered about his expression if her sisters hadn't arrived at that moment. Introductions were made again, the women helped with the meal amongst a conversation centering around Meg's guest. The men set the table, then Zeus, Lance, and Michael went into the living room with a mental promise from the latter two men to Meg that they would behave.

As usual in the Wolfe household, especially with mealtime, there was a lot of chatter. Everyone caught up on what everyone else was doing, humorous stories were told, and questions asked as well as general conversations carried on.

To some, it might have appeared a hectic or frenzied time, but for the Wolfes, as Zeus observed, it was a quiet, peaceful, informative, and relaxing time.

Zeus glanced at Meg, who was leaning toward one of her sisters and listening intently, then giggled at what had been said. His eyes moved on to the rest at the table, each either talking, listening, or eating. He smiled to himself and now knew what it felt like to be part of a big, loving family.

"Zeus?" He snapped out of his thoughts and his eyes met Lance's.

"Sir?"

"There are no formalities among friends . . . Lance will do."

"Yes, Sir . . . Lance."

"Your Eminence, really?" Carmen giggled.

Zeus shot a glance at Meg, who looked slightly uncomfortable. He was sure all conversation had stopped. He saw Lance roll his eyes as a small smile played at the corners of his mouth. He was also sure he hadn't missed Meg saying anything about the topic they had discussed with Clansey at Meg's house. What was going on?

Chapter Eleven

"Did your mother's love for Greek mythology bring about your name?" Lance asked.

"I doubt she has an affection for Greek mythology or my sister would have been named something like Athena instead of Tammy."

Suddenly, the silence felt different to him. A quick glance around the table and he saw what looked like . . . empathy on all the faces but one . . . Meg wasn't looking at anything in particular.

"Especially, being your twin sister."

His eyes went to Julie who had spoken, then snapped to Meg, who still was looking at nothing, yet he felt she was avoiding looking at him.

"Yes, especially." He answered.

"Zeus . . . God of Gods?" His eyes found their way to Bobbi, who hadn't uttered a word, yet he had heard her.

"Yes, though most think he's the God of War." Zeus informed her, presuming she must have spoken.

Bobbi continued making conversation and keeping Zeus' attention on whatever the subject was at the time. Still, from time to time, he would glance at Meg. He was certain she was avoiding making eye contact. He could wait.

Shortly after they finished eating, the men helped clear the table, then were ushered into the living room while the women went to the kitchen to prepare the dessert. This gave both the men and the women time to chat a little amongst themselves.

It was nine o'clock before Meg and Zeus started to leave. Everyone stood on the front porch saying goodbyes and telling Zeus he was welcome any time. They had just turned to walk toward the car when Michael spoke.

"Yeah, Meg, thanks for bringing your boyfriend over."

Meg spun around glaring at her brother. Something unspoken passed between brother and sister. Whatever it was, it didn't diminish Michael's expression of brotherly teasing. Zeus moved to stand behind Meg, his expression matching Michael's.

"Boyfriend?" He casually placed his arms around Meg carefully placing them to pin her arms down. Her head tilted back slightly as Michael's hand came up as if to ward off a blow while he laughed.

"Meg . . ." Bobbi's voice was a warning. Meg's body started to relax. She had been about to give her brother a mental shove, possibly even a headache.

"Didn't she tell you?" Zeus continued. "We got married last week."

"What?!" Meg's body tensed again. She tried to turn but Zeus held her firmly, bending his head he spoke in her ear.

"I said you weren't sorry, *yet*, didn't I?"

Michael's laughter rang out. The various expressions on everyone's faces disappeared as they laughed also. Zeus released his hold on her and stepped back. As she turned to face him, her brother called out to Zeus.

"Run!"

"You're right, you did warn me. You have no idea what you just started though. Consider yourself warned." She gave him a charming smile.

Meg walked to the car biding everyone good night as she went. Opening the door, she turned to look at Zeus.

"Coming? Or are you too scared?"

Zeus grinned, waved, and thanked them for the meal. He turned back toward Meg and the car.

"Coming, Dear." He caught her smile as she ducked into the car.

They drove a few miles in silence. Zeus sat, to all appearances, calmly. It would have been hard to tell that thoughts were tumbling around in his head faster than he could keep up with.

"How does stopping at the lake sound?" Meg glanced at the clock on the dash and her watch, checking one against the other.

"Tonight?" She considered the turmoil within him that she was feeling. "Sure."

Silence fell again and stayed until she had parked at the lake and both had gotten out of the car. Zeus shut his door and leaned over the top of the car. Meg merely stood by her closed door looking at him and waited. Thoughts still tumbled around in his head as he silently looked at her. Finally, he grabbed a thought and spoke.

"This is probably the most out of control you'll ever see me." His voice was deceptively calm. The following silence deep.

"Okay." She cautiously answered and waited.

"You're all freaking psychic!" He paused, then let the thoughts take form and fall off his lips in a rush. "Talking to each other without words . . . they knew . . . the conversation you, Clansey and I had . . . good sweet Lord, I'm talking like he's real . . . I thought I was going crazy . . . maybe I have . . . I . . ."

A strong breeze swirled around them. The shadows were flying around them, dipping and diving between them and toward him.

"Zeus." She spoke quietly, but firmly. He fell silent, looking at her. Finally he spoke, just as quiet, though confused.

"What?"

"Are you okay now?" He shook his head.

"You could have told me . . . warned me."

Meg looked at the shadows, watched as the breeze they created lifted his hair slightly. They had taken his raised voice as a sign of anger and were trying to protect her. She spoke to them.

"I'm okay." Zeus looked at her with confusion and anger.

"Well, I'm not!" Then, when the breeze stopped, realization hit him. His eyes opened wider. "Now who . . . what are you talking to?! Is Clansey here?"

"No, shadows. I'll explain later. I thought if I told you about my family beforehand, you'd be nervous the whole time you were there. If my siblings could have reined themselves in . . ."

"I'd be clueless?" Anger tinged his voice.

"You'd be more comfortable." She countered.

"When, exactly, would you have told me?" A little more anger was heard in his voice.

"Tonight." Anger surfaced in his eyes. "Check yourself."

"Check *myself*?" His voice rose an octave or two. "Who do you think . . ."

The breeze kicked up. Shadows swirled menacingly toward him. Meg couldn't see her, but she knew the dark spirit was there, taking advantage of Zeus' emotional state.

"Check your mood . . . surround yourself . . ." He glared at her. Realization started to come to him. Too slow.

"Zeus, I surround you with . . ." He joined in "the bright white light of love and divine protection."

The spirit took form. The shadows battered it with their shadowy forms. Clansey appeared, observed the battle, saw it was under control and stood guard by Meg and Zeus. Zeus saw a wind tunnel of swirling leaves, grass, and sand several feet away. There was not even a tickle of a breeze anywhere else, so he knew something was probably there that he couldn't see.

Suddenly, the wind tunnel stopped. Just as suddenly, he felt chilled, like he was in a cold air pocket. He looked at Meg, who was watching him

"What . . . ?"

"Shadows from the lake came to protect me when you started to lose control. They attacked the dark spirit, chasing it off. Clansey stood guard over us and now the shadows are surrounding us."

"Shadows from the lake?"

Meg explained about the shadows from the first time she had encountered them as a child to the present. Then, she thanked them for their assistance. Collectively, they inclined their heads in acknowledgment and returned to the lake. She then thanked Clansey.

"My pleasure." He nodded and looked out over the lake.

"Lake Shadows, dark spirits that effect moods, live-in ghosts. What chance do people have who are unaware of such things surrounding them?"

"They manage. That's why, at the very least, we all have Spirit Guides and Angels around us at all times."

"The *whole* family is psychic?!" Returning to their previous conversation.

"We all have our niches and it's mainly mom and us kids. Daddy, well, he has a connection with mom—with telepathy."

"And your mom . . ." He trailed off remembering something. "She's also a therapist—psychic—and uses it—like you? Is that how she solved that case?" Meg nodded.

He shook his head, looked off toward the trees, looked out over the lake and briefly looked at her. It appeared he wanted to say something, changed his mind, then got in the car.

Meg knew the look, though under different circumstances. She had seen it with clients. What needed to be done to better their situations seemed unattainable either because it was too much work or regardless of how much they worked at it, nothing would change or help. They simply couldn't deal with or handle the problem and chose to walk away from it. They were overwhelmed. This was the look in Zeus' eyes. He couldn't deal with it, didn't want to, and would turn away from it. It was too overwhelming and he couldn't change it. The "*it*" was the presence of ghosts, spirits, and ultimately, her.

Normally, this would bother her somewhat, and only briefly. Being psychic was part of her life and a part she couldn't, and wouldn't, change. People who didn't believe or couldn't cope with that had come and gone in her life . . . all of her life. It hadn't mattered much at the end of the day. And yet, with Zeus, it bothered her more. The fact that it bothered her more, bothered her and she didn't know why.

Then she realized that she did know why. Setting aside family, and Officer Barry, Zeus was the first adult to learn about her abilities and accept her as she was, asking nothing from her. Though that hadn't changed, his ability to deal with it had. They'd probably remain friends but there would be a distance between them from an unwillingness to put up with it. For him, and many others, ignorance was bliss.

"May I come up?"

Zeus' voice jolted her from her thoughts. She was surprised to see she had driven from the lake to her apartment building and even parked her car. She didn't remember any of it . . . no turns, other vehicles, stops, starts, red lights, acceleration, or braking. She glanced over at Zeus. He didn't appear scared to death so she must have done a good job driving on autopilot.

"Of course."

He gave her a quick nod and a weak smile. She returned the smile. Silence stayed between them until they entered her apartment. Once inside, the silence became heavy. Zeus stopped, his feet half in the foyer and half in the living room. His thoughts tumbled, disconnected.

"Tea?" Meg asked as she headed toward the kitchen. Once there, she looked back at him.

"Anything stronger?" He half joked.

"Irish Cream and brandy."

He hadn't moved. He hadn't blinked. Nothing about him changed, yet, she saw a spark as she said brandy and knew, at one time, he'd had a problem with alcohol.

"Tea will do."

He still hadn't moved when she carried a tray laden with teapot, creamer, sugar bowl, lemon slices, cups, spoons, and saucers toward the living room. He took the tray from her and put it on the coffee table as they sat on the couch. There was so much he wanted to say . . . to ask her. She poured them each a cup of tea, giving him time to let his thoughts settle.

"Are we alone?" His voice was quiet, conversational.

"Yes, we are."

"Clansey?"

"Not here." He looked a little surprised.

"I thought . . ."

"No. He comes and goes."

"What does he do when he's not here?"

"I have no idea. I've never asked him."

He gave a brief nod, mulling that over.

"So you do have privacy?"

"I'm a lot like anyone else. I'm not constantly surrounded by ghosts and spirits."

"But you can see then constantly."

"I see them when they're near and most of them simply acknowledge I can see them and go about their own business."

"What about dark spirits?"

"Those are rare. Mostly there are spirits visiting from the Other Side, some ghosts newly deceased, unaware they're dead, and others with unfinished business. They all cross over eventually . . . usually on their own."

"Even the dark spirit?"

"Yes, even her, though she goes elsewhere besides into the light . . . a limbo of darkness, hell, if you will, until she's reincarnated."

"Why hasn't Clansey . . . gone in to the light?"

"He doesn't know exactly. There's some unfinished business for him but he doesn't have a clue what it is yet. We've discussed it at length over the years and haven't figured it out."

"Years?" He digested that. "It must have something to do with you, right? That's why he hangs around you?"

"We don't know. We've gone over people I've known, people I've met, people I know of but haven't met . . . nothing rings a bell for him." He shook his head.

"I can't believe we're sitting here talking about dead people like . . ."

"We know them?" She finished for him. He sat very still, looking at her, realization dawning on him.

"You do know them! I know some of them!"

"Yes. It's rather like friends we know and talk to that other friends don't know, have never seen, and probably never will—geographically distant friends. Do your friends here know about your friends in other states or other countries?"

"I see your point." He paused. "So people aren't walking around with an entourage of ghosts and spirits following them they aren't aware of?"

"Just their Spirit Guide, Angels, and Spirit Totem."

"Spirit Totem?"

Exasperation started seeping into his voice. She had thought he was making progress in trying to understand it all. Perhaps this last thing was too much for him. She waited to feel him withdraw at any minute.

Chapter Twelve

He seemed neutral so she continued glazing over the new information, hoping not to overwhelm him any more than he already was.

"A Spirit Totem is an animal Spirit Guide. Regardless, we all have Spirit Guides constantly with us from birth to death—everyone, no exceptions. Some people also have one or more Angels with them at all times and some have all three—a Spirit Totem, a Spirit Guide, and an Angel. Usually Angels and Spirit Totems come when called or needed for extra protection."

"You've told me a little about this already, but please explain more about Spirit Totems."

"Do you have an affinity for any particular animal . . . a favorite?"

"As a pet, if I were to get one?"

"Not necessarily domesticated. Mine are hawks and wolves, though I'm also partial to big cats . . . panthers and pumas, mostly, though I find them all majestic and regal."

Zeus sat quietly for a long minute. He wasn't thinking but rather trying to decide if he wanted to answer her.

"Elephant." He finally blurted out, slightly embarrassed.

"Ah, the true king of the jungle!" He smiled at that.

"Should I have more? You have four."

"You have what you have." She shrugged.

"Why?" She shrugged again.

"Perhaps because of your past lives." She cringed when he rolled his eyes in exasperation. She should have left well enough alone.

"Past lives! What else is there? I'm still trying to comprehend invisible things following me around, nudging me to do things, making me have severe mood swings, and . . ."

"Perhaps we should save that for another time, *if* you want to continue."

"Maybe I should have some brandy to help me deal with it."

"A clear head works much better."

"A clear head? I have more *things* roaming around in my head than you can even imagine!" She smiled at him knowingly. "Well, maybe you can imagine!"

"My "things" roam around outside my head and they talk. Honestly, I don't know which is worse."

"How *do* you deal with it? Ghosts, spirits . . . walking around, coming to you, talking to you. Why haven't you been locked away for talking to people no one else can see or hear?"

"Lucky, I guess. I do try not to speak with them in public however."

"Is it constant? Do you see *all* of the ghosts and spirits that have passed?"

"No. Most cross over immediately. Of those that don't, I do see them wandering around. Some realize I can see them, acknowledge it, and keep going. A few ask for my help, either in crossing over or?. Some don't realize they're dead and others have unfinished business they need to deal with before they can go Home. With very few exceptions, I exist normally."

"Normally." He said the word, reflectively and a bit sarcastically. "You don't just see people . . . living people . . . you see their Spirit Guides and Angels . . . the ones who always with them, right? So when you meet someone for the first time or greet someone you've known for some time, you're meeting and greeting at least three . . . beings."

"No, I meet or greet the person. I acknowledge the rest but don't dwell on them."

Zeus thought about it and put it into perspective for himself. If he met someone . . . an old friend or new acquaintance . . . and they had a few people with them, unless introduced, he'd mainly center his attention on the one person. He thoughtfully nodded, understanding.

"That sounds . . ."

"Normal?"

"Under the circumstances, yes. However, I've seen and experienced beyond normal. Clansey's antics take a back seat to the dark spirit. Of all the ones I see just milling around on a regular basis, Clansey and the dark spirit are the exception to the rule. Clansey is usually benign. The dark spirit is rare."

He digested this information. She watched his expression change as he did so. He wasn't so much accepting everything he had learned as he was dealing with it. Finally, he just nodded his head and said, "Perhaps we *should* leave the rest for another time." She nodded.

"You have a question about my family?"

"Probably. I'm not sure what to ask at the moment."

"I do apologize for relaying to them personal stuff about you without asking you first. It didn't work very well but I'd hoped to prevent them from asking questions you may not have wanted to talk about, especially when they were still strangers."

"Like about Tammy?" She nodded. "Well, I opened that topic myself. What about the conversation with Clansey?"

"That was just funny. As a teenager I was into Greek mythology and Julie wanted to know if it was strange calling you Zeus. I told her about 'Your Eminence' and how Clansey found it funny."

"So, your family . . . you all . . . you're psychic?" This time he didn't sound as shocked. It was more like he was just checking.

"To one degree or another, yes. My mother sees things through touch, can hear people's thoughts, and projects thoughts. Michael has prophetic dreams. Julie can heal. And Carmen, when she settles down, will be very good at seeing the future and reading people, and especially animals. My sisters and I see and hear spirits regularly. My brother rarely. My parents not at all. We all use telepathy, though with daddy it's just with my mother."

Zeus slowly shook his head in disbelief with a small smile.

"You say that like it's an every day thing."

"It is . . . for us. How about this: Michael is a mechanic, Julie is studying to be a doctor, and Carmen hasn't settled down enough yet to know what she wants to do. The last I heard, she wanted to work with animals. She changes her mind like most people change their underwear."

"Maybe it *was* better that I had no idea when you brought me . . ."

"Into a den of wolves?" She grinned at him.

"Yeah!" He chuckled.

Meg had been right. Though they maintained their friendship, complete with his wonderful knack of irritating her, there was a subtle difference. They spoke on the phone and occasionally met to discuss the case, but there was a definite cooling off . . . a distance between them. Anything remotely close to the topic of psychic wasn't mentioned. There were no lunches, dinners, or even going for coffee. Apparently, he simply couldn't handle, nor want to acknowledge, anything to do with any of it.

This was nothing new for Meg. She had experienced it before growing up. Being psychic was so natural and common to her that she thought everyone could, at least, see and hear spirits. When she was labeled a freak, picked on, ignored and friends could no longer play with her, she realized she needed to keep it to herself. For the most part, however, the damage was done.

There had been a time in high school when she had a lot of friends . . . or so she thought. It soon became apparent that most weren't. They pretended to like her, asked her questions, and then went off to make fun of her with their own clicks. The rest . . . three girls . . . also outcasts . . . were her friends. Though at first non-believers, they eventually realized she wasn't faking or had actually convinced herself she could do, see, and hear things others couldn't.

Zeus was somewhere in between. He believed but didn't want to. He felt very out of control and didn't like it. What she failed to impress on him was that you were always in control. You didn't have to take your Spirit Guide's guidance. You could prevent attacks from dark souls and spirits. You have a whole league of Angels at your disposal waiting to help you, waiting for you to simply ask them.

What you're not in control of, on a daily basis, is life's conditions—weather, other people's actions, and time. Also, you can't control sickness or death, if it were meant to be. These things were out of people's control, though some were delusional enough to think they could control these things. All you had control of was what you charted for yourself, including the exit points.

People being uncomfortable with her wasn't new, but it still hurt and bothered her, more so with Zeus than anyone else and she didn't know why. She had her theories but that was all they were. She chose to try not to think about it. At least they were friends on some level. After they were finished with the case, ... well, that was something she chose not to think about until later.

In the meantime, she had other things to worry about. Child Protection Services had been trying to find a relative of Jasmine's in hopes of placing her with them and take her out of foster care. They hadn't had any luck for a long time, but now it seemed they may have finally found someone . . . Jasmine's mother's sister, an aunt.

There were a million reasons why Meg didn't think Jasmine should live with her only known relative . . . Jasmine didn't know the woman, the aunt lived a state away, and the bond Meg and Jasmine had as therapist and client would be broken. Jasmine would have to get a new therapist . . . one she may not like or open up to and then the case may never be solved. The odds of the aunt relocating just to keep Jasmine in a familiar setting seemed slim. She definitely didn't feel going to live in a strange place, with a stranger, would be in Jasmine's best interest. And, in addition to all these practical reasons, Meg loved Jasmine and had been thinking of the possibility of adopting her. With the aunt in the picture, Jasmine was not an orphan any more; unless the aunt signed her biological rights away, there was no hope of Meg adopting. Meg hoped against hope this woman wasn't a relative and yet felt bad about hoping such a thing.

Meg knew there was a chance that everything would work out wonderfully if this woman was related and Jasmine went to live with her. Jasmine could grow up to be a well-adjusted young woman and have a productive and full life. And though Meg would be extremely happy for Jasmine, Meg's heart would break and she would be very depressed.

Meg was torn between wanting to spend every spare minute with Jasmine and yet knowing she should slowly back off. The latter would be best both professionally and in preparation of Jasmine leaving. She couldn't help but wonder if this was the heartache a woman felt when she gave her baby up for adoption. She would want to keep her baby but knows it would be better for the baby to give it up.

When the call came that Jasmine's aunt, Erica Wells, was flying out to meet with Janice Powers, the CPS worker in charge of Jasmine's case, and with Mary, and of course,

Jasmine. After the call, Meg felt panic rise in her chest. She was losing her "baby."

Why her first thought was to call Zeus, she didn't know. She thought better of it, but too late . . . he had already answered the phone.

"Hello, Zeus, how's it going?" She stalled trying to find another reason for calling him.

"Okay." His tone was cautious. Lately Meg only called with information, gave it to him and ended the call. No pleasantries at all.

"Just okay, huh? I was hoping for news of some progress."

"Do you have anything for me?"

"Me? No, nothing. Sorry."

Now Zeus was getting confused. It appeared Meg had called to chit-chat, which was totally unlike her. Maybe . . .

"Have you . . . seen or heard anything?" Meg knew what he was asking but feigned ignorance.

"Like what?"

"Things most people don't hear or see."

What was she up to? What was wrong with her? She knew what he was talking about . . . he heard it in her voice.

"Oh, that. Uh-uh, no."

Was she trying to tell him something but couldn't come out and say it for some reason?

"Are you alone, Meg?"

"Yes, all alone. Why?"

There was something different in her voice just then. What he wasn't sure. His mind raced for a cause.

"How's Jasmine?"

"Fine."

Her voice had risen slightly. Whatever it was, he'd lay odds it had something to do with Jasmine. His mind raced again. If it was something serious she would have already said something, he was sure.

"Have you decided to step down and let someone else take her case?"

"*I* haven't." He heard a muffled sniff and he swore a squeak to her voice. She was crying.

"Tell me . . ."

"They're taking . . ." Another sniff. "They found an aunt of Jasmine's and . . ." Sobbing she couldn't finish the sentence.

"Are you at home?"

"Mm." It was an affirmative squeak followed by a loud sniff.

"I'll be right there."

Hanging up, Meg sobbed much louder. Tears flowed freely. She blew her nose. Her sobs grew more intense, her tears increased. Remembering Zeus was on his way, she managed to get enough control to stop crying, though tears were never far away. She blew her nose again and got a cold washcloth to put over her eyes. It didn't get rid of the redness and swelling, but it helped.

Red, puffy eyes were all there was left when Zeus knocked on the door. The facade crumbled when he stepped inside, compassion all over his face. She melted against him sobbing uncontrollably. His arms held her firmly. Not knowing what else to do, he just held her, one hand gently holding her head against his chest as he made comforting sounds and spoke soothing words. Meg could only manage words and unfinished sentences.

"They're taking . . . I love . . . never see . . ."

The phone rang and eventually went to voice mail. At the sound of the voice, Meg stopped crying, leaving sharp intakes of breath. The voice gave her hope.

"Meg, this is Janice. Erica Wells will be here Monday." Hope sank in Meg's stomach, leaving an ache. "Would you like to be present when we meet with Mary?"

Sobbing cut off the rest. Zeus felt helpless. There was nothing he could do or say to make her feel better. His mind turned logical to combat the helplessness he felt. His voice was gentle.

"You knew this was a possibility . . . you knew they were looking for a relative, didn't you?"

Meg heard the words and was positive about their meaning. Anger rose mingling with the tears. She brought her head up, meeting his eyes. He winced slightly when her fist hit his chest as she started yelling.

"You're right . . . how unprofessional of me. I never should have gotten emotionally involved. I know better. I'm sorry Jasmine couldn't have merely been just another client. I'm sorry her sad, frail mind and body got to me. I should have walked away from her and my emotions a long time ago. Maybe one day you can teach me how to feel nothing for anyone or anything. Go to hell you bastard!"

Chapter Thirteen

Temporarily out of things to say, some of her anger spent, silence surrounded them for a few seconds.

"Meg . . ." He rubbed where her fist had hit him. The punch had stung, but not nearly as much as her words.

"Thanks for coming over Zeus. You've been . . . very helpful. Good bye." She headed toward the door. He blocked her.

"Meg, I'm not . . ." His actions led her to believe he had no intentions of leaving. Her voice became slightly lower than normal and deceptively calm sounding.

"Get out."

"Meg . . ." He tried again. Her voice lowered more.

"Get out. Get the hell out of my house . . ." He moved toward the door. ". . . my sight . . ." He opened the door. ". . . my life!"

He stepped outside. She slammed the door with all of her strength, ran to her bedroom, threw herself across her bed and sobbed out all of her pain and anger until she fell asleep, exhausted, sucking in air at regular intervals.

They say things will look better in the morning. They didn't. Meg wasn't sure if she was glad she had the weekend to get herself together or if she wished she had work to keep her mind busy. Work. Monday. Jasmine's aunt would be there. Two short days. She packed an overnight bag and headed out the door. She needed her family. She needed their love and support and understanding.

As she pulled into her parent's driveway her cell phone rang. Digging it out of her pocket she saw it was Zeus. She turned it off, tossed it on the front seat, and got out of the car.

Meg had decided she'd sound as cheerful as possible when she walked inside. Instead her father greeted her, seeing she was upset about something, he opened his arms to her. She ran to him, letting him envelope her in the safety of his arms.

"Daddy!"

"What is it baby, what's wrong?"

"Daddy . . ." Tears slid down her face and into his shirt.

"Sh-sh baby, it'll be okay. What happened?"

"They're taking my baby!" She felt his shock and confusion.

"What . . ."

"Jasmine." He understood. "They found a relative. She'll be here Monday. I'll never see her again!"

"I'm so sorry honey. I know how much you love her."

He steered her toward the kitchen. She slid onto a stool while he made them each some tea.

"Where is everybody?"

"Michael and Julie are working, Carmen is off with friends, and your mother is shopping."

She accepted the tea as he sat on a stool opposite her.

"I don't know what I'm going to do daddy."

"I know I'm not much help but remember . . ."

"Nothing happens for nothing." She finished for him.

"Knowing that doesn't make it any easier, I know." He thought a change of subject would help. "How's Zeus?"

"He's an insensitive beast!"

"Oh . . . well . . ."

"His idea of comforting me is to remind me I knew it was a possibility."

"Well . . ." She heard his thoughts.

"I know he's right daddy, but he could have at least had the decency to keep it to himself like you did."

"You would have heard it even then." He reminded her.

"I know but thinking 'I told you so' and saying it are two different things . . . emotionally anyway."

"True." He patted her hand. "Your mom is coming."

"I know." Both had heard her mother's thoughts.

"Zeus' comment aside, or before he made it, how did you feel about him?"

"I don't really know. When he wasn't irritating me beyond belief, we got along fine."

"That's not what I asked."

"He's okay. A couple of times he was even enjoyable to be with."

"That's not what I asked either."

"What do you want me to say?"

"You don't have to say anything if you don't want to, but think about why you called him first."

"Because we're working on the case together and he knows how I feel about Jasmine."

"And?"

Meg's mother walked in through the kitchen door, placed the groceries on the bar and looked from her daughter to her husband.

"Thank you." She kissed his temple. "It's now time for the mother/daughter part to begin."

He came around the bar and kissed his daughter's forehead. She kissed his cheek and hugged him.

"Thank you, Daddy. I love you."

"I love you too, Meg. I hope I helped a little and think about my question."

"You helped a lot and I will."

Both women watched him leave the kitchen with love and admiration in their eyes. As soon as he was out of sight, they turned to each other.

"So, tell me."

"You already know, Mom."

"Yes, I do, but sometimes verbally saying it helps more than the mental."

Meg ran through the whole thing, including Zeus' part. Only a few tears escaped this time. Upon her mother's silent request, Meg handed her mother her teacup for a refill. Her mind wandered to her father's question. Her mother turned back to face her and slid her teacup across the bar.

"Definitely, seriously, honestly think about your father's question."

Meg nodded as she sipped her tea. Her mother replaced the Oolong her father had given her with relaxing, calming camomile.

"Now," her mother started, "this may not help now but remember you charted this for you to deal with and how it will turn out. Jasmine remembered. Plus, your attachment to her is because the two of you have been together in two past lives."

"Really?"

"The last two actually."

Neither had occurred to her. She had been too emotional to think she had charted meeting and losing Jasmine and it probably wouldn't have helped if she had. Somehow hearing it from her mother did help. Learning she had already shared two lives with Jasmine also helped.

"Was it the tea or my words that helped?"

"Mainly your words." She kissed her mother's cheek. "Thanks, Mom."

Meg spent the rest of the day enjoying her family. She had forgotten how carefree she felt being home. Life was constant there. She could count on her parent's love and guidance and being able to draw on their strength. She could count on Michael being a pain, Julie for sisterly chats, and Carmen to amuse everyone with her sixteen year-old way of seeing the world. At home she could be herself. She could talk to Clansey, her Spirit Guide and Angels out loud without getting strange looks from anyone.

She watched her parents and for the millionth time in her life saw the love and respect they shared. She caught the little looks, soft spoken words . . . verbal and mental, the gentle caressing touches. One day she wanted to find someone she could have something like that with. She gave a mental sigh.

She wasn't in a really big hurry though. She had plenty of time. And if she found somebody of interest she would take her time to make sure he was right. Take her time-that was funny to her in a sad way. She had dated Tony for eight years and still hadn't known him. It has been two years since she kicked him to the curb and she is just now starting to feel whole . . . for the most part.

"Abby." The use of her given name, rarely used, brought her attention back to the present. She focused on the caller, Michael.

"What?"

"Don't do that to yourself. Don't doubt and second guess yourself."

"When did you start hearing thoughts?"

"I haven't. I recognize that look though . . . you wore it for years. I still don't understand why you guys don't turn your attention on him and really mess with his mind."

"Because Michael," his father broke in, "two wrongs won't make it right."

"Don't worry little brother, I'm not about to fall back into that trap again."

"Let's play a game!"

Carmen flew off the to the game closet. Since they were young, the family had always played board and card games as a family.

"Don't you dare drag out Candyland!" Julie threatened.

"But we haven't played that in years!"

"There's a reason for that . . . we're not six years old anymore!" Michael added.

"UNO!" Carmen dropped the deck on the coffee table.

The card game was exactly what Meg needed to lighten her mood. There was laughter, groans, and empty threats from everyone as the game progressed. It was nearly midnight when Meg announced she was going to bed. For the most part, she felt better about the situation with Jasmine knowing whatever happened was the way it was suppose to be. That didn't make it less painful, however.

In the morning, Meg called Mary and asked if she could spend the day with Jasmine. Getting the green light, she told her family what she had planned, and after cleaning up after breakfast, she headed out.

In her car, she saw the cell phone where she had tossed it the day before. She turned it on, finding several voice messages . . . all from Zeus. She shut it off again and tossed it back on the passenger seat. Knowing it may well be her last day with Jasmine, she was determined not to let anything ruin it.

With mixed emotions, though putting on a brave front, she collected Jasmine and headed out for a day of fun. The morning was spent shopping since Mary had said Jasmine was quickly outgrowing most of her clothes. They ate at Denny's, per Jasmine's request. The same waitress served them that had served them and Zeus weeks earlier. She remembered them.

"Hello, there-where's your daddy?" Jasmine's face went through rapid emotions before she sweetly smiled up at the waitress.

"We'll see him later." Meg hoped that wasn't true.

"Girls day out, huh?" Jasmine nodded, beaming at her.

Lunch was ordered and eaten with a lot of chatter and giggling. They even shared a sundae before announcing they were officially stuffed.

They went to see a movie-some animated movie involving fairies. Meg found it hard to concentrate as her mind kept wandering back to when she and Zeus had gone to the movies. She remembered how funny he had been and how she had enjoyed being with him.

From the theater they went to a park. From the park, they went to the lake. The shadows silently greeted Meg, coming close to the waters edge, nodding to her, and smiling at Jasmine. Jasmine became excited, jumping up and down.

"Do you see them? Do you see them?"

Meg looked down at her and again wondered if this small child was psychic.

"Did I see what, honey?" Jasmine pointed up and over the lake where the shadows dashed and darted over the water.

"The eagles!" Raising her eyes above the shadows, Meg saw two eagles circling in search of food.

"Yes, sweetie, I see them."

"Aren't they beautiful?"

"Yes, they are."

"I like hawks better."

"They are beautiful, too."

They played for a couple of hours—digging holes in the sand until they filled in with water, building sand castles, burying their feet, and walking along the shore. Finally, both pleasantly tired and hungry, they prepared to leave. Discussing what they wanted to eat as they pulled onto the road, Meg had an idea.

"Why don't we stop at the store, go back to my place, and cook supper together?"

An excited squeal from the back seat told her Jasmine liked the idea. They wandered around the store, still not sure what they wanted. They finally settled on nachos.

The entire kitchen was a mess by the time they were finished, but they'd had an enormous amount of fun in the process. As they sat eating and chatting about their day, Jasmine suddenly changed the subject.

"I don't want to leave."

"You know I have to bring you back to Mary's, right?" Jasmine nodded.

"I don't want to live with anyone else 'cept you . . . and Mr. Garrett." She brought her plate to the kitchen, putting it on the shelf. Meg followed with her own plate. "Do I have to live with her?"

"You may like . . ." A knock at the door interrupted her, though Meg finished as she moved toward the entryway, "your aunt. And a new place could be fun and exciting."

As soon as she opened the door, Zeus stepped quickly inside, as though she might shut the door in his face . . . and she might have. There was no time for either to say anything as Jasmine launched herself at him. He caught her in mid jump, lifting her in his arms.

"Mr. Garrett, I knew you'd come!" Her little arms went around his neck as she kissed his cheek. Meg had a fleeting thought about her psychic abilities again. With a swiftness known only to an energized child, one arm encircled Meg's neck and pulled her toward them. They would have stopped inches from each others face except he continued moving until he could whisper in Meg's ear.

"I'm sorry."

Chapter Fourteen

Meg moved her head back, her expression unreadable. She felt the words didn't ever come easy for him but they were heartfelt.

"Are you hungry, Mr. Garrett? You missed supper. We had nachos. I can get you some."

"No, thank you, Hon. I've eaten."

Jasmine wiggled to get down. Before her feet were on the floor, she held one of their hands in each of hers. She led them to the living room where they sat on either side of her, their hands still firmly held in hers. Zeus was looking at Meg.

"I've tried to get hold of you since last night. I've been everywhere looking for you."

"I've been busy."

"I know. I think I've either been one step ahead or behind you all day."

Meg wanted to say something cutting. Instead she said nothing. Jasmine took up the slack in conversation.

"I may be leaving forever. Can you make her go away?"

Meg and Zeus looked at each other. She saw the question in his eyes, shook her head ever so slightly and looked away. There was nothing she'd like more than changing the aunt's mind, but she couldn't. That's also why she couldn't be at the meeting . . . she didn't trust herself.

"Will you be there tomorrow?" The question was directed at both of them. Without hesitation, they answered together.

"Of course I will."

Against her better judgment, Meg agreed to Zeus going along and even driving when it was time for Jasmine to go back. Personally, she'd have preferred he leave and she take Jasmine by herself, but she knew Jasmine would want Zeus to be with them. She also knew he wanted to talk to her on the way back. So, she had pushed her feelings aside.

Zeus unbuckled Jasmine from her car seat. When she got out, she raised her arms to be picked up. He obliged. She clung to him with both arms tightly around his neck. Meg watched this and fought the sting of tears behind her eyes.

Inside, Mary asked Jasmine to get ready for bed. As she left, Mary turned to Meg.

"She loves you and Detective Garrett."

"He's . . . we're not . . ." Meg swallowed. "Yes, she has become very attached to to him and to myself."

Mary nodded her understanding.

"She's not looking forward to tomorrow. I can't blame her. Her aunt is a complete stranger."

"Yes, I know. I tried easing her mind a little and I hope it's helped."

"Will you be here tomorrow?"

"Yes, we both will, at her request."

"Good. She'll need you."

Meg fought the sting of tears again. Jasmine joined them wearing her pajamas. The bottom part was as close to sideways as it could get and the top was buttoned haphazardly as though she had been in a hurry. She probably had been, plus she *was* only four years old.

Meg knelt down and straightened her pajamas, feeling Jasmine's sad eyes on her. With the top buttoned correctly, Jasmine put her arms around Meg's neck hugging her. After a few minutes Meg pulled back a little, forcing herself to look and sound excited about the next day.

"Tomorrow, you get to meet your aunt. I know you'll like her because she's your mommy's sister."

Jasmine melted into Meg, kissed her cheek, and whispered in her ear.

"I love you."

Before Meg could respond, Jasmine ran to Zeus who automatically picked her up. She kissed his cheek.

"I love you." moistened considerably. As fast as she could, Meg said good bye to Mary and left the house. She hurried to the car with Zeus close behind. She was determined not to lose control in front of him again. Before she got in the car, one tear rolled down her face. She wiped it away, sniffed, inhaled and got in the car.

They drove in silence for a while, each in their own thoughts. She wished it would continue, but knew it wouldn't. Especially now, she had no desire to talk. All of her energy went into controlling her tears.

"Can we talk now?"

"No . . . not now." He nodded slightly, understanding.

In the parking lot of her building, she had unbuckled before the car stopped. As soon as it did, she had opened the door and had one leg out. She stopped, staring at her foot on the pavement.

"Thank you." A hand on her forearm stopped her when she started to get out.

"Would you like me to drive tomorrow?" She pulled her arm away.

"No." She leaned forward to get out, then stopped. "Yes, that probably would be best. Thank you."

He watched her hurry to the building, fumble with the lock, then run to the elevator. He couldn't see it, but he knew she had been crying since she exited the car. He sat there a long time before finally driving away.

Meg allowed herself the luxury of crying for thirty minutes or so. She pulled herself together, reminding herself she had to maintain control. She could not break down at the meeting the next day.

The meeting. She had no idea when it was. Going through the messages left on the machine, skipping past the first three, she heard Janice's voice. She swallowed down the tears that were threatening her vision and shut off the machine as soon as she heard when the meeting would start. She *had* to make it through the meeting collected and in control.

With very little sleep, Meg rose early. There was plenty of time before the ten o'clock meeting. Too much time. She tried, mostly unsuccessfully, to convince herself everything would work out for the best. She had to believe Jasmine would like her aunt, and settle into and adjust to her new environment and life as quickly and pleasantly as possible.

Time flew. It seemed she had only been sitting at the table with an untouched cup of coffee for a little while. Her phone rang. She glanced at who the caller was and noted the time. It was eight o'clock. Two hours had passed since she had sat down. The time lapse surprised her and yet it didn't register. She flipped open her phone while sipping her coffee. She grimaced and swallowed.

"Hello." She croaked out.

"Good morning. Did I wake you?"

"No, I've been up." She heard his thoughts, wondering if she'd been crying. "I took a big swallow of cold coffee."

"I'll bring you a fresh, hot cup. When should I . . ."

"The meeting is at ten, give a half hour to get there . . ."

"I'll be there at nine."

"That's fine-sure-nine."

Meg dumped out her cup of cold coffee and poured another cup. Sitting at the table again, she absentmindedly stirred the dark brew, her mind going forward to the meeting. She tried to imagine the best . . . Jasmine would love her aunt and vise versa. She'd look forward to living with her and all would be well. She tried, but not so nice images kept intruding. She heaved a sigh and tried again, unsuccessfully.

She sipped her coffee, surprised to find it cold. She looked at the coffee maker. The red light showed it was on. She looked at the clock. Eight forty-five. Zeus would be there in fifteen minutes. She flew out of the kitchen and took the fastest shower of her life, second only by the speed of jumping into clothes. As she slipped on her shoes there was a knock at the door.

"Hot coffee, as promised." He handed her a medium-sized cup.

"Thank you." She carefully sipped it. "You have no idea how good this is!"

"How are you doing?"

"I'm okay, much better than the last time you were here."

She hadn't meant it to, but her words hurt.

"Did you dress in a hurry?"

"Kind of, why?" He pointed to the mispositioned buttons on her blouse.

"Oh, thanks."

She sat her coffee down, unbuttoned her blouse, then buttoned it correctly. Zeus watched her as she did so. Obviously, she wasn't doing as fine as she said or thought she was as she would never have done that in front of him. Even after she finished, picked up her coffee, and looked at him, she was unaware of her actions. He motioned for them to sit down.

"Would you like to go over possible outcomes?"

"I have and come up with nothing good. I have to stay in control today. I'm afraid, if I don't, I might try to change the aunt's mind."

"You're too honest to do that. You'll do fine in that respect . . . I have faith in you."

He hoped, if she was tempted, she'd remember his words and not impose any thoughts on the aunt.

The drive there was quiet. Meg was trying to center herself and be as detached as possible. She was also trying to believe everything would work out the way it was suppose to. After all, both she and Jasmine had charted the outcome. She had to trust in that.

They had arrived. Standing on the porch, Meg took three cleansing breaths. Zeus put a comforting hand on her shoulder. When she noticed it, she gave him a weak smile, then knocked on the door.

Mary let them in. It was clear, she felt strained, though she gave them a pleasant smile. Jasmine seemed to appear out of nowhere. She clung to Meg and Zeus, briefly, then took their hands.

"I will try to be very grown up, today."

"You'll do just fine." Meg assured her.

"I want you to be proud of me."

"I will, Sweetie. I'm always proud of you." She looked at Zeus, then back to Jasmine. "We both are."

"Jasmine, honey, why don't you help me in the kitchen?"

After Mary and Jasmine left, a woman appeared from the living room, followed by Janice. In the few seconds it took for both women to reach them, Meg assessed the aunt.

At first glance, with her short, thin frame and dark hair sticking up all over her head-which Meg suspected was done on purpose, or at least she hoped it was-and the thick makeup, Erica Wells looked seventeen or eighteen. A second glance and she might have been in her early twenties. Close up, she could see premature aging. Though she now looked to be in her mid-forties, Meg suspected she was actually in her late twenties or early thirties. She wondered if the rapid aging had come about due to the extended use of alcohol, drugs, or both. Her smile was too big. Her voice was too loud. Her hand shot out toward Meg like a bayonet.

"Hi!" Meg shook her hand. "You must be the head shrink."

"Yes . . . Meg Wolfe."

Quickly, Erica moved on to Zeus. Appreciatively, though inappropriately, looking him up and down. By her expression, she liked what she saw. Meg was irritated with the blatant flirting.

"I'm Erica. And you," she held her hand out to him, "must be the cop."

She hadn't bothered to give Meg her name.

"Detective." He shook her hand, then withdrew his with slight difficulty. He didn't bother giving his name.

"Well, let's get this meeting about the kid . . . . started."

"The meeting is about *you* not *Jasmine*." Meg had all she could do to not speak through clenched teeth.

"Right, right." Erica took a step toward Zeus, clearly aiming to walk with him to the living room. "Let's get this party started."

Zeus sidestepped her and placed an arm around Meg's shoulders. Erica ignored the obvious message.

"Yes, let's."

He maneuvered Meg and himself past Erica. Meg looked at Janice's hopeless expression and did her best to smile at her. Those three entered the living room together with Erica on Zeus' heels.

"Erica, if you would sit next to me."

Janice coaxed when she saw her plans to sit next to Zeus. Mary quickly placed Jasmine in a chair, nodding to one on either side of her for Meg and Zeus, then sat to Meg's left . . . the four of them facing Janice and Erica.

"So, what now?" Erica asked almost swinging her legs back and forth like an excited child. "Do I sign papers or something and get a license of some kind?"

Meg cringed, closing her eyes. Zeus reached over placing his hand on the back of her neck, hoping to remind her to stay in control. If Jasmine hadn't placed a hand on his leg, he might have lost his. Instead, when he spoke, his voice was deceptively calm and quiet . . . almost conversational.

"Erica," his voice dripped with charm, "if you'd like to adopt a puppy you're in the wrong place." Erica laughed.

"Oh, Detective . . ." She paused waiting for Zeus to give his name . . . at least his last name. He offered nothing. She gave him a coy come-hither smile, "you are so cute!"

"Yes, well . . ." Janice broke in, "let's get on with what we are here for!"

Zeus, who looked away. Janice continued.

"If you would like to take custody of Jasmine, being the only living relative, who we've found so far . . ."

"Oh, I'm the *only* relative." Erica assured her. Janice continued again, as if she hadn't been interrupted, "there are steps, rules and regulations that must be taken and adhered to."

"Like what?" That had put a damper on her tone.

"You must show that you have adequate and stable housing and funds to take on the responsibility of raising a child. You can't have a criminal record or record of substance abuse."

Meg felt any of those would disqualify her.

"Oh, *I'm* clean!"

Meg thought she heard something hidden in Erica's words, but couldn't put her finger on it just then.

"We will investigate you . . ." Erica winked at Zeus. ". . . your home, financial records, your job, your neighbors . . ."

"Hey, I'll get money for the kid, right?" Meg cringed.

"You can apply for assistance, yes." Erica's eyes lit up.

"Good 'cause I have a one bedroom now but I'll get a two bedroom so the kid can have her own room."

Meg stood so suddenly that the chair she had been sitting in slid back a few inches.

Chapter Fifteen

"I have to . . ."

"The restroom is down the hall to the left." Mary prompted.

"Thank you."

Meg hurried out of the living room, thankful for Mary's direction. It wasn't that she needed to use the restroom or directions to it. She knew where it was and Mary knew that. She knew Meg was upset and needed a few minutes to collect herself.

Meg made herself slowly and quietly close the door behind her. She paced the small room trying not to scream, trying not to forcefully suggest to Erica to go to hell . . . or at least go back under whatever rock she had crawled out from under. Erica didn't want a 'kid named after a flower' . . . she wanted an income. Splashing cold water on her face, then pressing a towel over it, she inhaled deeply three times, calming herself. She thought she'd hyperventilate before she could actually become calm enough to return to the living room. A little was better than nothing.

She returned to her seat, gave a slight nod to Zeus who looked at her questioningly, and took Jasmine's hand. Her calm cracked at Erica's next words.

"The kid *is* potty trained, isn't she?" Meg blew, quickly rising to her feet.

"The *kid* has a name. It's Jasmine. She's a four-year-old child who is housebroken just for your convenience. She's a little girl, not a . . ."

"Meg!" Zeus spoke her name with quiet authority and a warning.

She plopped back into her chair. Jasmine took her hand. Calm returned, somewhat.

"I apologize for my outburst."

After a few more questions, the meeting came to a close. Meg had shut down her emotions, solidly sitting in her chair, not moving but hearing everything. She kept her mouth shut. Mary walked them to the door, followed by Jasmine.

"I'm sorry. We'll have to talk later." Mary rolled her eyes in the direction of the living room where Janice and Erica remained. Meg nodded.

"How did I do?" Jasmine asked.

"You were very grown up!" Automatically Meg picked her up. "A lot more grown up than I was."

Meg wanted to run out the door with Jasmine and take her somewhere where she'd be safe and far away from Erica. She took a step toward the door. Realizing her body was following her thoughts, she gave Jasmine a hug and kiss then handed her over to Zeus. He hugged her for several seconds before handing her over to Mary.

"You'll come back?" Jasmine asked of them both.

"Yes, Baby," Meg answered, "we'll be back."

She wanted to cry. She didn't. She got in the car and made herself think analytically. No emotions. A hard outer mask.

"You okay?" Her mask started to fall. She crammed it back into place.

"I'm fine. You?"

"I'm angry. I intend to investigate her from birth to her most recent breath. I'll check under every rock, even the one she lives under!"

"Make your anger work for you. That's what I'm going to do."

"What are you going to do?"

"I'm also going to check her out. She showed some of her true colors today. It was unintentional for the most part, being her personality, I believe. What was intentional, particularly her name I believe . . . I don't know . . . there's something there . . . something in the way she said "*I'm* clean." I just got the feeling she meant the name she's using is clean, her real name isn't. Something like that."

"I picked up on that, too. My first thought was she meant she was clean but someone else, a husband or boyfriend, isn't. Erica Wells and anyone she lives with, within a hundred miles, will be under a high-powered microscope for a very long time. If I see so much as an ant at her place, I'll personally yank Jasmine out of there."

"You'll go to her place?"

"I will . . . officially or unofficially, but I will."

"Don't go alone. If what I saw today is a hint, she'll use you . . ."

"Jealous?"

"Of what?" Meg nearly snorted. "I mean if you piss her off or she finds out you're there unofficially or a dozen other things, like you're dissecting her life unnecessarily or not succumbing to her charms, she could scream sexual or physical assault, harassment, intimidation . . . there's quite a list she can pick from."

"In that case, I'll need a female partner. Would you like the job?"

"You should have someone impartial. You should ask your lady friend."

"I asked you."

"I don't think we can both, together, be unemotionally involved. If one of us thinks we found something on her, the other will feed off that and we'd look until we found something, even if there isn't anything there."

"No, we won't. We'll exhaust every avenue, every clue, regardless of how it's been covered up. We'll also push each other to check carefully and thoroughly so everything will stand up under scrutiny, in court, with no room for reasonable doubt. We will do that because we *are* emotionally involved and have the most to gain . . . Jasmine's well being and happiness, either way."

"I hope so."

"We'll keep each other on track. We'll constantly question each other until there are no more questions to ask."

"In theory, it sounds good."

"You already have the mindset. You're questioning me already. Will you work with me?"

She liked the idea if for no other reason than to have her thumb on the pulse of the investigation. She silently asked for guidance to stay on the straight and narrow.

"Yes."

"Unless I'm asked to investigate her, I can't work on it on company time. That leaves after work and weekends. I, personally, have nothing better to do. Will that put a strain on your free time?"

"Not really. Sometimes I take work home with me, but I'm sure that won't be a problem. Going home for supper with my family once a week may even be helpful. We could put our heads together and toss around ideas."

"During work hours we can still work on . . ."

"There isn't much I can do if Jasmine is gone. How is that going anyway?"

"Very slowly, almost a stand still and you never know, maybe you'll see something I missed . . . a fresh pair of eyes and all that."

Meg doubted Zeus missed anything. Somehow that brought his lady friend to mind. He should have jumped at the chance to work with her . . . after work and weekends. It was the perfect opportunity to be together, get to know each other. Did he really think she would do a better job? Suddenly, it hit her why he'd rather not work with his lady friend.

Avoidance. He always walked away from a relationship when it became too serious. Granted the previous relationships had gone a lot farther with more time involved, but with this one he seemed to be putting the brakes on before anything even got started. It did and didn't make sense. He was doing it because he was *very* interested in this woman, perhaps had even fallen in love with her already, and that was why he was, or had been, backing off. He didn't want to hurt her. He was thinking ahead and preventing pain . . . his and hers. True enough. However, he'd never get past his fear of abandoning a wife and family if he never tried again. What was she going to do with him? She couldn't ease him past the hump if he stayed on flat ground.

"We may as well go inside. We've been sitting out here for quite a while."

Meg looked around. They were in the parking lot of her building. She had been so engrossed in their conversation and then her thoughts she hadn't even realized the car had been moving. Thankfully, she hadn't been driving this time.

She had taken too long to answer.

"Unless you'd rather I didn't."

"No, no . . . come on up."

Clansey was there when Meg opened the door. He listened carefully, intently, as Meg and Zeus talked about their investigation into Erica Wells. Zeus called around to the different hotels and motels until he found which one she was registered at. From there, they went to a cafe just down and across the street from it. They ate lunch and watched to see if they'd see her coming or going. With no activity they left.

"I'd like to go to my place for a minute, if you don't mind."

"I'd like to see your man cave." She grinned at him. He grinned back.

"From a shrink's point of view?"

"Just plain curiosity."

He pulled up to an older, but well-maintained, brick building. As they entered, he warned her he lived on the second floor and there were no elevators.

On the second floor, he turned left going to the door on the end. He placed the key in the lock, then turned to her.

"I apologize for the mess and please ignore the porn magazines."

Meg entered expecting the worst. There was no mess, unless one coffee cup on the kitchen counter and a jacket laid over the back of the couch could be considered such. As for the porn magazines, there were no such things, just a Field & Stream magazine on a lamp table.

"Ugh, how can you live like this? It's absolutely appalling!"

"I thought if I gave you the worst scenario you'd overlook what mess there is."

Zeus turned on the laptop, typed something in and leaned his hands on either side of it while waiting. Again, she looked around to see if she had missed anything that could be considered a mess.

"Are you a neat freak?"

"Hardly." He typed something else.

"Unless your bedroom is a pig sty, I can' even stretch my imagination far enough to call this a mess."

Zeus remained leaning on the table. He turned his head to look at her with a very devilish grin.

"Are you asking to see my bedroom?" His voice held all kinds of mock insinuations.

"Is there anything interesting in there?" She wasn't about to let him embarrass her as he was trying to do.

"Not until I . . ."

His laptop beeped drawing his attention away . . . a fact Meg was glad for. She didn't know how far to go with their conversation or how far he would go. This was definitely a different side to him. On his own turf, he was definitely more relaxed. An idea came to her.

"Zeus, have you ever invited your lady friend here?"

"Just once." He seemed more interested in what was on his laptop. "If you'd like something to drink you can help yourself to . . . whatever is in the fridge. Otherwise, make yourself comfortable, I'll be done in a minute."

He had answered her and changed the subject. Clearly he didn't want to talk about her. She politely sat on the couch and thought how sad it was that he didn't even want to try having another relationship and that he'd opt to be alone instead. Momentarily, she realized he had finished with his laptop and was watching her, noting her sad expression.

"Sorry for being rude. I put in what information I have on Erica and the computer is working on it."

He went to the fridge, opened it, looked inside and closed it.

"I lied. There isn't anything to drink in there. No food, either. At least none I'd dare to eat anyway."

"You must eat out a lot."

"Yeah, or grab some take out on the way home." He paused. "Feel sorry for me yet?"

"Kinda." She admitted.

"Don't." He grinned. "I can cook if I want to. I just usually don't have, or want to make, the time."

"Still . . ." The thought of eating out or eating take out regularly wasn't very appealing to her.

"Okay, let's go shopping and I'll prove to you I really can cook." He challenged.

"That's not necessary. I'll take your word for it."

"Don't trust me?"

He was trying to goad her into accepting. He knew it and she knew it. She eyed him as she tried to decide if she'd allow it or not. She decided she would. Before she could answer, he used the guilt trip tactic.

"It would be only fair as you've cooked for me." Next came an option . . . the lesser of two evils. "And you let me spend the night."

Meg laughed at the ploys and how he was so blatantly unashamed of using them.

"Did you forget you're talking to and using mind/emotional tactics on a shrink?"

"Tactics?"

"Oh, please! There's no way it was a form of intimidation! You've used a challenge, trust, guilt and options to get me to agree to stay for supper. Have you even considered just asking me or are you afraid being that straight forward would be rebuffed?"

"Will you let me cook supper for you here, tonight?"

"Oh, Zeus, I'd love to! Thank you for asking."

"Why are women so complicated?"

"Complicated? Really? You just spent, at least, ten minutes on something that could have taken a minute, tops."

"It's still your fault, I'm sure."

His tone indicated he may as well have said, "a woman's place is in the kitchen."

"Still trying to goad me or trying to get me to change my mind about staying?"

"Yes. No." He grinned.

"If this is the the charm you use on women, you might want to rethink that charm, or do you prepare them for the worst so they are relieved to find you aren't so bad after all?"

"One hundred percent charm, baby!" His grin deepened.

"How's that working out for you?"

Meg wanted to bite her tongue off. Considering the problem he had with relationships, a comment like that about women probably not only hurt, but would cause a big change in his mood. She carefully looked at him to see what damage her words had caused.

Chapter Sixteen

He was still grinning as he raised a questioning eyebrow at her. She laughed softly, glad he had taken it as she had meant it. She shook her head in a mock sad gesture.

"Okay then, before you do change your mind, let's go shopping." She raised an eyebrow at him. "Okay, okay—you don't take orders and you can't be intimidated. I blame your clients for that."

"My clients?" She stood. "They're children."

"And children," he put an arm around her shoulders, steering her toward the door, "can be very intimidating."

"I can't argue with that!"

Meg was thoroughly enjoying the side of Zeus he was showing her. He was fun and funny, full of jokes and teasing. She gave as good as she got and he took it all in stride.

At first it appeared that he was tossing things in the cart randomly, but soon Meg realized that he had a list in his head. A variety of meat, as well as canned and fresh vegetables, fresh fruit, salad items, bread, milk, and juice were tossed in the cart. Potatoes, seasonings, condiments, and a six pack of beer went in. She was impressed; he hadn't gotten quick fix things.

She helped put the groceries on the conveyor belt at the checkout stand. As the items were getting rung up, he turned to her, nodding toward the food.

"What would you like for supper?"

"Chicken Alfredo, biscuits and gravy, green beans, and apple pie a la mode." For a few seconds, he gave her a blank stare.

"I said I could cook, not that I was a freakin' chef! How about baked chicken, mashed potatoes with gravy, spinach, apple pie and what is a la mode?"

"Topped with ice cream, usually vanilla."

"Well, then, two more stops before we go home."

The cashier was paid, groceries placed on the backseat, then one stop at a bakery and one at an ice cream parlor, and they were headed back to his apartment.

Of the five bags of groceries and the pie, Meg was handed the pie. Before he could stop her, she grabbed two bags. By the luck of the draw, both were heavy. She took off toward the building. Zeus said something from behind her, something to the effect of letting him take the bags. She ignored him and sprinted up the two flights of stairs.

She was leaning against the door jamb, breathing under fair control, when he rounded the corner at the top of the stairs.

"Remind me . . ." he sat a bag down, reached for his keys and unlocked the door, "to never run from you!" Her laughter echoed down the hall as she preceded him inside.

"You'd take it like a man, huh?" She helped him unpack the bags.

"Right on the chin." He tapped a finger there.

Meg giggled and had to stop herself from stretching up and kissing his chin. The notion shocked her enough to step away and sit at the table a few feet away.

"What can I help with?" She asked as casually as possible.

"I'm cooking." He reminded her.

"That leaves the salad."

Meg tore lettuce, sliced cucumbers, radishes and mushrooms, diced onions and green peppers, drained some black olives, and rinsed cherry tomatoes. She layered everything, ending with the olives and tomatoes on top.

She placed the salad in the fridge, and then watched Zeus rinse and season the chicken before putting it in the oven and setting a timer. He filled the sink with cold water and sprinkled salt in the sink, then added the fresh spinach. Finished, he looked at Meg.

"Impressed yet?"

"Very." She said in all honesty, then added, "You really know how to work the stove!"

He flicked water at her before drying his hands and taking two beers from the fridge. Opening both, he sat at the table, handing her one.

"So what was it like growing up with your powers?"

"They're gifts, not powers, and it was very lonely."

"Really? I'd think everyone would have wanted to be your friend."

"Quite the opposite. I was a freak and people didn't understand—they still don't."

"In this day and age?"

"In this day and age."

"Have you ever, or do you, do readings?"

"Carmen can read people, not me. And, we don't use our gifts for monetary gain." For just a second, her eyes had gotten distant, her jaw set, and her voice cooled.

"Did that question offend you? Does it have anything to do with the guy who hurt you—the one you don't want to talk about?"

Her eyes bore into his for several long seconds. In that time, she swept his mind for whatever thoughts were there. He hadn't been malicious with his questions. She relaxed.

"No, I wasn't offended. Well, perhaps a little. Your question just threw me back to a time I don't want to think about. And, yes, it has something to do with Tony." She sipped her beer, hearing his next thought, but couldn't swallow fast enough to reply before he asked.

"Do you want to talk about him now?"

He had used 'him' instead of the name she had just given, maybe intentionally, or unintentionally, to make the topic less personal. She shook her head, still unable and unwilling to discuss it.

"No, like I said before, not now, maybe not ever."

"Surely you know talking about it will help. And, remember, you had said one day, not 'not ever.'" She eyed him suspiciously.

"Shrink 101?" He shook his head.

"Common sense. Experience."

"Experience?"

"Yeah, this shrink badgered me until I faced the root cause of my problem with relationships." He smiled at her.

"And it helped?"

"Knowing what it was . . . no, I already knew, deep down . . . admitting it—saying it—thinking about it—I felt something crack open a little."

"So we should keep going!"

"I don't have enough beer to start that tonight." That distant look haunted his eyes briefly.

"I understand."

"One of these days we'll have to get totally snockered and get this crap out of our systems."

"Snockered . . ." She hadn't heard that word since college . . . since Tony . . .

"Shit-faced. Drunk." He thought she didn't understand.

"Such colorful wording."

Her voice was tinged with sadness, as were her eyes. He had hit another raw nerve. He decided a change of subject was needed.

"Okay, we're suppose to be having an enjoyable meal and pleasant conversation. We'll leave the past buried for now. Another beer?"

He glanced at the time as he retrieved two more beers from the fridge and nodded toward the living room. They sat on the couch, both positioning themselves so they half faced each other.

"Are you a light weight?" He nodded toward her beer. "Is there a point I should cut you off?"

"I know my limit. You?"

"I know mine, too, and will adhere to it."

"Do you push your limit often?"

"Not any more. Not in a long time. I prefer a clear head, unoccupied by demons."

"We would be a sad pair drunk."

"Crying in our pretzels, snotty noses, blubbering. Not a pretty sight."

"Definitely not!"

After several minutes of chatting, he stood up.

"Follow me, please."

Meg returned to the kitchen with him, sitting at the table as he rinsed the spinach and put it in a kettle, then added water, a diced onion, bacon bits. He put it on the stove. Opening the oven, he pulled out the chicken, uncovered it, then returned it to the oven. He brought the potatoes, a knife, a plastic bag and pan to the table where he proceeded to peel and cube the potatoes, putting the peelings in the plastic bag.

"Where did you learn to cook?"

"Mostly trial and error. Some cooking shows."

"A well-rounded man!"

"Except for the chink in my armor, I'm a pretty good catch."

"Really?"

"Definitely."

"No conceit at all . . . humble also—that's refreshing!"

"All part of my charm."

"And this—charm—is what attracts all the ladies?"

"Yup. I actually have to beat them off with a stick."

"I can imagine!"

Meg took a chunk of raw potato and popped it in her mouth. Zeus did the same as he took the pan, now full, and rinsed them, added water and salt and put them on to cook. She gathered the bag of peelings, put it in the trash, and rinsed off the knife. He replaced the foil, turned the oven to warm, then put the apple pie in. He checked the spinach, turned the heat down and watched Meg, appraising her as she washed off the table, her back to him. Her bottom wiggled slightly as she did so.

"I like this side of you."

When she had just finished wiping off the table, she heard his thoughts and felt his eyes. She slowly stood erect. His eyes traveled from her back side up until he was looking into her eyes when she turned to face him.

"Men usually stare at my breasts." She failed to embarrass him.

"They weren't visible at the time." He answered, nonplussed.

"How's your alcohol level?"

"Six or seven more should do it." He poured what was left of his second bottle down the sink.

Sitting down to eat, they carried on a conversation that touched on many topics. The atmosphere was easy and relaxed. He'd just asked her a question, and while she answered, she reached for the pepper shaker, needing to lean forward slightly. His mind returned to earlier in the day when she had unbuttoned and refastened her blouse in front of him. His eyes went to the slight swell of her breasts visible through the opening of her blouse.

The last thing she had said should have elicited a response from him. When none came, she looked up at him, realized what he was preoccupied with and got his attention.

"Zeus."

"Mm?"

"My eyes are a little higher."

His eyes slowly traveled up to meet hers.

"So they are." He agreed. "I was just checking out what most men stare at."

She should have been insulted. She should have been angry. She should have felt degraded or at least annoyed. She didn't.

"I see why they stare." She couldn't help but smile.

"So, you're a breast man?"

"I bought chicken breasts, didn't I?"

"You also bought thighs."

"And I was checking out your butt. I guess I'm a well-rounded man who enjoys a good view." He stated as a matter of fact. Meg decided to redirect the conversation.

"The meal was delicious."

"Dessert?"

"I'm afraid to answer that in light of the earlier topic."

"I'm only offering apple pie a la—something." He stood, clearing the dishes. "Coffee? Or will that keep you up all night? We could always . . ." He suddenly cut himself off, regrouped and continued, "drink decaf."

"Regular is fine."

Whatever had happened at the table, which was and yet wasn't, sexual, was gone. They ate their warm apple pie with French vanilla ice cream on top and drank coffee in the living room. The conversation easy and friendly.

Nine. Ten. Eleven. Eleven-thirty.

"Spending the night?" He asked casually.

"I can't—I didn't bring my PJs." He exaggerated a sigh.

"Then I should bring you home. We both have to get up early."

Meg laid in bed thinking how much she had enjoyed her afternoon and evening with Zeus. Considering the day hadn't started out very well, it was just what she had needed. She reached for the phone and called Zeus.

"Hello."

"I like this side of your personality, too."

"Ah, you're laying in bed thinking about me. I'm honored!"

"Maybe I was wrong."

"I'm laying in bed thinking about you, too." He paused. "I'm in bed—you're in bed—we're in bed together. Now go to sleep and at least get a few hours of sleep."

"A few . . . ?" She looked at the clock. "It's one-thirty! I'm sorry—I didn't realize. Good night." He chuckled softly.

"I do have that effect on women. Good night."

Chapter Seventeen

Off and on during the next day, Meg thought about the time she had spent with Zeus. She barely felt the fact that she had only slept a few hours. With her last client gone at three-thirty, she prepared to leave. Making sure her office was tidy and ready for the next day, she picked up her keys, pushed her chair up to the desk, then heard Luce buzz her from the outer office. Pressing the intercom button, she leaned on the chair.

"Yes, Luce?"

"You have a client out here. Daniel Newman wants to know if you can see him."

"Definitely. Give me a minute, then send him in."

Daniel Newman. She had only seen the teen once. He had more than vaguely matched the description of the killer of Jasmine's parents. She knew he had wanted to tell her something—something he knew about those murders, but he hadn't. He also hadn't made another appointment. Now here he was waiting to see her. She opened the door, smiling brightly at him.

"Come in, Daniel. It's nice to see you again." He nodded and walked in, his eyes darting around the room.

"How have you been, Daniel?"

"Okay."

"What can I help you with today?"

"Just," he shrugged one shoulder, "you know," and he quickly looked at her then away, "talk and stuff."

"We can do that."

She pulled out her chair and sat down, hoping he would sit also. He paced for a minute, then finally sat down.

"How's school going?"

"It sucks."

"Really? Why?"

"'Cause it's school."

"How are your grades?"

"They suck, too! Geez, can we talk about something else?"

"Sure. What would you like to talk about?"

"I dunno." He shrugged.

"Yes, you do, Daniel, or you wouldn't have come here. What's bothering you?" He gave a slight shrug and avoided looking at her. "I may be able to help." She offered.

"What if . . ." He started pacing again. "What if . . ." He stopped. "Ah, fuck!"

Daniel headed toward the door. As he reached for the handle, she imposed a thought.

"Stop." He stopped and turned toward her. She spoke to him. "Please talk to me Daniel. Getting it off your chest will help. What if . . . what?"

He looked at her. She could see in his eyes, actually just behind his eyes, that he was angry and scared. Mostly the latter. She calmly looked back and waited. He focused on her face momentarily then looked away.

"I was watching this show—you know, one of those cop shows—and this guy, well he didn't do anything wrong, but he knows a guy who did." He quickly looked at Meg.

"Sounds like a good show so far. What did the guy do?" She left it open for him to talk about either character.

"Which one?" He looked at her suspiciously.

"Either one—both." She continued to look back at him with just the right amount of calm and interest.

"Well, the second guy told the first guy what he did." He stopped. Meg let a few seconds tick by.

"Was he telling the truth or just making stuff up?"

"Oh, no, it was true 'cause there was blood everywhere!" He stopped short. Again—she let a few seconds go by.

"Goodness, if it were me, I'd be scared! What did the first guy do?"

"Nothing. Like you said, he was scared."

"Was he good friends with the second guy?"

"Yeah, almost like—brothers, I guess."

"Mm, that would be tough. Did he tell anyone?"

"No! I mean he loves his—friend—and he's a little afraid of him, too."

"Why is he afraid of his friend?"

"He—can be—can get—a little crazy sometimes."

"Violently?"

"I don't think so—not until then. You know, the show didn't really let you know."

"Shows do that sometimes. I guess they want you to figure it out for yourself. So, how did the show end?"

"It hasn't, yet—continued—you know."

"What do you think will happen?" Meg leaned forward, sounding excited, with a touch of conspiracy about the show.

"I've gotta go—homework and stuff."

"Okay. Thanks for stopping by Daniel. You'll stop by and tell me how the show ends, won't you? If you want to stop by before that, you're always welcome." He barely nodded and slipped out the door.

Meg sat in her chair, slightly swaying back and forth, thinking about what he had just told her. She hoped he would come back. Retrieving his file, she made notes. He knew the killer and was afraid of him because "he could get a little crazy sometimes." She had wanted very badly to mentally suggest he tell her everything. She sighed. If he wasn't ready and wouldn't tell her on his own, no suggestion would work. It might even scare him away, realizing he was about to tell all.

There was a light knock on the door and Luce poked her head in.

"I'm gone. Do you need anything before I split?" Meg glanced at her watch; it was after five. Daniel had been there an hour and a half.

"No, I'm heading out myself. See you tomorrow."

Meg heard the outside door close and lights click off as she put Daniel's file away. She glanced around her office, making sure it was still tidy. Her mind going over the fact that Daniel knew the killer, and knew him well—"almost like a brother." The killer was slight of build with vivid green eyes. Daniel was slight of build. Was the killer a teenager? Was his use of the word "brother" literal? Did Daniel have a twin? Did he have siblings? If so, was there a strong family resemblance?

With her mind flipping through questions, she opened her office door. Immediately, she audibly sucked in air, her hand went to her chest and she stumbled back. A huge man stood just outside her door, hand raised. Her mind froze.

Her mind started working again. It recognized Zeus and her thoughts that he was the killer disappeared. She smiled from relief and from the visual flight of fancy her mind had conjured.

"What are you doing lurking around? How did you get in? Crap, you nearly scared me to death!"

Adrenaline leaving her body, her legs started to shake. She sat in the chair that her clients usually use. Leaned forward and inhaled deeply.

"I'm sorry. Are you okay? I was about to knock. You also gave me a bit of a start, you know."

Meg started to giggle as she thought about what had just happened and the look on his face that hadn't registered at the moment but was now.

"Well, what a pair we are! In an emergency, we both have heart attacks!"

"Kind of blows 'To Protect and Serve' out of the water, huh?" She giggled louder.

"I'm just glad no one was here to see it. Let's get out of here."

"By the way, I wasn't lurking around and I came in as the secretary left."

"Great! I still have lumps in my underwear!"

A hearty laugh erupted from deep in his chest as he waited outside while she locked the front door. He walked her to her car, draping an arm around her shoulders.

"Did you—do something to me—when you saw me back there?"

She turned to face him after unlocking her door, trying to remember.

"I don't think so, why?"

"I literally froze. It wasn't from fear—I know how that feels. My mind and body just froze and for that second or two, before you moved, all I felt was like I was in a void—a bubble—surrounded completely by—well, it was like being in a vacuum of some sort—immobilized completely."

"I did do something—it was an automatic reaction, I suppose. In my mind, I screamed "No! Stop!" Maybe that was what froze you."

"It was an incredibly helpless feeling. I saw you stumble backward and wanted to reach out to steady you but I was stuck there."

"I've never done . . ." She stopped, thinking. "Yes I have! I was maybe eleven or so and Michael hid in my closet and jumped out at me when I entered my room. He'd taken the light bulb out so I was in the dark and I did something similar."

"What happened?"

"Like you, he froze. His arms were in the air like he was going to grab me and his face was contorted in mid snarl or something. As soon as I realized it was him, he became relaxed. His arms fell and his face returned to normal again, but he just stood there looking at me embarrassed."

"Embarrassed? Why?"

"He was only nine. It scared him when he suddenly couldn't move and then just as suddenly he could. He wet himself."

Zeus quickly took inventory to see if he'd done the same. He hadn't.

"Priceless!" He laughed.

"He was mad. He thought I made him do it."

"You should be a cop. You wouldn't have to chase anybody—just freeze them. By the time they thawed they'd already be cuffed!"

"I think I have to be scared out of my mind to be able to do it."

"Too bad."

"So, how was your day?"

"Interesting. I tried calling you, but it went straight to voicemail."

"I shut my cell off when I'm at work." She pulled it out of her pocket and turned it on. Three missed calls and three messages popped up.

"Or, when you don't want to talk to someone?" She ignored that.

"We can stand here all night or we can go to my place and tell each other about our day. I believe we both have information to tell the other."

"Or we could go to my place."

"Mine is closer. You know the way."

She was in her car and pulling away before he had unlocked his car.

They pulled into her parking lot, one behind the other and parked side by side, exiting their vehicles together.

"You had an interesting day, too, I take it." Zeus held the front door open letting her enter first.

"Oh, yes—especially the last part—*before* you showed up."

"So," they crossed the lobby and entered the elevator, "what happened?"

"I had an unexpected client stop by to talk."

"And that client was . . ." He prompted.

Exiting the elevator they went to her apartment. She unlocked her door and they stepped inside.

"Daniel." She tossed her keys on the bar and put the kettle on for tea.

"He came of his own volition? Of course, you said 'unexpected.' What did he say?"

"He just told me about a show he'd seen."

"What was the purpose to *that*?"

"It wasn't a show."

"I think I scared you more than either of us realized. You're not making any sense, Meg."

"If it wasn't a show, what would it be?"

He looked at her blankly for a few seconds before it came to him.

"Real life!"

"You got it!"

Zeus made the tea for them, bringing it to the table. When they were both seated, he sipped his, then leaned forward, elbows on the table.

"Tell me about this show."

"Well, there's this one guy who has this close, long-time friend. They're so close, he's like a brother. The second guy did something really bad and told the first guy about it. The first guy knows it's true because the second guy was covered in blood. The first guy was scared to tell anyone because the second guy gets crazy sometimes."

"And?"

"To be continued."

"That's all he said?"

"I'm afraid so. He said that's the way the show ended."

"Okay, so—Daniel definitely knows the killer. The killer told him what he did. He was covered in blood—blood splatter—he was standing close to at least one of the victims.

Close like a brother . . . I'll have to see who Daniel has for siblings."

"Especially one with vivid green eyes." She sipped her tea, hoping he would remember what she had previously told him as she couldn't give that information out now.

"Now, tell me about your day."

"I've been snooping around the area where Jasmine's father worked—coffee stands, fast food places, diners—any place he may have gone for lunch or whatever. A couple people in these places recognized his photo, but nothing more. On a gut feeling, I stopped at a newspaper stand just opening up. I showed the guy the picture of Mark Lutz and he remembered him because he used to buy a paper there every day, and he was with his wife. I showed him a picture of Elizabeth Lutz, but he said she wasn't the woman with Mark. He then described the same woman Jasmine had described and said that one time they had a kid with them. When I showed him a picture of Jasmine, it proved to be the same kid. The woman also had a rottweiler—a big, ugly dog, as Jasmine had also described."

Chapter Eighteen

"That's fantastic, Zeus!"

"That it is and what's even better, if I had stopped another day, I would have come up empty. The guy at the stand, Jimmy—only he pronounced it Jeemee,—is retiring and letting his nephew take over. Today is his last day."

"Wow, it's lucky you had that gut feeling!"

She wanted to remind him that feeling had probably been his Spirit Guide, but he didn't seem to want to think about anything psychic, so she left it alone.

"Okay, yes, I admit, I thought of what you've said about Spirit Guides nudging you when you get ideas out of the blue. And I did wonder if mine nudged me to stop today."

"Wow—nice!"

"I have his home address and phone number in case I need to speak with him again and he has my card in case he remembers anything else."

"I don't suppose he'd recognize the composite. There isn't much to go on with the ski mask. Just eyes really."

"He did say the woman bordered on beautiful and her eyes were an intense light blue—cornflower blue is how he described them—and that was about all he liked about her. In his words, she was a snooty bitch and, by her looks and attitude, could have or should have been, or possibly was, a model."

"There are a few modeling agencies around."

"I'll be checking those out tomorrow."

"You poor guy—all of those beautiful women and just one you!"

"Anorexic, and don't touch the hair and makeup—not my type."

"Will you bring your stick?"

"Stick?"

"To beat them off with."

"I won't need one. I'm not in the financial bracket that interests them."

"Voice of experience?"

"Life experience."

His tone indicated she should drop it. Verbally she did. Mentally she pieced together the possibility his mother had been, or wanted to be a model. She became pregnant and that alone, or coupled with being pregnant out of wedlock, ruined her career or caused it to never get started. A male caused that—Zeus was a male child—she was cool toward him.

"Where's Clansey?" Swift change of subject.

"Beats me. He's been gone a lot lately. When he has been here, he's been very secretive about what he's been up to. Ghosts, go figure."

"You rang, Your Eminence?"

"Oops, speak of the devil!"

"He's here?"

"Just arrived. He says hello."

"Hello, Clansey. What's up?" Clansey gave Meg a questioning look.

"He means what have you been up to—how are you doing."

"I've been doing fine and keeping myself busy."

Meg relayed the message.

"Staying out of trouble I hope."

"Always—usually anyway. If not," he shrugged, "what can you do?" Zeus laughed after hearing what he had said.

"What have the two of you been up to?" Meg ignored the suggestive expression on Clansey's face.

"We're up to our eyeballs with two cases—Jasmine's aunt and her parent's killer."

"Neither are what they appear."

"What's that suppose to mean?"

Meg held up a finger gesturing Clansey to wait and told Zeus what he had said.

"Just that." Clansey continued when she had motioned for him to continue.

"Just that." Meg repeated for Zeus. "That's not much help Clansey."

"Clansey." Zeus looked around not knowing where he was. Clansey placed a hand on his shoulder giving him a chill, "are you investigating on your own?"

"Jasmine is important to you two, so I'm trying to help." Meg repeated this to Zeus.

"Thank you, Clansey. Meg and I appreciate any help you can give us."

"You're welcome, Your Eminence. I'm gone."

Clansey disappeared in an instant. Meg let Zeus know, then looked at him as she contemplated something.

"Does it bother you that I have to repeat everything he says?"

"Not so much any more. I try to think of it as you're the interpreter for sign language."

"Okay, good. Both are not what they appear." Meg continued her analysis. "We are already fairly sure Erica isn't being totally honest with us, so that statement doesn't surprise us. But the killer—isn't what he appears. I wonder if he's talking about Daniel. We know he isn't the killer, but he knows who is."

"Could Daniel be talking in circles? This whole show story, particularly the brother thing—you think he's the brother and not the friend?" Meg thought about it for a few minutes.

"No, I believe he's the friend. He knows what happened but had no part in it."

"Just the fact that he knows may put him in danger. Friend or not, eventually the killer is going to start thinking that Daniel is the only other one who knows and can tell. Most people with something to hide, especially killers, don't like that."

"That may be a selling point. If Daniel shows up again and talks about the show—hell, even if he doesn't—I'll tell him the safest thing to do *is* to tell what he knows. It would be better if his friend is caught *before* he realizes Daniel needs to be dealt with."

"We've both got to be careful. If the killer is watching Daniel to see if he does anything out of the ordinary he may think he is, or is thinking about, talking. Seeing you is probably already a flag if that's the case. Anyone following him, talking to him, or that he talks to, is even more dangerous for him."

"How do we deal with that? Can you arrest him or at least make it look like he's been arrested . . ." Zeus shook his head.

"No. If he doesn't tell us anything, or even if he does, and we can't find the guy, he's screwed."

"There's got to be something we can do."

Meg busied herself with getting supper as she thought about it. A minute later, Zeus was beside her helping.

"Zeus," she stopped what she was doing, "what if the killer has been watching and has seen us together? Daniel's shrink and a cop, and puts a story together that isn't there? Even that aside, I do go to the station periodically. And what if he's followed me to Mary's and seen me—us—with Jasmine and . . ."

"Slow down, Meg. Jasmine was in a closet. Odds are, he doesn't know about her. You don't go to the station often enough to cause any suspicions. As for seeing us together—even that isn't constant. In the past month, we could have been seen together only a few times."

"In the past week alone—here, Mary's, a diner, your place, my work place, here again—that's not just a few times, and since the murder . . ."

"Okay, I get it. Do you suggest we stay away from each other?"

"Wouldn't that be the safest thing to do? I mean, sure, we have been seen together, but suddenly we're not, so obviously we aren't working on anything together, right?"

"Or, the damage is already done so . . ."

"Yes, the damage *is* already done and the more we're seen together the more damage will be done."

"Fine." He dried his hands, then turned to leave the kitchen.

"Zeus," for whatever reason, had been angered by her suggestion, "we can still communicate."

"Sure, I'll send you my thoughts." He strode toward the door. "See you." He opened it and looked back at Meg. "Or, maybe not."

Meg stood there, staring at the space Zeus had occupied before he had stepped beyond the door. She tried to reason it out and couldn't.

"What on earth just happened?" She asked herself. "He must see the sense."

She went back to preparing her meal as she tossed around possible explanations in her mind. A thought came to her as she left the kitchen to take a shower, leaving the food to simmer on the stove.

"No. It can't be because his male/cop ego couldn't handle the fact I thought of it first!"

She shook her head and the frailty of the male ego and stepped into the shower.

She got up the next morning and got in the car to drive to work. As usual, she shut off her phone as she entered work. Upon leaving, she turned it back on and listened to the message waiting for her.

"I'm sorry I walked out last night. I know you shut your phone off when you're at work. I just wanted to let you know that I don't know why I got so angry—yes I do—I felt . . . anyway, I wanted to say I'm sorry."

It didn't matter that he didn't finish how he had felt. She now knew. The word is "rejected." Meg drove home thinking how she should have known Zeus wouldn't have been angry because she had thought of the idea first. He wasn't that shallow.

She stepped out of the shower, put on a tank top and pajama bottoms. Her phone let her know there was a missed call. She checked it on the way to the kitchen. It was from Zeus. He hadn't left a message. She called him back.

"Hi, Zeus."

"Hi. What's your email address?" She gave it to him. "Now we can share information and work on things from our computers."

"Great idea. And, there is always the other."

"What other?" A few seconds went by. "The thought thing?"

"Yeah—that. We can try, anyway. I've never done it long distance. I've never had to. I mean I do with my family, but . . ."

"Not with a layman, I understand. Now?"

"No, I'm not doing it now."

"No, I mean shall we try now? I'll hang up so it doesn't come through the phone—or whatever."

"Okay. Who goes first?"

"You first. If you get something, try telling me what it was. If not, call me. Bye."

In less than a heart beat, she heard his thought and immediately answered with her thought.

"You are so naughty!"

"Sorry, that was the first thing that came into my head."

"*Typical male!*" She chuckled to herself. "*Pink thong underwear—really? Well, at least it wasn't an image of some porn magazine you warned me about.*"

"*I only read the articles, honest.*"

"*Uh—huh.*"

"*This is cool, but rather strange. I'm amazed I'm doing it, but I'm not sure I want you hearing my thoughts all the time.*"

"*I'm sure I don't want to!" Tell you what, when you want me to tune in, just think about those pink thongs.*"

"*My own personal ring tone?*"

"*Yeah, something like that—as sad as that is.*"

"*Perhaps we're not talking—you're just schizophrenic and you're hearing voices in your head.*"

"*I've already been down that road.*"

"*Okay, this is starting to feel weird. Call me and explain please.*"

Meg smiled, stopping her thoughts, and picked up her cell phone, entering in his number.

"I think we did quite well."

"Actually, though strange, it was almost natural if I didn't think about it. Now explain what road you've been down."

"Take a couple psych classes and as you read about all of the mental disorders, you'll swear you have most, if not all, of them. They stay in your mind, because you don't dare tell anyone. Which makes it your own hell, you're scared witless that you're crazy. I'm sure it was worse for me because I *do* see and hear things no one else can or does."

"How did you make it through?"

"I talked with Mom, first, then the professor. Though I had my doubts, off and on, I made it—more on the sane side."

"I think I'll continue to work with them, not think I'm one of them!"

"Smart move!"

"Change of subject. I'm sending what I have on both cases to your computer. When you get a chance, look them over. Let me know if I've missed anything or something gives you any ideas."

"Sure thing boss."

When they hung up, Meg decided she didn't feel like cooking after all. Instead, she made a large salad with strips of chicken left over from the night before. She settled on the couch with it and looked over what Zeus had sent to her laptop.

"Pink thongs." Came into her mind.

"Are you calling or looking at porn?"

"I think the idea of porn is to be naked so I must be calling."

"True—I guess. What's up?"

"I just wanted to say goodnight."

"Night Zeus."

Meg sat back smiling to herself. Maybe there was hope after all. She shut off the laptop and crawled into bed. Yes, maybe there was hope for them to be more than friends. She sat bolt upright. What was she thinking? Where did that thought come from? She was sure she'd meant to think they could be better friends as long as he was apparently accepting her as she was. How silly to think she meant anything else. How silly indeed! She must be more tired than she thought.

Eventually she fell asleep.

Chapter Nineteen

Meg's last client was Jasmine. She locked up her office, leaving early to be able to spend more time than usual with her. Her time with Jasmine was getting short, if Erica checked out as Meg thought she would. And Erica would check out fine as long as she kept whatever secret she had as well hidden as Meg thought she would. However, that was not going to stop Zeus and her from digging and poking around until they either found something or proved Erica was squeaky clean. Meg was torn as to how she wanted it to turn out.

Jasmine was happy to see Meg, yet there was a sadness behind her eyes. Meg tried to pump her up for the possible upcoming move. She told her how exciting it would be, the fun of a new place, new things to see and do.

"And your aunt is your mom's sister so she shouldn't be very different."

"I don't think so."

"You don't think so what?"

"I don't think she's mom's sister."

"Why not?"

"She's not like Mommy. Mommy was nice. I don't like this lady." She threw herself into Meg's arms. "I don't want to go with her!"

What could she say? Nothing. As much as she wanted to tell Jasmine she wouldn't have to go if she didn't want to, she couldn't. She also couldn't tell her that she and Zeus were trying to find something, anything, on Erica Wells so Jasmine didn't have to go. That would possibly give her a false hope and be more damaging if nothing came of it.

By the time Meg left, she was torn between whether their visits were harder on Jasmine or her not seeing Jasmine at all. Jasmine suddenly not seeing Meg at all could be very damaging.

She sent a silent prayer into the universe asking that Zeus would find something on Erica. Seeing how she hadn't tried to contact him directly, she was a bit surprised when she heard his voice.

"Yes?"

"Oh—hi!"

"You called, didn't you?"

"Not exactly, but as long as you're here, has there been any progress with the aunt?"

"Nothing definite yet—I'm waiting for information to come in. Your "voice" sounds different. What's wrong?"

"I saw Jasmine, today. I just left there in fact. She doesn't want to go with her. She also said Erica is nothing like her mother, which is a normal enough reaction, but it also coincides with our feelings about her—of something not being quite right. Am I hearing and seeing things because I want to?"

"I don't think so. I'm sure Jasmine has her reasons and like you said, it's a natural response under the circumstances."

"I just hate to think of her being forced to leave everything familiar to her again, with a person she doesn't know or like." She pulled into her parking lot. *"I'm going to go, Hon—I'm home."* She realized what she had just said and hoped he didn't read too much into it. After all, she calls a lot of people, Hon, from time to time. She couldn't see it, but on his end, he smiled.

"Okay. Look at what I sent you. Let me know what you think."

"Will do. Bye."

There wasn't much he had sent that was new. It did add to the files she had and collectively it now looked like a lot. As she was about to shut down the computer, it beeped letting her know she had incoming mail. It was from Zeus on the double homicide. Again, not much information to add to what she already had. The rest of the evening was the same—nothing new and she went to bed early.

Two days passed. She refrained from going to see Jasmine after work. She'd hoped Daniel would come by to see her and was disappointed. Zeus hadn't contacted her mentally, by phone or on the computer. She felt adrift as she went through her nightly rituals of showering, eating, and laying awake for a long time.

At the end of the third day, sitting in her car, she suddenly decided she would go to the station and fill Dr. Rose in on Jasmine, though there wasn't a lot to tell.

She checked the board and saw he was out. Searching out a computer not in use, she wrote a report, printed it, and left it in his mailbox. Now what? She didn't feel like going home, she didn't feel like going out to eat or seeing a movie. She felt—bored, not centered, and at a loss.

"Meg!" She turned to see Barry walking toward her. "I haven't seen you around for a while. How are you?"

"I'm feeling a bit lost at the moment. I feel it was an unproductive day at work. I came here to see Dr. Rose. He's out. It feels like nothing is coming together. I just feel—blah."

"Meg!" She turned at the sound of Zeus' voice, a smile lighting up her features.

"Well," Barry observed, "he certainly changed your mood!" She ignored the comment.

"Zeus!"

"What brings you to our office?"

"Actually, I came to see Dr. Rose, but he's out."

"That's good for me, then." He took her hands in his. "I have something to show you." He started pulling her toward him. For an instant, she thought he was going to hug her. If he was, Barry interrupted it.

"I'll get out of the way so you two can—talk." He melted into the background but not before noting both suddenly looked much happier.

Zeus didn't hug her. He continued holding her hands, walking backward, pulling her along with him.

"I have a few things to show you. Come to my office." He released her hands, moving so he was beside her and gently gripping her upper arm.

"I hope it's exciting news." He opened his office door letting her enter.

"Exciting—maybe. The point is, it's something," He shut the door. "And, it may lead somewhere."

Meg glanced around the office. It contained a large desk, a set of bookshelves, cement walls, no window, not even in the door. Just the bare essentials. He pulled out two binders, each with a case number and a name. He placed them on his desk in front of her and stood just behind her. Seeing both cases she spoke as she turned to him.

"Both?"

She hadn't realized how close he was standing to her. When she turned, she was barely an inch from her body touching his. He was looking down at her, an odd expression on his face. His head tilted slightly to one side. She knew he was about to kiss her. Her eyes moved to his lips. He inhaled sharply.

"Go to the last entry." He stepped back and moved to the other side of his desk. "You'll see what I'm talking about."

Meg took both binders to a side table, opened one, found the last entry, scanned through it, then did the same with the second one. She kept her head down, concentrating on their contents, while trying to appear as normal as possible. Her mind had been broadsided with information she didn't want to acknowledge.

Her eyes finally saw what she was looking at. They widened and slid over to the first binder and read what was there. She looked at Zeus.

"Daniel has a half sister, and Erica had a roommate who disappeared and was reported missing by Erica?"

"Yes and yes." Zeus answered. "I haven't found the half sister, yet, and with no obvious signs of foul play, nothing was done about . . . ?" Meg checked the information.

"Carla Rivers." She gave him the name he had been searching for. "Why not? Erica reported her missing."

"Carla is over eighteen and has all of her mental capacities, so she had every right to disappear if she wanted to."

"Her clothes—personal items . . . ?"

"Most were missing. It appears she packed and left—no forwarding address, no note—nothing."

"I suppose, if I lived with Erica, I'd do the same thing. Still," she glanced back at the report, "after three years it seems strange."

"Carla Rivers is out there somewhere and I'm going to find her. I'm sure she knows something."

"How do you find someone who obviously doesn't want to be found?"

"There's always some kind of paper trail—phone records—bank card activity—check activity—social security number used for renting cars, apartments, and major purchases. It's actually quite hard to disappear completely."

"Is there anything I can do at home to help with either case?"

"I'll see about sending you some stuff. Other than that, just read over everything and let me know if you see or think of something I missed."

"I will and I have been, but so far nothing."

"We just have to keep digging. I know there's something out there."

Edgar Cross, another detective, knocked lightly and poked his head in.

"Am I interrupting?"

"No, Ed, come on in."

"I'm going to run along now." Meg announced. "Thank you for the information, Zeus."

"No problem, Meg. Everything has been sent to you. Drive carefully."

"I will. See ya."

Meg slipped out the door Edgar held open for her. She concentrated on driving. She busied herself as long as possible when she got home. Eventually, she had to think about what she had been avoiding.

They had worked together before, she and Zeus. They had spent hours together discussing the cases, talking about his sister, had lunch and supper together, gone to the lake with Jasmine and spent hours there. He had been to her apartment, eaten supper with her, and had fallen asleep and spent the night on the couch. So why was now different? Could it have something to do with being shut in a windowless room with him? Why was he apparently suddenly acting like . . . what?

It seemed he had gone out of his way to lean close to her when he was behind her as she looked at the new information on both cases. When she had turned and found him so incredibly close to her, looking into her eyes, his head tilted, she thought he wanted to kiss her. Then, he had quickly moved, putting his desk between them. Had it been her imagination or was it just her?

In that brief amount of time, she had been able to smell soap and cologne, an enticing combination. She noticed his freshly shaven face—so tanned and smooth, begging her to reach out and touch it. His lips had been so close, so full, so soft looking. His eyes liquid pools of soft brown—suddenly hardening just before he moved.

It must have been her imagination. Even if he wasn't interested in someone else, by his own admission, he didn't let relationships get too serious. *If* she ever got into another relationship, she wanted it to be long term. Still, he had been so *hot*!

"Okay, enough!" Meg scolded herself loudly. "He is interested in someone else and even though that isn't going well at the moment, and if I hadn't imagined what just happened, I won't be Miss Right For Now until Miss Right works out! You're being absolutely ridiculous. How many times has he discussed his lady friend with you? For whatever reason, you're being foolish. He's attractive, yes, but he's not your type, so that's that—end of story!" Immediately following that came another thought. "What *is* your type—Tony? Heaven forbid!"

This was how Meg's evening went, until she was so mentally exhausted she couldn't think any longer. Her dreams, however, were filled with images of Zeus and Tony. One pleasant and confusing, the other nightmarish.

Chapter Twenty

She woke exhausted. Dragging herself out of bed and into the shower, she made her mind blank as she automatically washed her hair and body.

"Pink thongs." She dropped the bottle of body wash. *"Good morning."*

"Good—good morning," she stammered.

"I didn't wake you, did I?"

"No—no, I'm up."

"You sound strange. Are you okay?"

"Yes, I'm fine, but can I get back to you in a little bit?" There was a pause.

"Are you in the shower?"

For an instant she thought he could see her in the shower. She knew it didn't work that way. He could only hear what she wanted him to hear.

"Let's just say I'm not in a social position right now."

"You are in the shower!" He was having fun with her obvious embarrassment.

"Goodbye." Meg closed him out.

She hurried through the shower, then got dressed; feeling the whole time as though he could see her. She certainly wasn't in a hurry to contact him, certain he'd continue teasing her. After her thought from the day before, and her dream, she wasn't willing to go through that. She ate breakfast, cleaned up afterward, then called him on the phone. When he answered, he didn't bother with a greeting.

"Did you look things over last night?"

He was all business. Embarrassed? No, angry.

"Yes, a couple of times."

"See or feel anything?"

"No, just a strong urge to dig deeper into both cases."

"Same here. You must be heading to work. I won't keep you. I'll keep you in the loop."

He hung up. There was no goodbye or even time for her to say anything. She looked at the phone for a second or two before hanging it up. Checking the time she realized she had to leave. She didn't have time to analyze him, nor did she want to.

During her lunch break, Meg called Mary to check on Jasmine. She didn't like what she heard.

"Hi, Mary, this is Meg. How is she?"

"She's withdrawing and the nightmares have returned."

"Oh no! I'm so torn as to what I should do. I'm afraid slowly removing myself will make that worse, yet the more I see her, the harder it'll be on her when she leaves."

"I know. I hate to think of what the poor child will go through."

"I'll be over after work—around four or so, if that will be okay."

"I don't care if it's ten—she needs to see you!"

When Meg hung up, she felt depressed and anxious for her work day to end. Poor Jasmine, she wasn't dealing well with seeing Meg only during scheduled visits, and definitely not with leaving with a woman she doesn't know or like. She picked up the phone and called Janice, getting her voice mail, she left a message.

"Hello, Janice, this is Meg Wolfe. I was wondering if there have been any visits between Erica and Jasmine so they can get to know one another. Please let me know as soon as possible. Thanks."

By the time she made it to Mary's, she hadn't heard from Janice, so she asked Mary.

"Oh, yes, there have been visits set up, but Erica only showed for the first one and then she only watched soap operas. After that, she never showed up. She always had some excuse."

Meg's cell phone rang. It was Janice, who gave her the same information Mary had.

"I'm going to insist she start visiting regularly or she won't be able to get custody."

"Is that a prerequisite?"

"I'll make it one!"

Meg heaved a sigh, and as she hung up Mary's phone, she thought of Jasmine's name and sent off a prayer for her.

"I'm coming!" Jasmine shouted from another part of the house.

Mary and Meg looked at one another. The first looked confused since no one had called the child. The other knew what had happened.

Jasmine ran full tilt through the house and straight at Meg, jumping at her and being caught in midair. It was a toss up as to who hugged harder.

"Meg! Meg! You're here!"

"Yes—yes, baby, I'm here."

Meg walked into the living room still holding Jasmine. With the den full of kids watching TV or doing homework, the living room was the only quiet, private room. When she sat, Jasmine's arms around her neck tightened and she clung to her.

"I missed you, Meg!"

"I missed you, too, Hon. How have you been doing?"

"She doesn't like me. Do you think she blames me for Mommy being dead?"

"Of course not. Why would she?"

"Because I was in the closet and didn't do anything to stop it."

"You couldn't have stopped it, Honey." Meg hugged her closer. "Why were you in the closet?"

"I was scared and wanted to sleep with Mommy and Daddy. Mommy told me to go back to my own room, but I didn't. I sneaked into the closet, instead."

"What were you scared of?"

"I knew something bad was going to happen. I slept with them two times before. Mommy said I'm a thrasher and I couldn't sleep with them again."

That explained why she was in the closet. And Meg was almost positive now that Jasmine was psychic to some degree. There were lots of signs. Jasmine had known Meg was coming the day that Meg showed up unexpectedly to take Jasmine to the lake—she had known all day. At the lake, Jasmine knew Zeus was approaching before either of them saw his car. And, Jasmine had heard her name at Mary's house. Though no words had been spoken, Jasmine had answered as if her name had been spoken verbally. Time to test something.

"Jasmine," Meg thought, *"what did your aunt and you do when she came to visit you?"*

"We—she—watched TV—a grown up show. It was boring." Jasmine immediately answered verbally.

"You hear me—that's good." Jasmine leaned her head back to look at Meg. "Talk to me in your mind, Jasmine."

"Can everybody do this?"

"Not everyone—just a few. It's our secret, so don't tell anyone, yet."

"Why not?"

"Most people don't understand and probably won't believe us."

"Because they can't talk in their heads?"

"Yes."

Meg heard Mary walking toward the den.

"Now, Jasmine," she spoke as Mary passed by, "tell me about those bad dreams you've been having."

"I see the man . . ."

"No, Hon, out loud."

161

"I see the man who killed Mommy and Daddy. I know him, but I can't see him."

"Because his face is covered?"

"No. In my dream it isn't and it's fuzzy, but I know him. I've seen him before. I just can't . . ."

"It's okay, Hon. It's just a dream."

"I don't think so. He knows I'm there. He calls me a bad word while looking for me, then runs away."

"Were you thinking anything before he ran away?"

"I don't think so."

"Were you picturing anything in your mind?" Jasmine thought for a minute.

"Police cars—them catching him—and Mommy and Daddy being okay."

"Oh, baby, I'm so sorry." She hugged her closer, whispering softly. "If you have another bad dream, don't be scared. Watch it like it's a show on TV and remember as much as you can. Okay?" Jasmine nodded.

"I'll try."

The seed, the suggestion, was planted. All she could do was hope it worked.

"Pink thingies. Meg? Meg? Damn it! Meg?"

Meg heard Zeus, but couldn't respond until he quieted down. The cursing angered her. How dare he get mad because she didn't answer immediately.

"If you'd slow down I . . ."

"Damn it, Meg, Erica is clean. I can't find anything."

"Oh."

"Oh—what?"

"I thought you were cursing at me for not answering faster."

"What? No! This damn report just came over the fax—nothing, not a damn thing. There is something—I feel it in my gut!"

"Slow down. Calm down. Be level-headed, Zeus. You'll be able to think clearly."

She heard him quickly muttering with words of surrounding himself with the bright white light of love and divine protection. When he had finished, she told him to close his eyes and repeat it slower. Finished a second time, she spoke to him.

"Do you feel it? Do you feel calmer?"

"Yes."

"Next time you feel frazzled, just close your eyes, clear your mind and inhale deeply three times. That should help center you."

"I'll try to remember that. Thanks." There was a pause.

"Meg, I'm going down there. I want to speak personally with neighbors, people in the area. I want to hear it myself. Perhaps the right questions weren't asked or the wrong ones were."

"Make sure you're centered or you might ask the wrong questions, too—possibly leading ones. People might not want to be questioned again and they might say whatever you want to hear to get rid of you."

There was a moment of silence. At first he felt annoyed, leading to anger, thinking she was telling him how to run an investigation and interview people. Getting centered again, he realized she was right.

"I will." He hesitated. *"Care to come with me?"*

"Care to come over? We can discuss it and I can tell you about my day." She had shocked herself. She hadn't intended to ask any such thing! It was after six and all she really wanted to do was eat something and relax.

"What about us being seen together?"

He was right. Still, it hurt.

"You're right, of course."

"Tell me about your day?"

"I went to see Jasmine. She's having nightmares, again, and withdrawing. Erica has only been to one of the scheduled visits with Jasmine and then watched soap operas instead of visiting with her. Jasmine thinks Erica doesn't like her because Jasmine didn't stop her parents' murder."

"*That's a lot to shoulder, especially for a small child.*"

"*There's more. In her dreams—nightmares—the killer isn't wearing a mask, but his face is fuzzy. Basically, that is the only thing keeping her from knowing who it is. And, the killer knew Jasmine was there. He even called her a bad word while looking for her.*"

"*Why did he stop looking?*"

"*Here's an interesting development. When Mary told me Jasmine was withdrawing, having nightmares and Erica hadn't been interactive in the least with her, I empathized with Jasmine and mentally said her name. She heard me Zeus and came running.*"

"*Are you sure?*"

"*Very. She answered as if I had called her name out loud.*" She let that sink in. "*We spent some time "talking" and I suggested to her to remain calm when she had another bad dream—to watch it like a movie—and try to remember as much as she could. I think these dreams are trying to tell her what she doesn't want to remember.*"

"*Our little girl is psychic.*" He marveled. A small thrill ran through her at his words.

"*I've wondered off and on about certain things, but now I know for sure.*"

"*What certain things?*"

Meg went on to tell him the things she had noticed. She also remembered when Jasmine had said they'd see him later and he showed up that evening at her apartment.

"*Keep working with her about her dreams and her feelings for Erica. Perhaps with the latter, she has reasons for not liking her.*"

"*When she said she thought Erica blamed her for her mother's death because she didn't do anything to stop it, I assured her there was nothing she could have done to prevent it. Then I asked her why she was in the closet. Apparently, she had slept with her parents the previous two nights because she felt something bad was going to happen to them. And, because she thrashes around in her sleep, she was told to go back to her bed but she hid in the closet instead. I think that's the only thing that saved Jasmine as the killer was apparently looking for her."*

"And the killer knew about her, so he knew Mr. Lutz had a wife and a child, and intentionally went there to kill all three."

"Apparently."

"I wonder if the main target was the mother. She might have been having an affair, ended it, and the boyfriend went there to kill them all. Sure sounds like a crime of passion."

"That's a new angle!"

"Mm—yes, but—statistically men shoot boyfriends; women kill husbands and rarely use guns. Women seem to prefer knives or poison—more up close and personal, I guess."

"So, a boyfriend would have shot the husband, perhaps pleaded with the wife, then shot her when she refused—oh, but you said she was shot first."

"Right. So, she woke up—threatened to call the police—he shot her, then had to kill the husband—possibly didn't want to kill Jasmine, but take her—could be the killer is her father, not Mr. Lutz."

"Is there a way to check that now?"

"Yes, just a sample from Jasmine to cross match. Something still doesn't fit. There's either a missing piece of the puzzle or a piece from another puzzle altogether."

"Could Jasmine have been the target?"

"It's possible. I'll see if I can make a connection between recent crimes and Lutz's whereabouts."

"Zeus—I don't know why, but I am getting the feeling Jasmine was the target—the only target. Her parents were an afterthought because he couldn't get Jasmine."

Chapter Twenty One

"Meg, are you telling me what I think you're telling me?"

"Yes, a very distinct feeling—almost an image—that the killer was looking for Jasmine and only her."

"My God! That has to be the missing piece! Now why?" He spoke in a rush. *"You keep working with Jasmine and I'll make it my top priority to check crimes and Lutz's whereabouts. Don't hesitate, day or night, to contact me if you get any more feelings—or whatever. I'll work on this all night if I have to."*

"Same here."

Zeus was gone without another word. Meg did the next best thing to going to the lake—she filled the tub with hot water, sank into it, and closed her eyes. Centering herself, she cleared her mind and let thoughts and images come to her. More than once she had to center herself as her mind continued to come up with ideas and images. Finally, she gave it over to the Powers that Be and sank into a nearly unconscious dream state.

Not knowing how long she had been there, but realizing the water was lukewarm at best, Meg sat bolt upright, eyes wide.

"Zeus!"

"Yes, Meg, what is it?"

"Can I go to the crime scene?"

"Now?"

"That would be preferable, but probably not possible, huh?"

"I'll see what I can do. Be ready in case I can manage it."

Again he was gone without saying more. Meg quickly dressed, thankful this time he did not guess where she was, as her mind raced. She sent up a silent prayer for the help she had received.

"You're up late." The sound of Clansey's voice made her jump. She looked at a clock and saw it was after two in the morning.

"Clansey, there might be a break in one of the cases—the homicide. I think—no, I'm quite sure—Jasmine was the target, not the parents."

"Can you prove it?"

"Not yet. I have a strong feeling that I need to go to the crime scene. Zeus is checking to see if he can gain access right now."

"I'll go see how he's doing." Clansey faded out.

It wasn't long before she was surprised to open her door to find Zeus standing there. She hadn't expected him to come for her. She had rather thought they would meet outside the building of the crime scene.

"Did you see Clansey?" He gave her an exasperated look. "Did you feel him?"

"Should I have?"

"When I told him you were trying to see if we could get into the apartment, he said he'd see how you were doing."

"I didn't detect anything, but I was granted permission, suddenly, after the officer had been stammering about having to check with someone else. Must have been Clansey."

"I could have met you there. You didn't have to drive all the way here." He shrugged. "No matter, let's get going."

Meg and Zeus walked up the flight of stairs leading to Mark and Elizabeth's apartment—the crime scene. As he unlocked the door, she felt the fear and anger seeping through, surrounding her. When he pushed the door open, it came rushing out to meet her—a huge wave of despair that knocked her back a step.

"You okay?" She nodded.

"Yeah—just—let's go inside."

Once over the threshold, Meg was enveloped with sadness, fear, despair, and anger. She automatically laid a hand on his forearm to steady herself while separating the emotions into their own groups. This made it easier to deal with one at a time and to know who each belonged to. She closed her eyes, swaying slightly from the heaviness of the two prominent emotions—anger and fear.

"Meg?"

"I'm fine," she whispered, opening her eyes.

She walked through the apartment, living room first, feeling happy memories—laughter, togetherness, love. In the kitchen there was a feeling of hurrying, being tired. The bathroom felt relaxed. Jasmine's room—fear, the killer's anger, and confusion at not finding her there.

The master bedroom was next. Meg closed her eyes as the emotions swept over her—confusion, paralyzing fear, the killer's anger again. Then, Elizabeth woke and was shot between the eyes as soon as her eyes opened. Mark woke, sitting up with a flicker of an emotion before he was shot in the heart. There was a fleeting feeling of accomplishment. Anxious—searching for Jasmine—anger at not finding her. Fear—cops—gone. The closet—intense fear and anguish.

Meg opened her eyes. For a split second she saw the killer fleeing.

"Meg?" His voice startled her. The wispy vision evaporated. "Meg?"

"I'm fine."

"What happened? Did you see him?"

"Not really, but I did see Mark and Elizabeth get murdered. He *was* after Jasmine. Wait a minute—"

Something nudged the edges of her mind. She shook her head before continuing. She went back to the front door and closed her eyes. She felt the killer and moved through the apartment as he had done—the living room, the hall, a glance into the master bedroom, and then the bathroom.

Next, again as he had done, she entered Jasmine's bedroom, feeling shocked to find it empty. He searched her room. Nothing. Anger.

She retraced her steps as he had. At the master bedroom, she stepped inside. Quietly she stepped up to the bed. Elizabeth's eyes opened. BANG. Mark sat up. BANG. She looked around through the killer's eyes, then started to look under the bed. His progress halted by the thought of cops coming. She felt his fear, his heart pounding as he started to sweat. She watched him run.

"Everything except his face! I felt every emotion, traced every step. He looked in the master bedroom for Jasmine after finding her room empty. He may have left if Elizabeth hadn't opened her eyes—and that's all she did. Fear was just starting when he shot her between the eyes. Mark woke and was shot in the heart. He was starting to check under the bed when Jasmine's image of the police scared him and he ran. All that and he was just a black blur, except for those eyes!

Zeus didn't doubt Meg's ability to see, feel, and hear what had happened in the apartment. However, he was still amazed as she described things only the police knew. She stood in the now empty rooms knowing where the furniture had been, moving around where it had been as if she would bump into it. Standing by where the bed had been, looking down, seeing people now buried.

He realized Meg had done what he had, only she actually saw what happened. The best he could do was follow evidence—blood spatter, body position, and whatever else was left at the scene to make conclusions and educated guesses. Meg lived it. If it wasn't for the mask, they would know what the killer looked like.

"There's nothing else for me here."

In silence, they left the building. As they drove away, Meg was deep in thought going over in her mind everything she had seen and felt. When Zeus reached over, touching her arm, she looked over at him, half reviewing the apartment, half seeing him.

"Shortly after we met, I thought you were the murderer."

"Why?!" Her statement shocked him.

"At the store—in the parking lot—we shook hands, remember?"

"Yes."

"I saw two dead people and you reaching for Jasmine, who was cowering and beside herself with fear. I thought you had killed them, especially when I heard it on the news the next morning."

"How did you figure out that I hadn't done it?"

"After talking with Barry. Luckily your first name was all I needed and all I had. Then you appeared while we were talking so I knew it was you we were talking about."

"That would explain your sudden coolness that day. I thought, for whatever reason, you didn't want to be seen with me in public."

Meg had gone quiet again. Clearly her mind was wandering.

"You don't still . . ."

"No." She had heard his unspoken words before he could get them out.

"Are you still thinking about—back there?"

"Something isn't right." She sat in silence. "It's the eyes. There's something about Mark's and the killer's eyes. I can't put my finger on it, though." She concentrated, then shrugged. "Maybe, as far as the killer goes, it's because they're all I could see, but they just don't seem right—the eyes."

"Perhaps Jasmine described them wrong and you're seeing them wrong." A few seconds later, she shook her head.

"No. She described exactly what and how she saw it. I saw the same ones, but . . . there's something else. Something just out of reach." She exhaled heavily. "Now I'm trying too hard."

"Hungry?"

Meg started to take notice of her surroundings. It was starting to get light. Streetlights were just starting to blink off. She looked at her watch. Where had the time—hours—gone? Suddenly she felt exhausted.

"I guess a little." She was starting to feel her stomach grumble.

"My place is right around the corner. I can whip something up."

"Okay."

She didn't sound very enthused. He glanced over at her and saw why. She was having trouble keeping her eyes open.

"Aren't you leaving tomorrow . . . today?" Meg asked.

"I can always change flights if I have to."

"What time is it?"

"After eight." We were at the apartment for several hours."

"I really lost track of time."

"You'll feel better after you eat something."

"And after I shake this residual thing. This really wiped me out."

"Does it usually?"

"No, but I've never confronted so much emotion—strong emotion. It was like it had just happened."

"Don't forget, you were feeling intense emotions of four people."

"True—and all at once."

Even though Zeus made a light meal, it settled heavy with Meg. She became very drowsy shortly after eating. With a no nonsense tone, he told her she was going to lay down and ushered her into his bedroom, threw his pajamas on the bed, and shut the door.

Meg was too tired to argue, even though she had no clean clothes or a nightgown. On the bed, she saw his pajama top, so she stripped down and put it on. As she climbed under the covers, she could smell his scent on the pajama top. She drifted off to sleep with that on her mind.

Preparing to sleep on the couch, Zeus realized he had only the pajama bottoms in the clean laundry basket. He put them on and knocked on the bedroom door; then he cracked the bedroom door open and peeked in, softly calling her name. No response. He notice she was wearing his pajama top; her clothes in a pile on the floor. He tip-toed in, grabbed her clothes, turned out the bedside lamp, and quietly left the room.

In the hall bathroom, he added her clothes to the basket of towels and washcloths, took the basket and left the apartment. When he returned with clean towels, washcloths, and clothes, he also had a small bag. The contents of the bag were put in the bathroom, and her clothes, neatly folded, were left in the basket in the bathroom. Satisfied with a job well done, he laid on the couch and fell asleep.

Meg woke with the sun shinning on her face. She blinked and was momentarily confused. Where she was quickly came back to her. She sat up, looking around. Zeus' bedroom wasn't a pig sty. With a few out of place things, it was rather neat and orderly. She smiled to herself as she flipped the blankets back while sliding her legs off the bed. Where were her clothes? Fairly sure that she had left them on the floor, she looked around for a robe. Apparently Zeus didn't own one. She went to the door listening for sounds telling her that he was awake. All was quiet on the other side.

Slowly, quietly, she opened the door and stepped out. Immediately, she smelled food cooking. Her hope of quickly finding her clothes was dashed. Where would he have put her clothes?

"Sleep well?" She looked up meeting his gaze, but otherwise didn't move. "You look like a deer caught in headlights."

"Uh, how did you sleep?" She asked back, still a bit confused.

Meg was fully aware that his pajama top she was wearing went down to her mid thigh, and yet she felt as though she were wearing a little teddy. She was also very aware of Zeus wearing the matching pajama bottom, bare chested, in the kitchen looking *hot*.

"Quite well, actually." He grinned at her. "Ah, so you are the one who stole my pajama top."

"Want it back?" She spoke without thinking.

"Sure." His tone was conversational but she detected a slight dare. She fought the urge to accept it.

"As soon as I get my clothes, it's yours."

"Those you'll find in the bathroom laundry basket. I took the liberty of washing them with some of the towels so they'd be clean for you when you took a shower."

"That was very thoughtful of you. Thank you." He shrugged and grinned.

"Not that I don't enjoy the view of you wearing my pajama top. It sure looks better on you."

"I'm sure you would think so! Do I have time to take a shower before eating?"

"Sure."

His tone was carefully level. As she padded to the bathroom, she wondered if he was angry, or at least annoyed, as his tone had changed. Stepping into the shower, she found a bottle of body wash with a definite feminine scent. Her first thought was his lady friend had left it when spending the night. When she realized the seal was unbroken, she knew better.

Emerging from the bathroom, she found Zeus placing plates filled with food on the table. He looked up at her.

"Hungry?"

"Famished. It smells wonderful!"

"Considering it's afternoon, you should be hungry."

"Afternoon! I have really lost some time!"

"Enjoy your shower? While I was doing laundry last night, I decided you might not want to smell like a guy's soap so I bought the other for you. Did you like it?"

"Oh . . ." This revelation surprised her.

"You didn't think I used it, did you?"

"Not exactly. I thought it belonged to your . . ."

"Lady friend?' He finished for her, an odd half smile on his face. "Eat before your food gets cold."

Chapter Twenty Two

Zeus drove Meg home, then headed for the airport, catching his flight to Oregon. His thoughts centered around what Meg had done earlier at the crime scene and what lay ahead of him.

As for Meg she kept trying to decipher what hadn't been right at the crime scene, wondering if Zeus had found anything and hoping Daniel would show up again for another session soon. She didn't figure anything out, Zeus didn't contact her, and she'd have to wait to see if Daniel showed up the next day.

None of it really surprised her. She needed to relax and try not to think so hard about what was missing at the murder scene. She hadn't really expected Daniel to pop in and Zeus would contact her when he had time. In the meantime, she felt as though she was in limbo. That feeling intensified with not nearly enough to to keep her busy.

She showered, started supper, and sat in front of her laptop going over everything Zeus had sent her on both cases. She had already done this a few times and had come up empty. Perhaps this time would be different. With notepad beside her she opened the file on Jasmine's parent's murder. She read it again. She closed her eyes and went over the crime scene again. Still she felt something wasn't right with Mark Lutz and the murderer's eyes. If only she could . . .

Clansey's words came back to her—"neither are what they appear." The killer's eyes—vivid green. Mark's eyes—shock and . . .

"Damn!"

Frustrated, feeling she was so close, she had to remove herself for a few minutes. Checking on supper, her mind went over the time she had spent with Zeus, in particular, her dreams. His scent on the pajama top she had worn carried through to her dreams. She had smelled it while asleep and had dreamed about him—just snippets from the times they had been together, her growing feelings for him and the elusive lady friend of his who remained faceless in her dreams. A faceless woman. Her growing feelings for him. She wouldn't let her mind go there. She returned to the laptop.

Meg ate supper in front of the laptop. After eating she spent hours there. Briefly she glanced at the file on Erica Wells. Nothing jumped out at her. She went back to the murder file until she had to sit back, closing her eyes after rubbing them to give them a rest.

Her neck hurt. She had fallen asleep, her head lopping to one side. Stiffly she brought it upright, gave an angry look at the laptop and shut it down. Shuffling to bed, she slept comfortably for the few hours left before getting up for work.

She did her best to concentrate on her work, putting those files out of her mind. At noon she decided to go outside to relax and let the heat of the sun rest on her stiff neck. She closed her eyes reveling in the warmth, her mind spinning on the two sets of eyes from the crime scene, zeroing in on the green ones. What was wrong with them?

They were angry. Understandable—he was angry. Angry eyes looked at Elizabeth Lutz. Angry eyes looked at Mark Lutz. Angry and . . . a shadow passed over her. It didn't pass, it stayed. She cracked open her eyes and found herself looking directly into green eyes—angry eyes—no, not angry—scared.

"Daniel—hello."

"Ms. Wolfe, can we talk?" He looked around as if expecting someone to be there.

"Certainly. Come inside."

He followed her into the lobby where she told Luce to cancel her afternoon appointments. He followed her into her office making sure the door was closed.

"Please sit down."

He didn't. He paced. He cracked open the blinds looking out, scanning outside.

"What's up?" No response. "Is there more to the movie?" A slight falter to his step as he resumed pacing, but no response. "I've been thinking about how the second half would play out."

Daniel stopped pacing. For a heartbeat he looked at her, then paced some more.

"I'm thinking the first guy should definitely tell the authorities." He stopped again and stared at her. "I mean, considering the second guy gets crazy sometimes and being covered in blood, I'd say he killed someone." Daniel blinked quickly. She continued. "That being the case, and the first guy is the only other one who knows, well—it doesn't sound very safe for him, does it?"

Daniel continued staring at her. In his eyes, she saw fear and indecision. Fear won. He looked away.

"Daniel . . ."

His eyes met hers—his predominately angry—at himself.

"Oh, fuck—I gotta go!" He headed toward the door.

"Daniel." Meg spoke firmly halting his exit though he didn't turn around. "Talk to me."

His shoulders slumped as he slowly shook his head. He was out the door and gone in mere seconds.

"Damn it!" She spoke out loud, repeating it twice more in her head.

"*Meg?*" She looked up. No one was there. "*Center yourself.*"

"*Zeus . . .*" All of her frustration came out with his name.

"*Do it.*"

"*Where are you?*" Silence. "*Why the hell haven't you contacted me?*" Silence. She centered herself.

"Better now?" He asked.

"Yes." She grudgingly admitted.

"Good. What's going on?"

"I blew it! Daniel was just here and I blew it!"

"What happened?"

Meg told Zeus everything, even Daniel's pacing and stares, the fear and anger and his abrupt exit.

"You didn't blow it—you gave him something to think about and he will think about it when the fear subsides some."

"How do you know?"

"I've seen it before. He'll either come back or he'll go to the police. I'm betting he'll see you first."

"I hope so and before anything else happens."

"What else is going on?"

"Never mind that—did you find anything?"

"Erica's home."

"Really? She was suppose to have—I wonder if she's changed her mind—"

"It appears she had to return to work."

"Where does she work?"

"At a coffee shop. Carla used to work there also."

"And?"

"The neighbors had a bit of interesting information. According to them Erica and Carla, though not related, looked a lot alike. So much so they often weren't sure which was which when they met them in the hall and especially when Carla dyed her hair the same color as Erica."

"Wow—really—" Her mind turned the new information over a few times.

"Does your silence mean you feel something?"

"I'm not sure. What is the original color of Carla's hair?"

"A shade or two lighter, but still dark."

"Eyes?" Instantly her mind switched tracks. *"Eyes! That's it! I've got to go Zeus. I've got to try to contact Daniel. The eyes! It was right there in front of me!"*

Meg disengaged from Zeus. She centered herself. Keeping her eyes closed, she pictured Daniel and mentally called his name. She felt him close but couldn't cross the barrier. She gave a push, harder than she intended and like a strong gust of wind, she pushed into his mind. He was unnerved by the sensation so she waited for him to settle down. She took this time to decide how to approach him in this manner. She chose his thought process and listened in.

"What the fuck was that? Jesus, I'm going crazy! Maybe I'll get killed before I get too crazy. Maybe I'll be too crazy and won't care when D kills me."

Meg gently gave him a suggestion in the form of his own thought, wondering what name the "D" stands for.

"Shit, if I am going crazy I'd better go back to see the shrink. Wow, she's a knock out. I wonder if she's . . ." Meg took him back a couple thoughts. "Yeah, shit—at least she'd know if I was crazy and she's right, D is getting crazy paranoid and I am the only one D told, so . . ."

Meg left him then, letting the reasons to see her again pile up in his mind.

Having canceled her afternoon appointments, Meg relaxed in her chair, picking up where she had left off outside. What was it about the eyes? She had realized the eyes of both killer and victim held a message, and she almost had it. She searched her mind for a connection—anything that would show her what she had been missing. It was right there in front of her—if only . . .

"Daniel is here." Luce's voice came over the intercom. Meg sat up with a thud.

"Send him in please."

Daniel entered, plopped into the chair near her desk, a scowl on his face.

"Hello again . . ." He cut her off.

"I'm going crazy. I have to be."

"I certainly doubt that, but tell me, what makes you think so."

"I swear you were in my head earlier. Maybe it was my conscience."

"Has your conscience been bothering you?"

"Kinda." He hesitated so long Meg thought he was finished. "I know something. I should tell someone. I'm afraid to."

"What are you afraid of Daniel?"

"What I know . . . If I told . . . I could get hurt."

"If you don't say anything will you be safe?"

"I doubt it. I'm screwed either way."

"If it's that serious . . ."

"Oh, it is!"

"Then telling someone—the authorities—they can help you look over your shoulder so you don't have to do it alone." She saw on his face that he wasn't convinced. "Daniel, if you tell them—anything and everything—they can arrest them. Wouldn't you be safe then?"

"I suppose." She let him think it over. "Wouldn't I get in trouble for not saying anything sooner?"

"Honestly, I don't know, but I suspect, under the circumstances, you wouldn't."

"What circumstances?"

"Obviously, you're afraid for your life. You didn't help them or know about it beforehand, did you?"

"No—I found out right after though."

"Think about it Daniel. However, I feel the longer you wait, the more dangerous it'll get for you."

"Yeah, I know—they're freaking me out more and more."

"Getting paranoid?" He nodded.

"And suspicious."

"Then you really don't have much time, I'd say."

"Miss Wolfe?"

"Yes, Daniel."

"Who do I tell?"

Meg did a quick mind check with Zeus, then picked up the phone.

"Detective Garrett, I have someone here who would like to talk to you." She handed Daniel the phone.

"He—hello—Detective—Sir—"

"Hello, Daniel, right?"

"Y—yes . . ."

"Dr. Wolfe says you want to tell me something?"

"I . . . well . . . no, not really."

Daniel shoved the phone at Meg and headed for the door.

"Daniel."

He halted at her voice, turned his head to look at her, then bolted out the door. In that second, Meg saw everything she needed to. As before, Daniel's face morphed into the killer's, only much clearer this time. She saw a wispy cord attaching the two and knew the killer was related to him. The mystery of the eyes became very clear.

"Meg?" She looked down at the receiver in her hand.

"Zeus, it's the half sister. I know what was wrong with the eyes—she wore contacts that made her eyes vivid green—Mr. Lutz—what I saw that was mixed with fear—was recognition—of his girlfriend. Daniel's half sister is the girlfriend and the killer."

"I'm on it, Meg. Thanks."

Meg hung up when she realized Zeus was gone. She sat back going over all of the information she knew. Slight of build—feminine medium height—for a male—tall for a female. She wanted Mark to leave something—his wife and child—he refused. Cornflower blue eyes with green contacts—vivid green. Why was she after Jasmine? It made more sense to get the wife out of the way so the husband would be free. That would be logical; however, between killing to get what she wants and, according to Daniel, "a little crazy sometimes"—she wasn't logical or mentally stable.

With no afternoon clients, Meg went home. She poured over everything Zeus had sent her. The pieces of the puzzle fell into place, except one—what Jasmine had to do with it all. She went to the file on Erica Wells.

Besides what Zeus had told her about Erica and Carla looking a lot alike, he had sent other information to her laptop. She read the new things first, then everything together. Then read it all again.

"Pink thingies."

"Hi, Zeus. How did it go?"

"Quite well. We have a search warrant and I'd like you to come along."

"Me?"

"Yes, you. You'll get more there than the most seasoned CSI ever will—and faster."

Without saying anything, she knew that was true.

"Has the suspect, Simone Lenard, been brought in yet?"

"Not yet. We'll find her."

"Try the paper stand—plain clothes—each end. She knows or suspects. She's checking headlines."

"Now?"

"Now."

"Bye." He was gone. She contacted him again.

"Zeus."

"Yeah?"

"Look for a woman fitting Jasmine's and the guy at the news stand's description—tall, cornflower blue eyes—looks like a model."

"Got it. Thanks."

"Good luck. Let me know what happens."

"Will do. Bye."

Chapter Twenty Three

Meg made a light meal and waited anxiously for word from Zeus. It seemed to take forever, but it was actually just a little more than two hours before she heard a knock on her door.

"She's in custody on suspicion. There's a team waiting for us at her place. Ready?"

Within twenty minutes they were at Simone Lenard's residence. The husband, George, stood nervously outside. Meg greeted him, touching his arm. He knew nothing, deeply loved his wife, and was confused. She let calmness pass to him before following Zeus inside.

"Stay with me." Zeus handed her a pair of latex gloves. "Put these on. Only touch what you have to. Tell me everything."

It turned out Zeus stayed with her, steering her away from areas that hadn't been processed, yet. Still, she was able to point out where the gun lay hidden in an air duct and pick out the clothes Simone had worn the night of the murders. She also pointed to where the green contacts lens were hidden in a drawer, tucked into some clothes.

"Do you feel anything?" Zeus asked quietly.

"She is a strong minded person—controlling. She makes her husband's life hell if she doesn't get what she wants when she wants it—or before. She rules with an iron fist. She's a chameleon. She's what she needs to be to get what she wants."

"Jasmine said she wanted her father to leave something and he refused."

"You don't tell her "no." She'll do whatever it takes to get what she wants."

"Apparently! Though she lost this time. Mr. Lutz wouldn't leave his family, so she killed him."

"Don't forget, she was after Jasmine."

"I wonder if we'll ever know why?"

"Can I see her—talk to her?"

"I'll make it happen. Are you done here?"

"Yes, they'll find what they need now."

"We have an interrogation to go to, then."

Meg and Zeus entered the room. Simone looked at them with contempt, then looked away, dismissing them. They sat opposite her. Immediately she started ranting at them.

"I want the names of everyone involved in this miscarriage of justice. Each and every one of you will be prosecuted to the fullest extent of the law!"

"I am Detective Garrett and this is my colleague, Ms. Wolfe."

"Great, can I go now?"

"I'm sorry," Meg reached across the table placing her hand on Simone's, "this has to be very frightening for you, Diane." Simone's eyes flashed. She pulled her hand away.

"It's Simone. Simone Lenard." Her tone was that of someone speaking to a mentally challenged person.

"It is now, yes. However, you were born Diane Eunice Zimmerman. You changed your name to Simone Jewel LaFlare—now Lenard." Simone sniffed.

"So you've done a background check. Was that suppose to rattle my nerves or something?"

"Not much rattles you, does it?" Simone gave Meg a smug, contemptuous look. "Your parents, Rita and Wally, spoiled you rotten. About a month after wishing them dead, through no fault of your own, they died in a crash. You went to live with your grandparents—Wilhelmina and Bryce. They spoiled you as well, more since you were traumatized.

You weren't, were you? You realized your wish had come true—everything was working in your favor. You felt empowered, entitled." Simone's eyes widened slightly. Other than that, she held her emotions in check.

"Though not what you had planned, living with your grandparents wasn't too bad. They gave you whatever you wanted, doted on you, and bent to your tantrums. That aside, you knew they were old, not in the best of health, and wouldn't live very long. At that time, you'd not only get your inheritance from your parents, but your grandparents as well. What a win-win situation for you!" Simone's eyes narrowed.

"How dare you!"

"Skipping ahead now—you manipulated George into marrying you, saying you were pregnant, which you weren't, but once married . . . besides he was and is in love with you. Skipping ahead again—Financially you've drained him. With that ride coming to an end you went in search of someone to take his place—not that there weren't many in between. You found Mark Lutz. The fact he was married, and had a child, was a minor speed bump.

You got him drunk and waited for him to pass out. Crossroads Motel, Room 316, wasn't it? As far as he knows, the two of you had sex. When he wouldn't continue to see you, you fabricated, again, that you were pregnant. He still wouldn't leave his wife and child. You were beyond angry. Should I continue or would you like to finish this?"

"You're absolutely crazy!"

"Is she?" Zeus spoke up. "We've ransacked your house, gathered what we need. People lie. Forensics does not."

"Then I definitely don't have anything to be concerned with."

"Really? You should be quite concerned, Diane. We have the gun from the air duct . . ."

"Gun? George's gun?" Her eyes widened. "George did this? Oh, my God, that's why he's been acting so strangely!"

"Nice try Diane, but we also have the clothes, gloves, and mask, as well as green contacts. Gunshot residue—GSR—will be on the clothes and gloves, as well as your DNA. The gun will prove to be the one used to kill Mr. and Mrs. Lutz. The contacts will also have your DNA. None of these things will have your husband's DNA, but you already know this, don't you? Like I said, you should be very concerned, even scared, especially with an eye witness."

Simone's face remained calm. Her eyes registered shock, quickly turning to anger. She locked them on Meg.

"You see the brat, don't you?"

The only brat I see is in front of me. Why were you after the child?" What did she do to you?"

"What did she do?! Mark would have left that pathetic wife if it wasn't for that snotty-nosed brat! Once she was out of the way, he'd run to me and *our* child!"

But there is no child, is there?" Zeus asked.

"Yes, there is. I'm pregnant!"

"A simple test will prove otherwise." Meg stated.

"I *was* pregnant. I lost the baby."

"Again, a simple test will . . ."

"I thought I was, okay!" She hit the top of the table with her palm. "I would have killed that little bitch, too, if I'd found her."

"But, you couldn't. So what did you do?"

"The next best thing—I killed the big bitch!"

"So, you shot Elizabeth as soon as she opened her eyes?"

"Yes!"

"With her out of the way, why did you shoot Mr. Lutz between the eyes?" Meg tested Simone.

"He pissed me off and I just knew he'd call the police, so I shot him in the heart, not between the eyes! The heart that should have been mine!"

"What would you have done if the child had been there?"

"If everything went as planned, they would have found her with her throat slit! Then, he would have left that bitch and ran to me and *our* child!"

"Looks like you lost all the way around this time." Meg stood. "You're going away for a very long time."

Bitch!" Simone lunged at her.

Zeus moved quickly and had her planted back in her chair before Meg could blink. Two officers came in and secured Simone with handcuffs to the chair.

"Hey, bitch." Meg ignored her. "Ms. Wolfe . . ." She turned back toward Simone. "How did you know all that stuff about me? Are you psychic or am I crazy?" Meg smiled at her and walked away.

George Lenard and Barry Kerbs exited the room behind the two-way mirror. The first looked devastated. The second smiled at Meg and Zeus, before turning his attention to Mr. Lenard.

"You're free to go, Sir." George simply nodded.

"Mr. Lenard," Meg stopped him, offering her hand. He shook it. "Thank you very much for coming down. We all appreciate it."

"How could I not have known? I suspected about the infidelity and she was preparing to leave me, but—the rest . . . She'd always been controlling and threw fits to get her own way—I just never knew how twisted her mind really was."

Meg placed a hand on his shoulder, absorbing some of his pain. She ached for the heartbreak he was feeling.

"Nothing happens for nothing, Mr. Lenard. At least now you'll know what to avoid in a woman."

He nodded, sadly, and walked away. Meg, Zeus, and Barry heard Simone screaming at, then pleading with, her husband. The three moved closer to observe the scene. George just stood there, looking at her until she quieted down.

"You'll get me out of here, won't you honey?"

"Goodbye, My Dear. I don't expect you'll see me again."

He walked away, followed by screaming obscenities aimed at him. Once George was gone, she quieted and looked around. Suddenly, she was screaming again.

"I'm innocent! You have the wrong person! It's mistaken identity!" She was led, dragged, then pulled away.

"That was pretty." Barry dryly observed. "So, what's next?"

"I have one more case to solve." With an arm around Meg's waist, he pulled her to his side. "With my sidekick here—actually, I'm more like her sidekick."

"I see." Barry eyed them both. "Be careful."

As Barry walked away, Meg watched him, but her mind was somewhere else as she spoke softly to herself.

"Wrong person. Mistaken identity. Not who they seem."

"What? You don't think Simone can use that, do you?"

"No, that case is locked down tight." She turned to Zeus. "Clansey said 'neither is who they seem'; remember? We thought the killer was a man."

"Okay, so Erica . . ." With his arm still around her, Zeus suddenly propelled her toward his office.

He closed the door and released Meg. He went straight to his computer and began typing as Meg pulled out her cell phone and dialed a number. They both had had the same thought.

"Janice, this is Meg. Do you do DNA testing to make sure a relative *is* a relative?" She listened. "Can we make an exception?" She listened again. "Yes, that's what we're thinking. Can we meet and I'll explain everything? Okay, see you then." She hung up.

"Will she do it?"

"She'll do everything in her power to get it done. She'll tell Erica a DNA sample is needed either way."

"I imagine Erica won't make it easy—unless she really is Erica."

"I'm sure she'll try to talk us out of it, but only to stall long enough to figure a way around it."

Both Meg and Zeus met with Janice. Being late, they met at a restaurant. Though Meg had eaten, the light meal had worn off. All three ordered and got down to business right away.

"Okay," Janice started, "explain why you think Ms. Wells needs to be tested." Zeus answered.

"Erica had a roommate, Carla Rivers, who disappeared one day. To all appearances, Carla packed most of her things and just left. This happened less than a week after Jasmine's parents were murdered.

According to neighbors, Carla and Erica looked so similar they often had trouble telling them apart—especially after Carla dyed her hair to match Erica's.

Erica doesn't seem the type to want a child hanging around, though she's very anxious to get money for having her. That's just my personal take, however. That aside, Erica suddenly wasn't as good at her job as she was before the murders and had to "practically be retrained" according to coworkers and her boss."

"Stress." Janice interjected. "She'd just lost her only living relative, save Jasmine."

"True, and people do react to stress in odd ways. However, it would take a very dedicated person to completely disappear—name, social security number, bank account—all have to be changed. Why would she do that? And, if she did, she didn't and hasn't touched her bank account. Erica, however, opened a second bank account, leaving the first with over four hundred dollars in it and nothing has been done with it—no deposits, no withdrawals.

Explanations: Carla's account only has fifty dollars in it. Erica's first account has a fingerprint on record, but who's? That's being checked out. I believe DNA would be quicker, especially when I have a friend who could make it a priority.

However, I don't think we'll even need a sample, just the threat of needing it."

"Very compelling, Detective."

"Now, I'm sure Erica will have excuses for not giving us DNA. I'm sure she'll think we need a blood sample. I'll bet she's horrified of needles. We'll try without success to get one and give up. To calm her nerves, she'll be given something to drink—saliva—DNA—will be left on the container."

"Very sneaky, Detective. What if she *is* Erica?"

"Then we're whipped, unless you can come up with something."

"Okay, I'll get to work on my end. Hopefully, within the week we'll have our sample."

"Thank you, Mrs. Powers."

Chapter Twenty Four

After three days, Zeus got a call from Mrs. Schwartz, one of Erica's neighbors. As he was hanging up his office phone, his cell rang. The caller ID said it was Meg.

"Seems odd talking to you on the phone. What's up?"

"We've got to go to Oregon. Clansey says something is going on there."

"Does he know what?"

"He won't say."

"I'll check into a red-eye flight. You coming?"

"I wouldn't miss it!"

"I'll call you right back."

Twenty minutes later, he called to say he was on his way to get her. They had to hurry or miss their flight. Meg didn't look, but she was sure they bent some traffic laws—possibly broke a few. They were both exhausted and slept on the plane.

Minutes after landing, they were in a car he had rented ahead of time. As they were driving towards Erica's apartment, Zeus started an explanation.

"I was about to call you when you called."

"So, what's going on?" Meg asked.

"Mrs. Swartz, one of Erica's neighbors, called just before you did. She said there was a lot of angry screaming, all one-sided, coming from the apartment. She could hear it from her own apartment, and better still, when she took her trash out. Erica saw her dropping the trash down the chute and thought Mrs. Swartz was spying on her—which she was.

Anyway, Erica ran out and started cussing at Mrs. Swartz, calling her names that Carla used to call her, especially when Carla was drunk. Mrs. Swartz swore she was confronted by Carla, not Erica."

"Wow! I bet this was brought on by the request for DNA testing. Janice said that Erica was just contacted about it, today. Apparently, she kept her cool while talking to Janice."

"We're in for a bumpy ride, then."

Contrary to what they expected, all was quiet as they approached Erica's door. Mrs. Swartz's door cracked open. The crack widened enough for her to expose half of her body and motion for them to come her way.

"How long has she been quiet?" Zeus asked in a hushed voice, thankful for nosy neighbors.

"Twenty-thirty minutes maybe."

"Did she leave?"

"No, it just went quiet all of a sudden."

"When you saw her in the hall, were there obvious signs she'd been drinking?"

"I didn't smell anything and she seemed to be walking okay. She was just mad as hell."

"Did she say anything besides what you told me—anything that might be a clue as to why she was so angry?"

"Not to me, but I heard bits and pieces when I took the trash out."

"Like?"

"Just stuff like "those people," "nosy SOBs," "leave me alone," and "how the eff will I . . ."—no full sentences. I'm sorry I can't be more help."

"That's fine, Mrs. Swartz, you've been very helpful. "Please stay in your home."

Meg and Zeus quietly went back to Erica's door. No sound came from the other side. Zeus put his ear to the door, then shrugged.

"Now what?" Meg whispered. In answer, he knocked on the door. Silence. Shuffling.

"Who is it?" Even though Zeus was sure Erica had already looked through the peephole, he answered her.

"Detective Garrett and Ms. Wolfe. May we come in?"

The door had already opened after he had said his name. On the other side, stood Erica, looking calm and unruffled, sober and sane.

"Detective" she gushed. "To what do I owe the pleasure?"

Zeus stepped forward, followed by Meg, as though Erica had invited them in. She had two choices—block them or let them enter. She chose the latter.

"I was told you were made aware there was a DNA sample needed."

"Well, yes, but I thought I had to go . . ."

"Change of plans. We saw no sense in disrupting your life any more than was necessary. We don't want you to lose any more work."

"Very thoughtful, Detective . . ."

"Garrett." He offered only his last name.

"I'm . . . I'm very squeamish about blood and needles and all that."

"There's nothing to it, Miss Wells. You won't feel a thing."

"Yes, yes, I know, but . . ." Her eyes darted around. "You will catch me if I faint, won't you?" She smiled flirtatiously at Zeus.

"Of course I'll catch you." He smiled.

Zeus slid his hand into his coat pocket. Erica's eyes rolled back as if she'd faint. Meg noticed the slightest of smile at the corners of Zeus' mouth.

"Detective Garrett," Meg broke in, "obviously Miss Wells won't be able to do this . . ." Erica's eyes refocused instantly. "There has to be another way."

Zeus slid his hand out of his pocket. Meg looked at him as though she were thinking. He finally looked at Erica.

"Your hair brush and toothbrush will do. Would you please get them for me?"

"Yes—yes, of course."

Erica left the room. Meg and Zeus smiled at one another. Then they waited. It was taking Erica a long time to return, considering it shouldn't take long to grab both items. Zeus looked at his watch, then raised an eyebrow at her. They both heard a click. The sound meant nothing to Meg, but just as the sound registered with Zeus, Erica had already entered the room with a gun pointed at Meg. Zeus reached for his gun. Erica pointed hers at him; he stopped.

"Why can't you people just give me the brat and leave me alone?"

"Carla, put the gun down." She laughed.

"How long have you known?"

"Almost from the beginning." He lied. "Why did you kill Erica?"

"She was getting in the way of my dealing." Carla shrugged. "If she had minded her own business when she found the stuff, she might be alive now."

"What did you do with her body? Where is she?" Carla grinned.

"Here and there—mostly there." She laughed at her own joke. "The two of you will be joining her, though it'll take me a little longer—two bodies—one huge and delectable. Too bad—I would have liked to mount you. Maybe I still can . . ."

"There's not a snowballs chance in hell," Zeus chuckled sarcastically.

"Too bad." She looked at Meg, turning the gun toward her. "He's a good mount, isn't he? I can tell these things. He's big and rough and . . ."

"You disgust me!" Meg nearly spat.

"You bitch . . . neither of you will stop me!" Carla pulled the trigger.

All at the same time, Meg saw Zeus pull his gun as the bullet left the barrel of Carla's gun and headed toward her. Then Carla aimed at Zeus. He flicked the safety off with a thumb. Carla's finger started to tighten on the trigger.

"No! Stop!" Meg screamed.

Nothing moved. Zeus was motionless, his gun a breath away from being fired. Carla stood with her gun held out just as close to firing. A bullet had stopped half way between the barrel and Meg. Not sure how long this would last, Meg moved quickly. She snatched the bullet out of midair, pulled Carla's gun from her grasp, moved Zeus' gun off target, and removed his finger from the trigger. She found a pair of handcuffs attached to his belt behind him.

"If you can, Zeus, help me."

His body reacted. Holstering his gun, he took the cuffs from Meg. Then he walked over to Carla, pulled her arms behind her, and locked her wrists into the cuffs. It was then when Meg felt safe and Carla regained control of herself.

"Meg, that was—man!" Zeus started.

"What—what just happened?" Carla croaked. "How did you . . . right out of the air!" She tried to sit, but Zeus kept her on her feet.

"Stop babbling, Carla." His tone was gruff, but from behind her he smiled and winked at Meg as he pulled his cell phone from his pocket and called the police.

Once Carla was in custody, Meg and Zeus left. The apartment was now a possible crime scene. As they stepped out onto the sidewalk, they both inhaled deeply.

"If you weren't you, Meg, we'd be dead."

"Don't remind me."

"That was the oddest feeling and I was just as flabbergasted as she was!"

"That makes three of us, then. I was scared to death it would wear off before I was finished!"

"You didn't stop it . . . I mean, on purpose?"

"No, it just . . . happened and I didn't know for how long."

"We'll have to hone this gift of yours so you're more in control of it."

"Definitely!"

They got in the car. Meg melted into the seat, thankful she didn't have to hold herself up any longer.

"We will need to go to the station, tomorrow, first thing, to give our statements. In the meantime, we can fly home, tonight, or get a hotel room and stay here."

"It doesn't make much sense to go home."

"Hotel it is, then."

"I have a great idea—let's get something to eat—I'm starving—then buy some clothes for tomorrow." Meg suggested.

"I'm good."

"Well, I'm not. At least we'll need clean underwear."

"Why, did you soil yours?" He chuckled.

"I may have." She grinned at him.

"I'll bet Carla did!" They both laughed. "I'll tell you what—I'll pay for our rooms, then I'll pick out your underwear and you can pick out mine."

"Who pays for that? The department will pay for the rooms—at least yours."

"I'll pay for your room and your underwear. You pay for the food and mine." Meg told Zeus.

"Deal. Now let's eat!"

They settled into a booth at a family restaurant. As she ordered, he sat listening with one eyebrow raised. She hadn't been kidding when she said she was starving. She ordered a sampler appetizer consisting of onion rings, spicy chicken wings, fried mozzarella sticks, and potato wedges. Then, she ordered supper—fried chicken, mashed potatoes with gravy, biscuits, spinach, coleslaw, and milk. He ordered the steak special and coffee. She noticed him looking at her.

"What?"

"You forgot dessert." He teased.

"I didn't forget . . . I just haven't ordered it, yet."

"I'm not rubbing your tummy tonight."

"I'm not asking you to."

Their food arrived, and without further ado, Meg proceeded to eat every bit of her meal plus a second glass of milk with a slice of silk chocolate pie with whipped cream on top.

"Full?"

"Satisfied."

"We'd better hurry getting your room—I'm sure you're going to crash soon."

She grinned at him.

Their accommodations for the night didn't go as planned. Due to some convention in town there was one room available in one hotel, and it had one queen bed. They looked at each other.

"I'll behave if you will." He grinned.

"You'll behave, regardless." She countered.

Zeus secured the room, then they left the hotel.

"Does that mean you have no intentions of behaving?"

She had realized her mistake of speaking before thinking.

"We have some shopping to do."

"Oh, yes, and now my selection has suddenly broadened!"

"Watch it, buddy, or you'll find yourself frozen stiff all night!"

He didn't need to comment. His deep laughter said it all. She turned crimson, despite herself. As they parked at the store, then exited the car, he took her elbow.

"Just so you know, when I have to, I wear boxers." He paused. "And no cheating—keep my thoughts out of your head."

"Too late—your mouth has already given your thoughts away." They stopped just outside the store.

"Let's meet right here in one hour, and no sneaking up on me."

Entering the store, they went their separate ways. She headed for the men's section and he went to the women's. She appropriately picked out a pair of boxers that happened to have a police badge design. Then she asked a floor sales person for help.

"Do you have any pink thongs for men?"

"Pink . . . Oh . . . I don't know. Let's look. What size?"

"I've no idea. If I show you who it's for, could you guess?"

They made their way to where Zeus was searching for her items. The sales person looked at Meg with genuine surprise.

"You want pink thongs for *him*? I never would have guessed. He's such a hunk—what a waste!"

"A waste?" Mystified, Meg followed her back to the men's section. What the sales woman was implying, finally registered with Meg.

"Do you have a style in mind?"

"Style?" She didn't know shopping for men was as time consuming as shopping for women. "I suppose just something that will hold his—junk—securely in place."

It took a while, but they finally found a pair of fuchsia thongs with a fuzzy bunny on what there was of a front. With a store bag hanging on her arm, filled with his boxers and pink thong, a pair of jeans and a T-shirt for her, and pajamas for them both, she stepped outside.

Chapter Twenty Five

Meanwhile, Zeus had his own problems. Finding what he was looking for was easy. Figuring out the size was another matter as he found he had to buy a set. He approached a sales person.

"I know what I want but not the size."

"Do you know her height, weight, and build?" Zeus looked around. Spying a woman about the same size as Meg, he pointed to her.

"She's like her, but with bigger . . ." He held his cupped hands in front of his chest.

Between the two of them, they found what they thought would be the right cup size. Pleased with his purchases, he left the store, finding Meg waiting outside.

"Find everything okay?" She asked.

"Yup, and the sales woman wasn't too bad either." Meg laughed.

"I wouldn't suggest you shop for a date here."

"Really? Why not?" She laughed again.

"They think you're gay." He stopped her in mid stride.

"Just because I bought women's underwear doesn't make me gay. Besides, they're clearly not my size. Men buy their—women such things all the time."

"True." She giggled and proceeded walking.

"*What* did you *do*?"

"I just bought you some underwear."

"Meg!" It was a mock warning.

"You'll see." She ducked into the car and shut the door.

Entering the hotel, Meg grabbed his arm, gently pulling him toward the elevator.

"Come on, I can't wait for you to see what I got!"

"Mr. and Mrs. Garrett?" They turned toward the voice of the desk clerk."

"Yes?" Zeus answered as Meg opened her mouth.

"Your daughter called while you were out."

"Did she?" Zeus spoke first again. "Did Jasmine leave a message?"

"She misses you and please call."

"Thank you."

Meg was going to say something as soon as they were in the elevator but on second thought decided no harm was done.

"I'll call *our* daughter."

Meg opened her mind, closed her eyes, and called Jasmine's name; she got an immediate response.

"Shouldn't you be in bed?" Meg asked.

"I am in bed." Jasmine replied.

"Okay—shouldn't you be asleep, then?"

"I miss you and Mr. Garrett."

"We miss you too, Honey. We'll see you tomorrow and we have a surprise for you."

"What is it?"

"You'll have to wait until tomorrow. Now go to sleep."

"Okay. I love you."

"I love you, too. Night."

"How is she?" He asked as soon as she opened her eyes.

"She misses us. I told her we have a surprise for her and we'll see her tomorrow."

Stepping inside their room, Zeus shoved the door shut.

"I think, considering, you should model what I got for you."

"It never pays to do your own thinking, Big Guy."

"Okay, okay—just show me what you bought for me, then, and get it over with."

With as serious an expression as she could muster, Meg took out the thongs and handed them to him.

"Pink thingies." She proudly displayed.

"Oh my—no wonder they thought I was gay! How does one—how does a guy—it can't work."

"I was assured your junk would be secure." She laughed at his dubious expression, then handed him the boxers.

"That's more like it!" Next she gave him the royal blue silk pajamas.

"Jammies? I was going to go commando."

"Sucks to be you, doesn't it?"

"Anything else?"

"I bought jammies for myself."

"*One* of us has to go commando!"

"Keep it up and one of us will be sleeping in the lobby!"

"You'll look divine sleeping down there in this." Zeus pulled the bra and thong out of the bag. "Pink thingies."

Meg wanted to say something smart but the set was beautiful. Both were made of pink lace—very feminine and delicate.

"They're beautiful!"

"Are you going to model them?"

"In your dreams."

"Okay, but I have less control then."

"You really are naughty."

As Meg showered, turning down the offer to conserve water by showering together, and got into her pajamas. She couldn't believe she had sparred with Zeus in such a manner. She really wasn't sure who had started it, but suspected it had been mutual. Another surprise was her lack of embarrassment. His voice came through the door.

"You won't let me sleep commando. You won't. And not even a sexy nightie. Considering we've been married five years and have a four-year-old daughter—I just expected more."

Exiting the bathroom, her return comment was forgotten as he tossed something at her. Immediately she knew it was the pajamas she'd bought him. She was afraid to look at him, considering their earlier bantering.

"The top doesn't fit. You keep it as a souvenir of our trip." She silently heaved a sigh of relief.

"Go take a shower."

"Would you like me to model my thongs?"

"If you do, I swear I'll take pictures!"

"How about the boxers?"

"Sure, why not?"

"Hey . . ." His face lit up, then fell as Meg responded to his thought.

"Nope, the cuffs are at the station."

"Another time, then." He disappeared into the bathroom.

The impact of their predicament hit her. She had to center herself. The kind of bantering they had been doing had to stop. She fell into it way too easily. And, considering they would be sleeping together, it couldn't continue. Tomorrow, sure. Tonight—no.

She folded the blankets down, then sat on the bed. She wasn't sure if she should get in before he came out or wait. She didn't want to look too—what? Inviting? Anxious? She jumped off the bed as though it were full of snakes and started pacing.

She pulled back the curtain, looking out over the city below. Traffic flowed. Lights flashed. People walked along knowing who they were and what they were doing. She had no idea about herself. She did know she had to be very careful though. If she wasn't, if she let her guard down, she was in jeopardy of falling in love with Zeus. Being honest with herself, that process had already started.

A movement caught her eye. She watched his reflection in the window against the darkness outside. His hair was mussed, his chest bare—clad only in the pajama bottoms. She closed her eyes and the curtain, reining herself in.

"Still awake? I thought you would have fallen asleep immediately. You weren't waiting up for me, were you?" He grinned.

Control. Don't get sucked into it.

"You should have brought your lady friend—this would have been perfect."

"I should have skipped the shower—it cooled off out here considerably."

"I'm sorry, Zeus. I didn't mean to give you the wrong impression . . . to lead you on."

"I haven't been led anywhere, Meg. I meant what I said—I'll behave. I didn't mean to imply, because we're sharing a room, that I expected—anything. I fully expected from the beginning to sleep on the floor, so just toss me a pillow and I'll get the extra blanket and bunk down."

"You don't need to sleep on the floor!"

"*You're* not going to!"

"Well, no—I thought we were adult enough to share the bed." She saw humor flash across his face. "We are, aren't we?"

"We are."

They both got into bed. Zeus got comfortable in the middle of his side of the bed. He imagined she jumped when he spoke.

"You're so close to the edge, *if* you fall asleep, you're liable to fall off the bed. Relax—scoot back."

Center, Relax. She scooted back. Center again. Breath. She wasn't worried about him. She was worried about herself. She did what had worked before.

"So, how is—your lady friend? I haven't heard you talk about her, lately. I guess considering today's events, it's good I came instead of her." *Shut up, you're babbling.*

"She's—fine, I think." She heard the smile in his voice. She deserved him laughing at her. "I've been rather busy, lately, and haven't had a chance to talk about her. And, yes, I am lucky you're here."

"Have you taken her out—you know—like a date, yet?"

"Mm—I've even bought her a gift."

"That was sweet. She must know you want to be more than work buddies, then, right?"

"I'm still clueless about that. It seems no matter how hard I try, she doesn't get it."

"She kept the gift though, right?"

"So far."

"If she wasn't interested she would have refused it."

"Maybe not. It was a gift of necessity."

"Oh." She couldn't fathom what kind of gift that could be. "Well, then, try the direct approach. Just tell her how you feel and let the chips fall where they may."

"I might just have do that."

"I know you have concerns about relationships. I want you to know I'll help you in any way I can if you want me to."

"I'm counting on that. Now go to sleep." She yawned.

"Okay. Night."

Meg fell asleep while he laid awake for an hour or two tossing her words around in his mind. He looked over at Meg and thought about his lady friend, falling asleep with a smile on his face.

Giving their statement at the station the next morning went faster than Meg thought it would. Before she knew it, the plane home had landed and she was heading toward her apartment. Neither had said much on the way back, mainly because Zeus seemed to be deep in thought. She would have loved to listen in. Instead, she was content assuming he was thinking of his lady friend and their conversation about his friend from the night before. She saw that as a very good sign.

Meg had to find something to distract herself. She poured herself into her work. She met with Daniel and found he was very relieved his half sister was in jail. He was definitely a much happier young man.

Then she went over to meet with Janice Powers. Now that Jasmine really didn't have any relatives, and no one claiming to be a relative, Meg was earnestly seeking to adopt her. As Erica had, Meg had to go through consultations, court dates, and an investigation. With Janice backing her and giving her recommendations, Meg was sure the process went a lot smoother and faster than it would have otherwise.

It was the final court date. The judge would either grant her guardianship or take her dream away. How she wished Zeus was there with her—for support, if nothing else. She sat as patiently as possible, waiting for the judge to appear. Mary brought Jasmine in. As they sat down, Meg looked at Jasmine, this small child in the large courtroom, sitting in a large chair, her feet dangling, her eyes huge—she looked scared.

The judge entered. Everyone stood. At that moment, Jasmine shrieked when she saw Meg and darted across the aisle, launching herself into Meg's arms.

"Meg! Please don't make me live with that lady! I love you Meg!" Everyone looked at them, then sat down. Meg and Jasmine sat as one. Jasmine refused to release the hold she had on Meg's neck.

"Young lady." The judge checked a paper in front of him. Meg tried to put Jasmine down. She clung to her.

"Jasmine." The judge said. She hugged Meg tighter.

"Look at the judge, Honey, and answer him." Slowly, Jasmine turned her head to look at the judge. Meg failed at another attempt to dislodge her.

"It's okay, Jasmine, you don't have to get down. I'd like to ask you a few questions, okay?"

"Yes." Her voice was so quiet. The judge leaned forward to hear her.

"Who is the woman holding you?"

"Meg and I love her!" She spoke clearly and louder this time.

"Yes, so I heard when I came in. Do you know why you're here?"

"To make me go with that bad lady."

"The bad lady is gone. You'll never have to live with her. Who would you like to live with?"

"Meg and Mr. Garrett."

"Who is Mr. Garrett?" The judge asked Meg.

"Detective Garrett . . ."

"Ah, yes, the detective on the case. Is there . . ."

"No judge."

"I see." He looked at Jasmine. "Jasmine, would you like to live with Meg permanently . . ." At her confused expression, he clarified. "Forever?"

"Oh, yes! Can I really? Can you do that judge?"

"I can and I will. Jasmine, you are now Meg's little girl."

"Forever?"

"Forever," he banged the gavel, "and ever."

Jasmine wiggled down and ran toward the judge. He met her half way. She hugged him and whispered in his ear. He nodded and sent her back to Meg. Standing behind the bench, he raised the gavel in the air, waving it like a wand.

"Meg, I hereby make you officially Jasmine's mommy, per her request!"

"Thank you, judge." Her voice quivered.

Meg cried. Jasmine cried. Mary cried. Even the judge wiped away a tear or two before leaving the courtroom.

Chapter Twenty Six

"Can I go home with you now?"

"Sure—we'll just go to Mary's . . ."

"I brought all of her things with me. I knew you'd win!"

"Oh, well then, let's go home Jasmine!"

"You will bring her by during the day while you're at work, won't you?"

"Yes, of course, Mary."

It didn't take long to transfer Jasmine's things from Mary's car to Meg's. Meg noticed, even for a four year old, that her belongings were sparse, to say the least. As she drove home, with Jasmine chatting away in the back, she made a mental list of what she needed to get for her—more clothes and toys, bed and bedding—where would she put the bed? She supposed, for now, Jasmine could sleep with her. As for an extra room, she had been apartment shopping, but as of yet, hadn't found one she liked.

Meg glanced in the rear view mirror. No, a child needed a yard to play in. She'd start looking for a small house first thing in the morning. A swing set, sandbox . . . her mental list grew by leaps and bounds. She looked again in the rear view mirror.

"Jasmine, do you want to go out to eat to celebrate?"

"I want to eat at home!"

"Okay, then home it is!"

She had to admit, that did sound very nice. With Meg's arms filled carrying two boxes, the two made their way to the apartment. Jasmine did her best to help put her own clothes away. Another mental note—child-sized hangers. A drawer was cleaned out for her pajamas, socks, and underwear. The box of toys found a spot in the living room. Another mental note—toy box.

Together they prepared supper, eating at the small table. Meg was beyond thrilled—she had been granted custody, but there was something missing—Zeus. She hadn't even thought to call him afterward to tell him the good news. She supposed, when things quieted down—

"Call him." Meg looked at Jasmine. "Call Mr. Garrett."

"Think his name—like you're calling him from another room." Meg told her.

Meg could tell when he answered by the way Jasmine's face lit up. She watched her expression change as they talked and smiled to herself.

"He says join us."

"What? Oh." Meg had been deep in thought about Jasmine's feeling for him. *"Zeus?"*

"I'm here."

"Jasmine?"

"I'm here, too."

"Congratulations, Meg."

"Thank you. I was going to call you later. I'm sorry for not calling sooner—I've just been so busy with . . ."

"No problem. I understand. Do you have a game plan?"

"Actually, I need to make a list. There's so much I need to do and get. I'm going to look into buying a house with a big yard tomorrow. Then we have to go shopping for clothes and toys and . . ."

"You're not going to spoil her, are you?"

"Not more than necessary."

"Good!" He chuckled. *"Why don't you call back when things quiet down?"*

"I will, I promise."

"Okay, Jasmine, I'll talk with you later—maybe tomorrow."

"When will we see you?"

"Hopefully, soon. Until then I want my two best girls to stay out of trouble, okay?"

"Okay, we love you."

"I love my girls, too."

They disconnected. Jasmine finished eating. Meg nibbled. She was thinking about Zeus' words. The two of them were attached to one another and she should include him in her life as much as possible. Was that a good thing? She didn't really know. Zeus has his own life. And, if things worked out with him and his lady friend, would he have time for Jasmine? Would his lady friend want him spending time with her—them?

"Will I sleep on the couch?"

"I was thinking you'd sleep with me until you have your own room."

That seemed to please Jasmine. While they did dishes, Jasmine chatted about her dolls and what kind of a house they'd get, what her room would look like, the trees in the backyard . . . Soon Meg realized she was picturing everything Jasmine was describing. It sounded and looked wonderful.

As promised, as soon as Jasmine was in bed and asleep, Meg called Zeus on the phone—regular style.

"How's my girl?"

"She's finally asleep. I think she talked non-stop since we left the courthouse. I'm so mentally exhausted; I had to call on the phone."

"She'll settle down. So, do you have any idea where you want to live?"

"Nothing specific right now. Jasmine has it all figured out, though. She has described the house and the yard to me in great detail. I hope she's not too disappointed if I can't find that exact house."

"I'm sure as long as she's finally with you she won't care."

"She'd be thrilled if you came with us tomorrow. Or, you can meet with us at my parent's house later for supper."

"Yes to both. What time?"

"Probably ten or so. I think I'll have her fed and dressed by then. I don't even know when she gets up. Oh boy, I have a lot to learn."

"It'll all come together, and I believe quite naturally. Go to bed, get some sleep. I'll see you in the morning."

"Okay. Night Zeus."

Sleep? Right! Meg had forgotten Jasmine is a thrasher. That had been the reason Jasmine had told her she wasn't sleeping with her parents on that fateful night. Meg was jarred awake several times during the night by flying arms, legs, and feet. Just when she decided to sleep on the couch, Jasmine settled down and Meg was finally able to get uninterrupted sleep.

She felt the bed move. Jasmine must have rolled over. She sank back into sleep. The bed moved again. A small hand brushed hair out of Meg's face. Jasmine was awake.

"You okay, baby?" Meg asked, without opening her eyes.

"Can I call you Mommy, now?" The question was starting to register.

"Yes, Honey, if you want to."

"Then, Mommy, Mr. Garrett is here."

"He'll be here around ten, sweetie. Go back to sleep."

The bed moved as if someone had sat on it. She furrowed her brow. Jasmine was already on the bed. Who . . . ? Jasmine's words came back to her. It couldn't be. She slowly opened her eyes.

"Hi." Zeus greeted her.

"What?" Confusion. He wasn't suppose to be there until ten.

"It's afternoon."

"Afternoon? How did you . . ."

"It's okay—she asked who it was first."

"How much later than noon is it?"

"One something."

"How long have you been up, Jasmine?" Realizing Jasmine couldn't tell time, she was about to ask her something else when Zeus spoke.

"She contacted me somewhere around eight-thirty, said you were asleep, so I came over. We ate breakfast together and played some games."

"I'm a thrasher." Jasmine chimed in. "I think I should sleep on the couch. You slept better when I got up."

"Okay—wait—"

"There's coffee waiting for you. Come on, Jasmine, let's let her wake up a little."

Meg watched them leave her room hand-in-hand. It gave her a warm feeling. Donning a robe and heading for the kitchen, things started to come together. She must have fallen into a deep sleep when Jasmine got up. Jasmine had called Zeus because she hadn't wanted to wake her up. He had come over and taken care of her. Some mother she was turning out to be!

"I'm sorry, Jasmine. I should have gotten up with you. Wake me up next time. And Zeus, thank you for coming over."

"My pleasure. I'm always available whenever either one of you need me."

Jasmine wandered into the living room while Zeus made breakfast for Meg. He sat with her as she ate. Soon his cell rang. He spoke for a few minutes, then hung up.

"I took the liberty of calling a realtor. She has a couple places for us to look at."

"I emailed one last night. Maybe he'll call me today, too. When can we look at yours?"

"As soon as you're ready, I'll call her back."

"Oh!" Meg started to get up.

"Sit. Eat. I'll get Jasmine dressed."

"Clansey!" Meg and Zeus turned their heads toward the living room when they heard Jasmine giggle.

Breakfast forgotten, Meg went to the living room, followed by Zeus. Clansey acknowledged them with a wink and went back to telling Jasmine a story. Meg watched Jasmine listen with rapture as Clansey made the characters come to life and laughed at his antics. Zeus just saw Jasmine watching and listening to something—Clansey—and wished he could see him, too.

"I feel left out. I'm the only one who can't see or hear him." Meg felt bad for Zeus. He was excluded in that area. "Oh, well," he seemed to brighten, "go get ready, Meg."

While she dressed, a call came from the realtor she had emailed. Zeus had been cleaning the kitchen. When Meg reappeared, he told her about the call and she called the realtor back. Meanwhile, Zeus got Jasmine dressed. Clansey had already left, going shortly after his story was done.

"Well!" Meg turned when Zeus and Jasmine joined her. "Aren't you the prettiest girl in the world! Thank you, Zeus."

"No problem." He nodded towards the phone in her hand. "Realtor?"

"Oh, yes. We're going to be busy today; we are looking at three houses, at least."

Their day was set. The afternoon was spent going from one house to the next. None of them were quite right, however. Leaving the realtor and heading toward her parent's house, the three discussed houses, room sizes, and yards. Jasmine had definite ideas and told Zeus about the same house she had described to Meg.

As they neared her parent's house, Meg worried Jasmine would feel shy around a bunch of grown-ups she didn't know. Her worries were unfounded as Jasmine met them with openness and as if they had always been her family. Michael couldn't resist teasing his sister, smiling as he directed his thoughts toward her.

"What a nice family, Meg—daughter—husband!"

"Not yet, Uncle Mike." His smile faded as he looked at Jasmine who had mentally spoken. The smile returned as he looked back at Meg.

"We have a talker!" Meg had turned pink after Jasmine's comment—something about her and Zeus. "And you, Zeus, you heard that? You're not a father, yet."

"I'm a surrogate, for now."

Meg turned red—had Zeus heard everything? She groaned and went to the kitchen. Jasmine followed.

"Hello, there!" Bobbi greeted Jasmine. "You must be Jasmine." Nodding, Jasmine asked her own question.

"Are you Meg's mommy?"

"Yes, I am."

"Can you talk in your head, too?"

"Yes, I can." This pleased Jasmine immensely. "Would you like to help with supper?"

Jasmine climbed up on a stool and was soon folding napkins and lining wicker bread baskets with checkered cloths. Meg buttered croissants while Jasmine told her mother all about the judge making Meg her mommy, moving to Meg's, and their afternoon looking for a house. Once more she repeated her version of what kind of house they would get. Every detail was exactly as it had been before.

At the table, there was the usual chatter, bantering, story telling, and general chit chat. Silence descended when Jasmine spoke up in a lull of conversation.

"Can I call you Gramma and Grampa?" Lance and Bobbi looked at each other smiling.

"We would love it if you would." Lance answered.

"I almost have a whole family!"

Meg knew exactly what she meant. She looked at Zeus who just gave her a lop-sided grin. She was too tired to even try to figure out its meaning. Her lack of sleep, an afternoon of looking at houses, and a full stomach were more than she could handle. Staying awake took all of her energy.

As they prepared to leave, Meg handed Zeus the car keys.

"I'm beat. Would you mind driving home?"

He took the keys and nodded his head in agreement. She wasn't a lot of company on the way back. For a short distance, she listened to Zeus and Jasmine. After that, she dozed, then fell asleep.

She must be dreaming, but if she was dreaming . . . She dragged herself from sleep. Zeus and Jasmine were still talking. She started to slip back to sleep. Something wasn't right. There was no movement, no motor lulling her—what was confining her left hand—compressing it—someone was . . .

"Mommy."

Mommy. Was she dreaming? The voice didn't sound like her brother or sister when they were small.

"Meg?" Her hand was squeezed and lightly shook. "Meg."

"Hm—what? She mumbled.

"We found your house."

"We're home—k." Her eyes cracked open, then widened considerably.

"Where are we?" She sat up. Zeus nodded in front of them.

"Look familiar?"

At first glance, it didn't. It was just an empty house. Slowly things fit into place. Everything Jasmine had described for the house she wanted was there in front of her.

"Where are we? How did you find this place?"

"Jasmine directed me. It's close, very close to Crystal Lake, I believe."

"Is it for sale?"

"The sign by the road said it is."

"Absolutely . . ." Meg looked back at a beaming Jasmine. "Incredible!"

"I have all the information in my phone. We can leave a message and ask to officially see it Monday, but let's poke around tomorrow. We'll be at the lake, anyway." Zeus assured them.

"We will?"

"If you don't mind because Jasmine and I were talking about it just before she directed me here."

"Unbelievable!"

Meg was still looking at the house that so very closely fit what Jasmine had been describing all along. She hadn't remembered a sign being anywhere along the road when they passed by on their way to her parents. On such a long stretch of road with nothing except grass, trees, and bushes, a sign would have stood out. There hadn't been a sign earlier, of that she was sure.

Sure enough, when Zeus called about the house the next day, he found out that it had just gone on the market the day before while they were at Meg's parent's. What were the odds, Meg wondered, of that happening just when she was looking for a house, one that looked almost exactly like what Jasmine had been describing all along, and in a price range that Meg could afford. To say nothing of the fact that Meg had never been aware, in all the time she had been going to the lake, that there even was a house there.

Things moved fast after Zeus had called the realtor's. By the end of the month, the house was hers. Two weeks later, with the help of her family and Zeus, rooms were painted, Meg's apartment was cleaned out, packed up, and contents brought to the house. Everything was unpacked and put away. A bedroom set and an outside play set were delivered and set up. Curtains, blinds, and pictures were hung. Even steps leading down to the lake through the woods were installed. Lake rights were exclusively hers.

A large cookout was planned. What started out as roughly thirty people, quickly grew as her guests invited their friends and relatives. Thankfully, it was potluck. The weekend before the cookout, Zeus arrived early, kicking Meg and Jasmine out for the day. He answered no questions; he only gave them strict orders to stay away until six that evening and to eat light while away as he also had supper planned.

They did as he requested, first heading into town to do some shopping as there were many things needed for the cookout. They not only needed a ton or two of food but large folding tables, lawn chairs, paper plates, plastic eating utensils, paper towels, cups—the list stretched on and on. As long as they were at it, Meg bought a fire pit, lawn ornaments, and plants.

Exhausted, but not yet the assigned time to return home, they headed for Meg's parent's house. There they relaxed with cool drinks on the deck while explaining that Zeus had kicked them out for the day. Whatever he was up to, he had given them instructions to go home hungry. A whole day of cooking and Meg could just imagine what her new kitchen would look like!

"How are you and Zeus getting along?" Meg's mother asked.

"Okay, I guess. He's been very helpful with the moving and renovating. Sometimes I feel guilty about the amount of time he spends there, though."

"Why would you feel guilty? He seems like a nice enough guy . . . and you know Jasmine adores him."

"I believe the adoration goes both ways." Meg commented as she watched Jasmine playing on the lawn. "However, Zeus has a life of his own. I'm afraid the time he's spending with Jasmine is cramping that."

"He's also spending time with you." Her mother pointed out.

"Well, yes, of course, which makes it worse. There's someone he's interested in and he's either going to let that go because of the time he spends with us or we're his excuse to stop that possible relationship before it really gets started."

"If it's the latter, he must have a good reason."

"Mm," Meg began, "relationship—intimacy issues."

"Oh, dear!"

"Exactly. On the other hand, if he does return to his lady friend—spend more time with her and on that relationship—Jasmine won't understand his lack of attention to her, with her, and all that. As it is now, all the time he's spending with us is only feeding her desire for us—Zeus, me, and her—to be a family."

"Oh Dear! Have you spoken with him about it?"

"Basically he verbally pats me on the head and tells me everything will work out."

"Is it possible he's already broken it off with his lady friend?"

"I don't think so—whenever I ask about her, he speaks positively about the relationship. I've even given him hints—ideas—to further it along and offered my help if he feels the urge to run when the relationship gets too serious."

"Has he come to you for help, yet?"

"No, but he's said he's counting on my help when he needs it, so," Meg shrugged, "we'll see, I guess."

"Keep your eyes and mind open." She looked at her mother, thinking her advice had seemed odd. She would have asked about it if Jasmine hadn't diverted her attention.

"Mommy!" Jasmine ran to Meg taking her face in her small hands. "Mommy, can I be your flower girl?"

"My—what?" Her mind raced. "You are my flower girl—my *Jasmine flower girl!*"

Jasmine scowled, thinking it over. A smile lit up her face. She kissed Meg and ran off to play again.

"What goes through their minds is boggling!" Meg stated.

"And, interesting." Her mother commented with some sort of understanding.

By the time Zeus contacted her, supper was already cooked at Meg's parent's house. He sounded so tired from his day of whatever he was doing that he was invited there and gratefully accepted, admitting he had bit off more than he could chew. He arrived just in time to sit down and eat.

"You look beat." Lance observed. "Only hard, honest work does that."

"It was honest and hard and I'm very pleased with myself."

"What have you been up to?" Meg asked.

"You'll see." He changed the subject. "Bobbi, this meal is absolutely wonderful—much better than what I had planned!"

"Thank you, Zeus."

"Take it to heart, Mom—Zeus doesn't throw compliments around." Meg added.

"Then, I'm doubly honored!"

Carmen and Julie had come to dinner; they passed a thought to each other, then giggled. When they looked at Zeus, who was the topic of their thought, they found him smiling at them. Michael heard what was going on and also smiled.

"Uh—oh . . ."

"Be careful girls—I can hear you." Zeus spoke out loud, enjoying the shades of pink the girls turned. Carmen sniffed.

"It's not polite to eavesdrop."

"It is when it's about me." He countered.

Meg sat watching all three. She had heard her sisters and had just been thinking she was glad Zeus couldn't hear them, when he spoke. She was surprised and a little disappointed. She thought what she and Zeus shared was just between them—like her mom and dad—something special that only the two of them shared. She supposed it was only natural . . . if he could hear her, he could hear others, too.

"Hey . . ." Meg looked at Zeus. He winked at her, then continued eating.

Full, tired, and the car repacked; Meg, Zeus, and Jasmine prepared to head out. Lance had watched Zeus' blinks getting longer and longer as the meal progressed. He held his hand out to Zeus.

"Hand over the keys. Ride with Meg and I'll personally make sure your car is delivered to you tomorrow. You're exhausted and would probably fall asleep behind the wheel." Zeus hesitated.

"Don't argue with Dad," Michael interjected. "He'll win."

"Thank you." Zeus handed over his keys.

With a final farewell, Meg pulled out of the driveway and headed toward home.

"Would you like me to bring you home or would you like to spend the night?"

"I'll spend the night whenever I can. Besides, your dad has all my keys."

"Leave it to dad!"

"I know you were wondering if I heard your sisters—I didn't. The way they kept glancing at me, I knew they were discussing me."

"Have you ever tried listening to them—or anyone?"

"No, I'm happy just hearing you and Jasmine. They can hear me though, right?"

"It's never come up, but I would imagine so."

"So, you and I couldn't have a private conversation—there?"

"Not if they eavesdrop, which is frowned upon. There's always accidental, though, which can happen in any conversation. Decent people don't listen in on the whole thing, though."

"Do you know what they were saying?"

"Are you asking if I eavesdropped?"

"Well . . . that would be suggesting you're not decent, wouldn't it?"

"It would. I heard enough, though—you're a hunk."

"Humph!"

Zeus unloaded the car while Meg gave Jasmine a bath. They both tucked her into bed, then relaxed in the living room. Meg expected he'd want to get to sleep but he seemed to want to talk—or at least sit up with her.

"What *did* you do, today?" She hadn't seen anything different in the house.

"I'm too tired to show you tonight. You'll have to wait until tomorrow."

"Does that mean you're ready to go to sleep?"

"In a while."

"Do you want to watch TV?"

"Not really."

"Do you want to talk about anything in particular?"

"Now that you mention it, yes."

She waited. When he said nothing, she raised a questioning eyebrow. He smiled.

"You really don't listen in, do you?"

"Not unless I have to." Knowing what he wanted to talk about was something she was sure she didn't want to talk about. She quickly changed the subject. "How's your lady friend? I haven't heard you mention her in a while."

"She's fine."

"Has she come around yet?"

"Not really. I'm wondering if she's even interested. Just when I think things are going smoothly, she goes neutral on me."

"Maybe she senses your—commitment issues. That could be a problem unless she's looking for here and now and nothing long-term."

"That's possible, but I'm more inclined to think she has an issue that keeps her from letting go—an issue about someone who hurt her deeply—possibly ruined her trust and faith, and gave her fear of commitment."

"Fear of putting her heart on the line again." Meg spoke more to herself than to him.

"Any suggestions, Doctor?"

"Just keep at it. Keep showing her you can be trusted and won't hurt her. Unless she's scarred too deeply, she'll start to see it."

"Okay." He gave her a crooked smile. "We've depleted that subject for now. So, this would not be a good time to talk about Tony?"

He watched her inhale and stiffen at the mention of his name. An anxiousness passed through her eyes. Obviously, just his name brought back the pain and fear as if whatever had happened was minutes fresh.

"How long has it been?"

"Two years."

"How long did it last?" Her eyes darted to him and quickly away.

"We were together eight years. It was bad for three and a half."

"Ow! What kind of bad?" She gave him an instant irritated look.

"How bad does it have to be? Is physical abuse worse then mental abuse because it leaves scars? How about emotional abuse? Spiritual?"

"They all leave scars." He quietly commented. She stared at him until her irritation and anger ebbed.

"It was mental, emotional, and spiritual."

"Tell me about it."

"I just did."

"You told me of it, not about it."

"We spend too much time together."

"Why do you say that?"

"You're starting to sound and think like me."

"And you're avoiding the subject." She rolled her eyes.

"Okay, I guess I'll tell you. In a nutshell—he accepted my gifts—thought it was cool and all that. Then he had me help some people—using my gifts. It was just a few at first, those who really needed help according to him. Then in college, it was almost like a job—people came out of the woodwork, as they say, asking for my help. It cramped my studies, but I didn't mind—I was helping people who truly needed it. Then I found out he was sending people to me after they paid *him* a lot of money for *my* services. All the while, he told me people were mad because I hadn't helped them at all. I'd see them again—he got paid again. Repeat business was great for his wallet—he charged more for the follow-up appointments and people willingly paid."

"How did you find out what he was doing?"

"One of the people mentioned my sessions were expensive, but well worth it and they'd be willing to pay even more for a third session. I used my gift on this person and found out what he was getting charged by Tony. I used it later on Tony. He knew I didn't use it unless I had to. I felt I had to at that point. Apparently—and according to what I read in his mind—I wasn't bright enough to ever figure out what was going on. Honestly, I don't know if I even would have suspected anything if it hadn't been for that one person."

"How did he react when he found out?"

"He used it all on me—guilt, mental and emotional abuse, and even bartering. He was willing to share the money with me. Of course, what he said he was getting and what part I would have gotten wasn't anywhere near what he was really getting. I went home for spring break and switched schools and my major."

"What had you been studying?"

"I wanted to be a teacher."

"And you switched to psychiatry." She nodded. "Have you seen him since?" She shook her head. "Do you know where he is?" She shook her head again, then looked at him, suspiciously.

"Why?" He shrugged. "Don't even entertain the thought of contacting him! Leave it alone, Zeus."

"Don't you think he deserves—something?"

"Yes, I do, but I believe "What goes around, comes around.""

"Karma?"

"Karma."

"Sometimes that's not fast enough."

"Now you sound like Michael."

"Great minds . . ."

"What goes around, comes around." She repeated.

"And you charted that for yourself?" He sounded unsure.

"Nothing happens for nothing. I never would have gone into psychiatry, otherwise, and I wouldn't be where I am today."

"And you wouldn't have met Jasmine—or me." She sighed.

"The ripples one small pebble makes in a pond . . ."

"It's all starting to make sense now. Dark spirits aside, I couldn't understand why it upset you when it appeared I had accepted you being psychic. To me it seemed you should have felt relieved, not suspicious. Then I thought about what it was like for you in school and thought you were thinking I was making fun of you behind your back. My mind has bounced all over trying to figure it out; but I never would have thought you'd been exploited—that someone had taken chunks of your soul . . ."

His words, the fact that he really did understand that what Tony had done took pieces of her very being, her soul, her essence, made her look at him differently. At that exact moment, she was no longer falling in love with him—she *was* in love with him. Tears of love and regret fell down her face. He wasn't hers to love.

Chapter Twenty Seven

He reached for her.

Suddenly she was on her feet.

"Okay—enough of the soul searching! We'd better get some sleep. Night Zeus."

Meg hurried to her room and shut the door. Her mind was whirling. Oh, no, sheets! She had to go back out there. She grabbed a pillow, a flat sheet, and a blanket. Just as she was about to open the door, Zeus knocked on it.

"Meg?" She pulled the door open, shoved the bedding at him and shut the door. "Thanks."

Sleep didn't happen for either one of them. By morning Meg looked unrested and frazzled. Zeus and Jasmine, on the other hand, were quite chipper. Noticing the blinds on the sliding glass door were still closed, she went to open them. Perhaps letting sunshine in would help her feel better.

"Not yet, Meg, leave them closed for a little longer."

"I just wanted to let some sun in."

"Come help us in the kitchen. We'll eat out there."

"But . . ." He handed her a tray laden with food.

"Mr. Garrett has a surprise for us!" She carried a plate of bagels.

Zeus held another tray with juice, bowls, and silverware. Balancing the tray, he opened the blinds, then the glass door. The three stepped outside. As Meg and Jasmine stood staring, he relieved them of their burdens, placing everything on the patio table.

Meg stood staring at a large deck that hadn't been there before—or the patio set, plants, stone grill center, and awning.

"Look!" Following Jasmine's gaze to the right side of the backyard, Meg saw the jungle gym set, the sand box, and a swing hanging from a tree branch.

"Zeus . . ." Meg was at a loss for words.

"Is it okay girls?"

In answer, Jasmine flew down the steps toward the jungle gym, squealing with excitement as she went. Meg still stood on the deck trying to take it all in.

"Meg?"

Her eyes finally met his. Thoughts, partial ones anyway, tumbled through her mind. He put his hands on her shoulders and looked into her eyes.

"Slow down. Center yourself."

She looked at him helplessly for a few seconds, then closed her eyes and inhaled deeply. Her problem wasn't a lack of words. Exhale. Her problem was the words she nearly said. Inhale. Her problem was she didn't want to just stand there. Exhale. She wanted to let her feelings for him out. Inhale. She wanted to hold him and tell him. Exhale. She moved away from him at the same time.

"Zeus, all this . . ." Her arm moved to encircle everything. "It's all so beautiful and thoughtful. How can I ever repay you?"

She sank into a chair. He sat beside her taking one of her hands.

"I'll think of something." He winked and smiled at her.

He called to Jasmine promising her he'd push her on the swing after eating breakfast and getting dressed.

"You know," he handed Meg a bagel with strawberry cream cheese, "there are steps leading to the lake through the woods. With a little work, I could place lights down the steps."

"We can walk to the lake!" Jasmine exclaimed.

"Never go by yourself. *Always* have an adult with you Jasmine. Understand?" Meg insisted.

"Yes, Mommy." Meg took her hand. "I'll never go to the lake by myself again."

"Again!" Both Meg and Zeus said together.

"When did you go to the lake?" Meg asked.

"Before."

"Before—when?"

"You know."

Meg tried to remember when she could have possibly gone to the lake alone. She couldn't remember a time Jasmine hadn't been with her unless she was in bed. She couldn't have gone down there in the middle of the night.

"Did you . . ." Something about the way she was looking at her. "Oh, then."

"When?" Zeus asked.

"In a past life. This is our third life together. She drowned in one."

"You remember?"

"She does and Mom told me we'd been together twice before."

"Wow—I mean, you told me about past lives but I never thought any of us knew each other in them."

Meg had a curious thought but it got interrupted when her phone rang. She went inside to answer it.

"Hi, Mom."

"Your dad has a splendid idea. He's out grilling meat. I'm making the rest. We'll bring all of it over when we return Zeus' car."

"That will be great, Mom. I can't wait to show you the surprise Zeus had for us!"

Meg told Zeus about the plans for supper. She helped set up tables for lunch that her parents were bringing over.

"By next weekend, this one," he nodded toward the stone grill he had made, "will be ready for use."

They fell into a discussion about the coming weekend and how fun and busy it would be as well as trying to guess how many people would actually be there. Then they all got dressed. As promised, Zeus pushed Jasmine on the swing for a little while, then all three followed the steps to the lake. They spent a couple hours walking along the shore, building sand castles, digging holes in the sand until they filled with water.

Eventually, they made their way back to the house. Sitting on the deck, they discussed the placement of tables for the following weekend. Just as they finished planning where tables would be placed, which ones for guests and which for food, Meg's family arrived. With a flurry of activity, the meal was brought from the car to the tables on the patio. Everyone admired the deck, barbeque pit, yard, toys, and lawn ornaments.

Meg seemed unusually quiet for the first few minutes of the meal. Zeus glanced around to see if anyone else was also quiet—and checking to see if Meg was 'talking' to someone there. The rest were engaged in eating and talking. Apparently Meg was reflecting on something.

Once she started participating in the chatter surrounding the table, he glanced around again. To his surprise, her mother was watching him, a motherly smile on her face. Now he wondered if mother and daughter *had* been communicating after all.

Zeus flipped back and forth the rest of the afternoon as to whether they had been communicating. If they had been, what they had been saying peaked his curiosity. After Meg's family left, he decided he'd just ask her.

After Jasmine had played until she was silly, they ate leftovers from lunch, then gave Jasmine a bath. They were tucking her into bed when she asked if Zeus was going to be there in the morning. He paused only briefly before telling her he had to go back to his own place so he'd be able to get ready for work. Jasmine offered a solution.

"You could bring your clothes here."

"That's true," he conceded, "however . . ."

"And if you slept on Mommy's bed you'd be more comfortable."

"Jasmine . . ." Meg was mortified.

"And," Jasmine continued as if Meg hadn't spoken, "if you bring your clothes here you wouldn't have to leave."

Jasmine put their hands together and held them there. Zeus had a slight grin, fighting to keep it from getting wider. Meg was beyond mortified.

"Now you two go think about it."

Zeus squeezed Meg's hand tighter as they stood and left Jasmine's room. To say he was enjoying Meg's discomfort was an understatement. Entering the living room, his face split with the grin he'd been holding at bay. Any of his thoughts about asking her if she and Bobbi had been communicating was lost.

"Like I said, she has a very focused mind! She also has a point, you know."

"Just because she used to be my grandmother doesn't mean she's right!"

"Your grandmother? Really?" Meg didn't answer. She just looked at him, noting his grin and looked away. "When did minding your elders go out of fashion?"

"Let me know when you're finished."

"Have we ever shared a life?"

"You and Jasmine?" She knew who he was referring to.

"You and I?"

"I have no idea."

That wasn't exactly the truth. She didn't know for sure but she had a feeling they had.

"How do we find out?"

"PLR." He looked at her questioningly. She clarified. "Past Life Regression—being hypnotized and brought back to your past life or lives."

"Can you do that?"

"Yes, but someone neutral should do it so nothing is imposed unintentionally."

"Do you know anyone . . ."

"I can check into it tomorrow if you'd like, but for right now, shouldn't you be heading home before it gets too late?"

"I take it Granny's suggestion is out then?"

"Yes and Granny and I need to have a talk!"

"Is it strange knowing that little girl used to be your grandmother?"

"Only when she acts like it."

There was something in her voice that told him she didn't want to talk about it. This made him more curious but he took the hint.

"Well, I suppose I had better get going." He stood and she followed him to the door. "We'll talk sometime tomorrow."

Meg laid awake for a long time trying to sort her emotions out. She had a feeling that she and Zeus had shared a previous life. Or, it could be that she just wished it. But—*if* they had, how would that effect their relationship? Would that fact bring them together; whereas otherwise they wouldn't even think about it? Well, he couldn't—he already had a heart interest and she doubted he'd be swayed away from that person.

She could always ask her mother. The information wouldn't change how she felt about Zeus. Unless . . . What if they had been married before and he beat her or murdered her? That would certainly change at least how she reacted around him. But, even if that were true, he's nothing like that in this life. Maybe he wasn't like that in that life either—at first.

Such were the thoughts that kept her awake half the night. The other half was spent tossing and turning from dreams running along the same themes as her thoughts about Zeus. At the first hint of daylight, Meg gratefully got up putting an end to her dreams. Her thoughts, however, bombarded her as she drank coffee on the deck. Would knowing really be better, especially if they had shared a life together? What if? That was what kept going around and around in her head. She hadn't realized how long she had sat there until she heard Jasmine's voice.

"Mommy?" Meg dragged her mind away from her thoughts.

"Good morning. How did you sleep?"

"Fine. Why didn't Mr. Garrett stay?"

"Honey, he has his own place."

"He doesn't want to move here? I'll sleep on the couch—or we can make the other room his bedroom."

"Jasmine . . . sweetie . . ."

"He likes us, I know he does!"

"Yes, he likes us, but . . ."

"Not 'enough' again."

Jasmine slowly walked away as her word "again" pounded in Meg's mind. Now she was almost positive. She followed Jasmine inside.

"What would you like for breakfast?"

"Cereal, I guess."

Jasmine was upset and Meg had no idea how to comfort her. She was also afraid to ask her what she had meant—what she knew.

She thought about it, though, as she brought Jasmine to Mary's for the day, and again as she drove to work. "*Not 'enough' again.*" Had Zeus had commitment issues then, too? Perhaps he and Jasmine shared a past life and he had left her with a broken heart. She wanted very badly to know. Or did she? Perhaps it would effect how she saw Zeus and how she felt about him and not in a good way. To know he had hurt

Jasmine, even in a past life, would make her protect Jasmine that much more.

She felt miserable all day. Her clients picked up on her feelings and consequently didn't have good sessions. This made her feel worse. Unsure of herself, she was glad for her work day to end. She would be equally glad when the entire day was over as she dreaded hearing from Zeus and the questions he would ask and the answers he wanted. Then, there was Jasmine. She prayed she wasn't still upset about Zeus not spending the night.

Arriving at Mary's, she found a much happier Jasmine playing and enthralled with a new foster child who had just arrived that day. Jasmine greeted Meg mentally, but didn't make any moves to greet her physically because she was enjoying playing in the living room with the new child.

"Jasmine really likes the new arrival!"

"They've been inseparable since he got here. They hugged like they knew each other their whole lives. Jasmine even called him by name—Christopher. She has been taking care of him all day. Sometimes that child of yours is much older than her years."

"What's his story?"

"Basically he's awaiting adoption. Parents passed away and no relatives. He's the sweetest little boy. Jasmine had been taking care of him all day, like I said. They even took a nap together."

"Mommy!" Jasmine stood, waiting for Christopher to stand, then took his hand. Together they went to Meg. As soon as she saw his face, she knew she had known Christopher before. "Look who's here—Christopher!"

"See what I mean? It's like they've been friends forever and have just been waiting to see one another again."

Meg nodded at Mary's comment but she couldn't take her eyes off the small boy heading her way. From somewhere in a past life she recognized him. He smiled at her and crawled into her lap, then hugged her. Apparently, he also recognized her.

"Mommy." He sighed while hugging her. It was as if he was happy to be reunited again.

"Hello, Christopher." She hugged him back. "How are you?"

"I knew you'd come."

Chapter Twenty Eight

"Do you know him, Meg?" Mary was astonished at his greeting.

"I'm sure Jasmine told him all about me."

That was all she could say. Explaining about knowing him in, at least one past life, wasn't an option.

"How old are you, Christopher?" Meg asked. He worked hard to hold up the correct amount of fingers.

"Three."

He said the words, but the look in his eyes as he looked directly into her eyes, said he was much older.

"What a big boy!"

"Are we going home now?"

Meg was taken back by his question and was at a loss as to what to say to him.

"Honey," Mary spoke up, "Jasmine is leaving but you're staying here."

"I want to go home, too!" Christopher pouted with an attitude.

Meg and Mary looked at one another, neither knowing what to say. Jasmine took his hand, waited for him to slide off Meg's lap, then led him back to the living room.

"Oh boy," Mary stated, "he must think he's suppose to go home with Jasmine."

"It would seem so." Meg felt the same way.

"They're like siblings who only have each other and no one else."

"I hope he'll be okay when we leave."

Jasmine and Christopher came back out to where Mary and Meg were.

"It'll be okay, Mommy—he understands now."

Meg looked at Christopher who just smiled reassuringly at her. Jasmine gave him a hug then he hugged Meg and kissed her cheek.

"Bye." He spoke quietly. Suddenly she felt as though she were abandoning him.

"I'll bring Jasmine back in the morning."

He nodded and gave her a small smile. It would have felt completely normal to take him with them. She felt imprinted with him as though she were his mother. Leaving him there, watching her leave, was very heartbreaking for her.

"I promise we'll be back in the morning Topher." Meg told him.

She had no idea why she'd called him that but upon hearing it his smile broadened.

"Love you much." He spoke softly.

Meg couldn't take any more. In order to keep from snatching him up, she took Jasmine's hand and made herself walk out the door and to the car. Almost mechanically she buckled Jasmine into the car seat, got behind the wheel, and pulled onto the road. A mile down the road, she pulled over, rested her head on the steering wheel and willed herself not to cry.

"It's okay, Mommy—don't cry—be brave."

Meg suddenly sat up looking into the rear view mirror, tilting it to be able to see Jasmine. Except this Jasmine looked different—only the eyes were the same. Beside her was Christopher clinging to her side. She was holding them tightly as she knelt in front of them. They were in a cottage of some sort and flames were all around them. There was no way to escape. She held her children, crying.

"I love you Topher and Darlene."

"It's okay, Mommy—don't cry—be brave."

The fire consumed them.

"Would you like to go to Gram and Gramp's?"

"Yea!"

Meg not only wanted, but needed, to talk to her mother. She had to know how Zeus and Christoper were connected to Jasmine and her.

Meg's father didn't have to hear her thoughts to know she was distressed—it was so prominent in her eyes it jumped out at him. Jasmine ran to him hugging him.

"Hey, Jas, let's go find some trouble to get into."

Taking her hand, he led her away as Meg found her mother in the living room, a tray of tea waiting for them. Meg sat in her father's chair unsure where to start or how to begin. Accepting tea her mother passed to her, she stirred it once then looked at her.

"Have Zeus and I shared a life?"

"Yes—your last ones."

"Christopher? He and Jasmine were with me in my last life?"

"Zeus, too." Meg closed her eyes and inhaled three times.

"Elaborate please." She exhaled the third breath.

"Zeus was your lover. He was married and at that time there was no divorce. He didn't love her, nor her him. He was her possession. He fathered Darlene and Topher—now Jasmine and Christopher. He couldn't be with you but spent as much time as he could with the three of you. His wife found out. She had him followed. She had your small cottage set on fire—all around the outside so you couldn't escape. All three of you died that night. The next day Darius killed himself—the Darius who is now Zeus."

Tears were streaming down Meg's face. She told her mother of the vision she saw, about meeting Christopher, how he and Jasmine seemed to know one another, how he had called her mommy and wanted to go home with them.

"He's three, right?" Meg nodded. "He remembers like it was yesterday."

"Would he recognize Zeus? Would Zeus recognize him?"

"Perhaps. Zeus, or Darius, wasn't around constantly so naturally he was more attached to you."

"What am I going to do? He thinks he's coming . . ." She stopped, her mind whirling. "He's waiting to be adopted—I'll adopt him! That's what this is all about, right. This is why I have been reintroduced to the kids, right?"

"It will happen as the three of you have charted it."

"Don't breath a word of this to Zeus. Whatever happens I want to know he did it on his own."

"Like what?"

"He's interested in a woman who is giving him a run for his money. I don't want him to think, because of our past lives, he should drop her for us." Her mother smiled.

"He'll be with the one he's supposed to be with. In the end, it will all turn out for the best. He won't leave the one he's supposed to be with." She patted her daughter's hand. "I won't say a word."

That was what Meg wanted. Hearing Zeus would end up with his lady friend, however, didn't make her feel better. Could her day get any worse?

"We'll be right back." Her father announced as he and Jasmine entered the room. "We need to get supper ingredients!"

"Oh, no!" Meg exclaimed. "With those two drumming up supper, there's no telling what we're having!"

"I'm sure your father talked her out of having cake, cookies, and ice cream for supper with candy bars for dessert."

"Even though that may be, you know how much daddy loves pie."

"Hm, yes—you have a point there." Her mother smiled at her.

Much later, after chili dogs and potato chips, washed down with soda, Meg and Jasmine headed home. As Jasmine sang songs in the back, Meg's mind went over the conversation she'd had with her mother. Just before the driveway came into view, her mind wandered to Zeus and how it was strange he hadn't called her yet. Perhaps he had a change of mind and didn't want to know if they had shared a life together. Stranger, yet, was turning the bend in the road and seeing his car with him leaning against it. She pulled in, parking beside his car. He unbuckled Jasmine lifting her out as she told him all about Christopher then supper with her grandparents. Hardly giving him time to comment, she dashed off to play in the back yard.

"She's wound up!" Zeus exclaimed.

"Blame my father. Soda, really!" They fell into step as they followed Jasmine.

"I hate to sound like a suspicious husband but why is your phone off?" Meg groaned as she pulled it out of her pocket and turned it on.

"I forgot to turn it on when I left work. How long have you been here waiting?"

"An hour or so."

"I'm sorry, Zeus. It's been a tough day."

He reached for her keys still dangling in her hand. After getting her settled on the patio, he went to the front of the house, let himself in, poured them some iced tea and joined her in the back.

"What made your day tough?" She shrugged.

"Just nothing went right at work. Then, at Mary's, Christopher thought he was leaving with us. It nearly killed me to leave him there. But there's hope . . ." She paused. "Listen to me going on and on." She paused again. "How was your day Zeus?"

"A breeze compared to yours! Tell me about the hope and who Christopher is."

"Hope? Oh, yeah. Christopher is a new child at Mary's. He just got there today. He's waiting to get adopted and I'm going to get him."

"Are you sure you want to do that Meg?"

"As sure as I was about Jasmine."

"Do you ever plan to have your own children?"

She thought about Jasmine and Christopher. They were her own children . . . and his.

"It's possible." Not wanting to elaborate, she changed the subject. "Have you eaten?"

"Not yet. I'll grab something on the way back." He gave her a crooked smile. "You do realize you can't adopt every child in need, don't you?"

"Would that be such a bad thing?" She didn't wait for him to answer. "I'll whip something up for you."

Hurriedly she went inside and rummaged around in the fridge and cupboards until she had enough for a meal. In less than thirty minutes, she brought a tray to the patio. She sat at one of the tables with him as he ate, watching Jasmine and carrying on a conversation with Zeus.

By the time he was finished, it was time for Jasmine's bath, then some quiet time before bed, which she spent on Zeus' lap chatting away about shows she'd seen, a movie she wanted to see, and her doll, Annabelle. An hour later, she was winding down and yawning.

Among her, "I'm not tired" protests, Zeus carried her to her room. He and Meg tucked her in, still under protest that she wasn't in the least sleepy. They suspected before they left the room that she had already fallen asleep.

"I think I've got this kid thing down. You just ply them with sugar, let them run and play themselves silly until they wind down, a nice bath, and boom—they're tired."

At first Meg was horrified at his comment, then she realized he had to be joking.

"Using that recipe sounds good on the surface. But once your nice and warm and asleep in your bed you'll get jarred awake by a child with a tummy ache, or they're throwing up, or they have diarrhea—or all three. That'll tarnish the polish quickly. Then there's cavities and . . ."

"Okay, okay—I get it!" He chuckled.

"Good because I wouldn't hesitate to make you take care of any and all of it!"

"In a round-about way that brings us to our next topic. Have you found anyone who can tell us about our past lives?"

"Yes." She answered honestly, dreading the conversation. Worse, however, was the excited interest on his face.

"When can we talk to them? I can't wait to find out if we knew each other—before!"

"She pretty much already told me everything without PLR. We did know one another."

"Really? Were we married?" She picked her words carefully.

"You were—I wasn't."

"Oh." He sounded disappointed. "But we knew each other?"

"Yes—we ran into one another from time to time."

"So we were friends—kinda like now." He mused. "Did I have any kids?"

"Two—a boy and a girl."

"How did I die?" Meg swallowed hard.

"You committed suicide."

"I killed myself? Why?"

"You were depressed."

"Why was I depressed?"

"The love of your life and your children died in a fire."

"That would do it—my wife and kids, all at once—man!" He reflected on that briefly. "How about you? How did you die?"

Meg's eyes had filled with tears. She sniffed and wiped them away, shaking her head.

"Can we please stop talking about it?"

"Yes, of course. I'm sorry, I didn't realize it would still bother you . . . that you can still feel it."

"It's just so tragic . . ."

"We'll get it right in this lifetime."

A comment meant to make her feel better had only made her feel worse. It was obvious she carried her feelings over from that life to this one, but he hadn't. Zeus didn't fully understand her tears and didn't know what she needed. He moved closer to her, wrapping her in his arms without speaking.

She knew he was trying to comfort her. The problem was, it wasn't working. She tried to put on a brave front by pretending to be cheered when she actually was feeling rather pathetic because, even though it saddened her—his arms around her, the feel of his body so close to her, also felt good. She wanted so much more and couldn't have it but was willing to take what she could get. The fact he was only being a friend—that his heart belonged to someone else . . .

"We should get to bed—it's getting late and I've had a taxing day."

They stood together, walking toward the front door. He stopped, looking down at her with concern.

"Will you be okay?"

She nodded, afraid if she spoke he'd hear the sadness in her voice and perhaps ask questions.

"Sure?" She nodded giving him a weak smile.

"Call me if you want to talk or whatever."

She nodded again. He kissed her forehead before he left. As the door clicked shut, she squeezed her eyes tightly shut and let the tears falls.

Chapter Twenty Nine

Zeus called in the morning to see if she was feeling better. She told him she was and hoped she sounded convincing. As for the rest of the day, she painted on a smile and infused herself with as much enthusiasm as possible. Most of her clients bought it.

Her next hurdle was going to get Jasmine. Leaving without Christopher would be more painful than the day before. Trying to steel herself, she headed for Mary's, partially cheered by the thought that soon the adoption process for Christopher would be started and with any luck it would progress quickly.

Meg was greeted by both children with hugs and kisses before they went off to play. Once alone, Meg asked who Christopher's case worker was; it was the same person as for Jasmine. Meg told the case worker about her plans to adopt him.

"I may have to open an adoption agency myself, or you'll put me out of business!"

"That might make it easier for me!"

"I'm sure you'll have no problems. Certainly nothing like before."

"Let's hope not. We'd better get going. I'm not particularly in a hurry but it breaks my heart when I have to tell Christopher he can't come with us so I want to get it over with."

To their surprise, he didn't ask to go with them this time. He simply hugged her tightly, kissed her cheek and whispered "soon" in her ear. When she put him down, he held her hand as she spoke with Mary. Simultaneously, there was a knock at the door. She felt a thrill of excitement pass through Christopher and into her. She glanced up as Mary opened the door and saw Zeus just entering. Christopher ran to him. Zeus automatically picked him up. Christopher's face turned serious as he placed a small hand on either side of Zeus' face and intently looked into his eyes. Suddenly he smiled and shouted, "There you are—hello again!" For just a second Zeus was mentally off balance.

"Hi, Little Man. How are you?"

"Hungry."

"Come on, Christopher," Mary spoke up, "I'll get you a snack."

He squirmed out of Zeus' arms and took Mary's hand.

"We'll just be on our way, Mary."

"Okay, see you tomorrow."

Jasmine ran to give Christopher a hug and whispered something in his ear. He turned his head and smiled at Meg and Zeus, gave a little wave with a chubby hand, then followed Mary smiling back at them.

Outside, Zeus followed Meg and Jasmine to their car. He buckled Jasmine in, then turned to Mag.

"What was *that* all about? He acted like he knew me and I swear when he looked at me he was looking into my very soul!"

"He does make you feel like that, yes."

"I can't explain it, but when he was looking at me like that I felt as though I'd known him a long time."

"Yes, that, too."

"I understand how you feel about leaving him with here."

"Actually, today wasn't as bad—he didn't ask about going with me." She opened her car door. "But I still want to get out of here before I change my mind and go back to get him. So, supper—my house?"

"I'm right behind you."

While Meg and Zeus prepared the main part of the meal, Jasmine asked if she could help. Zeus opened a bag of pre-made lettuce salad, retrieved a large bowl, sliced the rest of the ingredients for her, put her on a stool, and told her she could toss the salad.

As he turned back to finish helping Meg, Jasmine asked, "Really?"

"Yes, toss the salad."

"Um . . . Zeus . . ." Meg began.

Salad ingredients started flying through the air. Some hitting them. Meg started to grin.

"What are you doing?!" Zeus asked.

"She's tossing the salad." Meg answered. A tiny chuckle erupted from her. "Children are quite literal," Meg explained.

"Okay, Hon, thank you." He helped her down, then she scampered off to the living room.

"I was going to warn you after I realized how you had worded it, but too late. It's best to show them what you mean or find a wording they'll understand."

"I guess I'll just have to live and learn as I go! Not everyone has gone to college for this."

"I did learn about kids in college, but it probably wouldn't have been retained unless I'd experienced it—which I did with my younger siblings."

"That definitely leaves me at a disadvantage. My only sibling was my age."

After supper the three of them cleaned up. Meg noticed Zeus chose his words carefully whenever he gave instructions to Jasmine. This made her smile.

"Has Clansey been around lately?"

"He comes and goes but he hasn't been here nearly as much as he was before we moved."

"Do you think it has something to do with your moving?"

"I don't think so. He's just been busy with something and hasn't felt like sharing what it is. When he is here he spends a lot of time amusing Jasmine."

With the kitchen clean, they moved outside. Jasmine played while Meg and Zeus sat on the deck. Eventually they strolled through the woods to the lake. As they walked along, he brought up putting lights and perhaps even a railing in. He suggested putting in a dock and getting a row boat.

As he spoke, Meg almost forgot his presence with her and Jasmine wasn't permanent. It bothered her that she so easily forgot that more and more as time went on. She tried to deter him from committing himself as much as possible. Not only should he be spending his time with his lady friend and working on their relationship, but she feared she would come to depend on him.

"I'd rather get the spare room ready for Christopher first."

"You're giving *my* room away? Jasmine will be so disappointed!" He grinned at her. "I like her back up plan better anyway."

"Taking her room and she sleeps on the couch?"

"That was plan C."

"What was plan A?"

"Sleeping with you!"

Meg stumbled, both mentally and physically. Zeus took her arm, steadying her, leaving his hand on her arm as they walked along.

"Do the two of you discuss this when I'm not around?" He laughed but didn't answer her.

Momentarily, they made their way back to the house. Zeus seemed content to walk along in silence while Meg thought about how to ease him out of her life. He spent too much time there for someone with a love interest elsewhere. Perhaps he was using her to break away from his growing feelings for his lady friend.

"How are you and your lady friend doing?" They had just stepped onto the lawn.

"Fine. We're actually seeing more of each other, lately." They crossed to the deck.

"How is that possible—you're always here?"

"We manage." He grinned at her. "Tea?"

He disappeared inside leaving her to think. When he returned, he changed the subject.

"I brought juice instead." He sat across from her. "How's your love life?"

The question surprised and mildly shocked her and it showed.

"What?"

"You ask about mine all the time," he shrugged, "I thought I'd ask about yours. So, how is it?"

"I manage."

"Really? Anything serious?"

"Definitely not—just friends." She was talking about him.

"Playing the field, huh? Any benefits?"

Benefits? What was he talking about? What benefits? Her face flushed as it hit her.

"Zeus! I don't ask you about *your* sex life. Mine is not open for discussion!"

"I'll tell you about mine, if you like."

"I don't like."

"Too bad—it could be interesting—from a shrink's point of view."

Meg finally caught on. He was teasing her and enjoying her discomfort. She was only mildly irritated.

"As a client, that's fine. As a friend—too much information!"

"I just thought—you know—since we'll be sleeping together you might want to know."

"Plan A will never happen."

Zeus stood. He watched Jasmine on the jungle gym briefly. Turning his attention back to Meg, he moved to stand beside her, bending down to whisper in her ear.

"Never say never."

He quickly joined Jasmine, leaving her to wonder about the meaning of his words. Was he being general or specific? She rejected both ideas, deciding instead he was teasing. She threw a mental thought at him

"Get to know your lady friend better!"

He looked up at her, his brow knit. She maintained eye contact with him. Suddenly his brow relaxed. He smiled and winked at her, then continued pushing Jasmine on the swing.

Meg watched them for a while. When the scene before her eyes changed she didn't know. She found herself smiling as she watched them together—*them* being Darius and Darlene. Absently, she rubbed her belly, looking down at the rounded swell. She was in her eighth month. From the beginning she knew it was a boy. She'd already decided on a name—Christopher.

A squeal of laughter caught her attention. Looking up, she was suddenly seeing Zeus spinning around in circles with Jasmine in his arms. Darius and Darlene were gone. She inhaled sharply, left the deck, and entered the house. She paced the living room several times before going to the kitchen. Absentmindedly she started chopping fruit, not stopping until she realized the fruit bowl contained one apple and another bowl was filled with fruit salad. She put some in three bowls, a spoon in each bowl, and put the large bowl in the fridge.

"Mommy, I'm hungry." She handed Jasmine a bowl. "Thanks, you're the best!"

Zeus took the bowl she held out for him. He couldn't help noticing the sadness in her eyes as she stared at him. He wished he could hear what she was thinking—maybe. Had their earlier conversation depressed her?

"Join us?"

Meg preceded Zeus into the living room with her bowl of fruit salad. They sat on the couch. Whatever was going through her mind was serious enough so she didn't realize they were breaking the rule of no eating in that room.

"Mommy?"

"Yes, Baby?"

"Is it okay to eat in the living room now?"

"No . . ." She looked at them. "I'm sorry, my mind was somewhere else. Thank you for reminding me honey."

Back in the kitchen, sitting at the counter, Meg sat with Zeus and Jasmine. The latter were chatting while she picked at her fruit. Having past life visions could only mean she was too close to Zeus—bringing back past memories. It had to stop. She needed to make a clean break between Zeus and herself. She looked at Jasmine. How would she take it? How would she explain it to her? She looked at Zeus. He would be confused and hurt. She couldn't see another way around it.

"Penny for your thoughts." Meg smiled at him. "What, not enough?"

"My parents have a thing about that. They've used it for years. They have the original sixteen cents."

"Sixteen cents?"

"A penny for your thoughts, a nickel for a kiss, a dime if you tell me that you love me. It's from some old song. It started when they first met and they've kept it going all these years."

"That's nice! I like to see older people still in love. It gives me hope."

There was something in his voice. A message perhaps. She didn't dwell on it. Instead she presumed he was thinking of his lady friend.

"Me, too."

She would have added 'she wouldn't settle for anything less than what her parents had' but she decided it was a moot topic for them and would only inspire a conversation she didn't want to open or participate in.

Once Jasmine was in bed, Zeus poured them each a glass of wine and they relaxed in the living room. Meg enjoyed their quiet time together at the end of the day. She was getting too comfortable having him around. She planned meals, events, weekends for three. Sadly, it had to stop.

"Tell me about your love life."

"Are you still on that?" He just looked at her expectantly. "There's nothing to tell."

"No boyfriend—men friends?" She shook her head. "Why not?"

"No time. No interest. No desire."

"Why not?" She shrugged. "Have you given up?" She shrugged again. "You're too young and beautiful to give up. Please tell me that's not the case."

"I haven't given up." Her tone partially suggested otherwise.

"Then, why isn't there someone in your life?" When she didn't answer, he continued. "When was the last time you were on a date?"

"A few months ago."

"Where did you go?"

"Applebee's and a movie." There was a moment of silence.

"Besides with me?"

"More than a few months then." He waited expectantly. "I've been on three dates in the past year—two with the same guy."

"Why not more with either one?"

"One is better left as a friend—the other . . ."

"Go on."

"He thought, because I hadn't dated in a while I'd be—desperate for—affection. He wasn't happy to be turned down and the date terminated."

"I'll wager that was your last date." She nodded. "Why not try again?"

"No one has asked me."

"Why don't you ask someone? That's perfectly acceptable these days."

"There really isn't anyone I want to ask."

"There *really* isn't anyone—which means there *is* someone you're interested in. Ask him."

"I can't."

"Can't or won't?"

"Both. Zeus, please . . ."

"Why?" He demanded.

"He's—not available, okay."

"Does he know you like him?"

"No."

"You're really stuck on him, aren't you?" She avoided looking at him.

"Yes, now drop it!"

Zeus became very quiet. He went to the kitchen, returning with the bottle of wine, refilling their glasses.

"I'm sorry."

"For what?"

"Asking. Pushing. Knowing."

"Me, too."

Chapter Thirty

He flipped on the TV, scanning the menu, turning to a movie. They watched in silence for an hour. Meg hadn't been in the mood for watching anything, but the storyline caught her attention, drawing her in.

"Good movie, huh?" Zeus asked during an ad.

"Yes, it is. I'd never have chosen it though."

"That just goes to show you—never say never."

"I've heard that somewhere before recently."

"No doubt from a wise man." She rolled her eyes.

"Shh, it's back on."

"You'll love this next part where they get hopelessly lost going in circles and the killer zeros in on them . . ."

"Stop!"

"You haven't seen this movie before?" He looked a little too innocent.

"No and I don't need to now, thank you very much!"

"I'm sorry."

He chuckled as she hit him with a pillow and grabbed for the remote, which he moved out of her reach.

"There's no sense in finishing the movie now." She attempted to grab the remote again, failing again.

"What if I was lying?" He smiled at her.

"Were you?"

"Maybe. You'll just have to watch it to see, I guess."

"Fine, but not another word, understand?"

It turned out he was only half lying so the movie wasn't completely ruined. All in all, she enjoyed the movie. Between them they had finished the wine. She was relaxed and comfortable by the time the credits were rolling. He moved, adjusting his position. She looked over at him wondering if he'd moved a little closer to her.

"So, did you enjoy the movie?"

"The parts you didn't ruin." She teased.

"Ah, come on." He placed a hand on her knee. "I didn't ruin any of it."

"If you think I'm going to admit that," she patted his hand, "you're crazy."

She swore he ever so slightly squeezed her knee. She laid her head against the back of the couch, looking at him. His beautiful eyes, sensual lips, strong jaw—sensual lips again. She wondered what his lips would feel like. It would be so easy to lean over and kiss them, to feel them, soft and warm and . . .

She caught herself, reining in her thoughts. Had she started to lean in his direction or had she imagined it? Either way, she stood, took their glasses and the empty wine bottle, and brought them to the kitchen. When she glanced back at him, his lips were curled up ever so slightly. He must have seen her thoughts on her face. He followed her to the kitchen, stopping at the counter, leaning an elbow on it.

"Plan A?"

"Humph!"

"Do you snore?"

"Yes, very loudly. I even wake myself up."

"How charming. I can adjust, though."

"Luckily, you won't have to."

"Why fight, according to Jasmine, the inevitable?"

He was irritating her. The fact, not long ago, her thoughts had run along those same lines didn't help.

"Why don't you spend less time here and more time with your lady friend?" She snapped, instantly sorry she'd worded it so bluntly.

"I spend as much time with her as I can."

"She doesn't mind you spending time with a single woman and her child?"

"She's very understanding." He grinned at her.

"I presume, at some point, the two of you will spend more time together—perhaps even have a more permanent relationship."

"That's what I'm hoping for."

"When that happens, you'll be spending a lot less, if any, time here."

"Will you miss me?"

"Of course I will," she answered analytically, "but I was thinking more of how Jasmine will miss you and not understand your absence."

"Mm, I see." He looked into her eyes, resting his forearms on her shoulders. "I promise I won't abandon either of you."

"Are you trying to sabotage your relationship before it can really get started?"

"Quite the opposite, actually."

"How do you figure that? Oh, wait! The less time you spend together, the less chance of fighting and possibly breaking up—is that it?"

"The way your mind works," he shook his head, "is awesome."

"If that isn't it, then it's the other way around. If you're not together much she'll break up with you so you won't have to do it."

Zeus moved away from her, which was a relief to Meg. She was enjoying the closeness and the feel of the weight of his arms on her shoulders. She had actually been half thinking that if she turned just right his arms would fall around her and then . . .

"We aren't really together, so we can't break up."

"Why aren't you together? Don't tell me you still haven't let her know you're interested!"

"I've tried—sometimes she seems interested—sometimes she doesn't."

"Be blunt Zeus. If she isn't interested in being more than friends, there's no sense wasting your time." He gave her a sideways glance.

"I'm kinda stuck on her."

"But, if she isn't interested . . ." He looked away.

"She may be—in someone else."

"Oh, Zeus, I'm sorry. You definitely have to come out and ask her, then go from there. Do it now before you invest any more time and emotions."

"I'm thinking that if he isn't interested in her—perhaps I can switch her affections to me."

"You don't want to be second best—a stand-in—while she's waiting for him to notice her."

"I'll take what I can get." He silently regrouped. "Okay," he moved closer to her, "what if it were you? You're more than interested in me, I'm more than interested in someone else. You and I are friends and you just hang in there, as my friend, be there for me. Eventually, I'm liable to lose interest in the one who doesn't see me and change for you—the one I can see and who sees me, right? However, if you tell me how you feel, I'll back away thinking I'm leading you on or your feelings are out of sympathy. Just be there and if it happens, it happens."

"Is she worth all this Zeus?"

"I believe she is."

"Do you think you can stay committed to her?"

"I know I can! She's what I've been looking for, even though I didn't know it until I met her."

Tears sprang to her eyes. She definitely didn't stand a chance. All she could ever be was his friend even if he never got together with . . .

"Meg?" As she looked up at him, first one tear, then the other, slid down her cheeks.

"Don't mind me," she swiped the tears away, "I'm just being sentimental—wine induced, I'm sure." He kissed the corner of her mouth.

"It'll work out for us. It has to."

"It will for you, I'm sure."

"If it works for me, it'll work for you."

"Will you shut up!" Tears flowed freely. He pulled her to him.

"Let it all out."

"I may do this all night!"

"Then I'll hold you all night." He squeezed her a little tighter. "Plan A and all that."

That made her smile and let out a small laugh. She gently pushed away from him.

"Go home, Zeus. I'm fine now. Thank you."

The next time she saw him, he was waiting in her driveway as she pulled in. She'd had a full day between work, family court, and visiting with Mary and Christopher. On her way home, she heard her car making a strange sound.

Zeus was leaning against the driver's side door of his car, arms folded over his chest, waiting. When she pulled in, he pushed off the car, letting his arms fall to his side. As she stopped, he walked to her car and got Jasmine out, setting her down, then turned to Meg.

"How long has your car been making that noise?"

"Just since leaving Mary's."

"How has it been steering?"

"It pulls a little to the left. I noticed that yesterday."

"Mind if I take it out for a spin?"

"Not at all. Do you know what it is?"

"Possibly."

She handed him her keys and watched him drive away. She went inside with Jasmine and started supper. As she turned to get something out of the fridge, she saw Clansey was standing there. She jumped, bringing her hand up to her chest.

"Clansey! Don't sneak up on me like that! Are you trying to give me a heart attack?"

"No ma'am." He grinned at her. "I'm just checking in."

"Checking in? Where have you been anyway?"

"A little bit of everywhere. I'm getting close to figuring out why I'm here—I think."

"That's great, Clansey! Is someone or something keeping you here?"

"Both—I think."

"Is it something left unfinished?"

"More like something I have to see through—make sure it comes out right—for someone."

"Sounds mysterious."

"How is Jasmine?"

"Very good."

"How is Zeus?"

"Good. Confused, but good."

"If he's confused it must have something to do with a woman!" She nodded. "Figures! Females can mess with a man's mind!"

"Now, now, Clansey—we're not all like that."

"That's true. You seem to be decent. If I was a little younger, I'd court you." Meg giggled.

"If you were, oh, a hundred years younger . . . but, no, it would never work."

"No? Why not?"

"You're dead." She smiled at him as Zeus walked in.

"Either I did something terribly bad or you're talking to Clansey."

"It's Clansey." Meg said. He nodded his head in greeting. "Hello, Clansey."

"I think I'd rather talk to him." Clansey looked in Zeus' direction. "If only he could hear me. Guess I'll go amuse Jasmine. I love that child!" He disappeared.

"He's gone." She informed Zeus.

"What are you smiling about? What's Clansey up to now?"

"That's what I'm smiling about. I was just hit on by a ghost!"

"Oh really?" He puffed out his chest in mock jealousy. "Do I need to put him in his place?"

"Slow down Turbo—he's at least a couple hundred years old—and dead. I don't think there's anything to worry about."

"Is, um, is he who you're stuck on?" Her laughter rang out at the thought.

"No, it's you, silly. You beat out a two hundred year old, needless to say, dead ghost!"

Meg quickly turned toward the counter fussing with the dishes and gathering ingredients for supper. She hadn't meant to blurt out the truth.

"Well, that just makes me feel—terrific! I beat Clansey because I'm alive. My grandfather could have passed *that* test!"

"Your grandfather is alive?" She sounded interested.

"Oh, no! I won't be beat out by my own grandfather!" He chuckled. "Anyway, besides giving me that thrill—do you have any rags I can use?"

Meg went to the laundry room, thankful her words hadn't been taken seriously. When she returned, she had a half dozen rags, which she handed to him.

"Really? You're stuck on me, huh?"

He grinned and winked at her. As she opened her mouth, not sure what she was going to say, he walked away.

Meg returned to the task of getting supper. While her hands did the job, her brain was working overtime on her recent problem. That she was in love with Zeus wasn't in question. What was in question was her ability to keep that information from him. It seems that just as she had decided they needed to spend far less time together, the more her feelings were showing and the more her thoughts turned in that direction.

Obviously, she needed to keep herself in check. She had to watch where her thoughts went and be very careful of what came out of her mouth. Her subconscious mind seemed to do whatever it wanted to without checking with her first. She needed to stop thinking about him in a romantic way.

Yeah, right! Like that was going to happen!

Chapter Thirty One

An odd thing happened when Meg went onto the deck to set the table. Maybe it wasn't so odd after all. Just before she left the kitchen, laden with plates, glasses and eating utensils, she started humming a tune titled, "*Jesse's Girl*." Basically, it's about a guy wishing he had his best friend's girl. That made her think of Zeus, but in reverse; she wanted the guy—his lady friend's guy—Zeus. Then as she stepped onto the deck, she could hear him half singing and half humming the same song. It was either a coincidence or she had projected the song into his head. Either way, it made her sad.

"Such deep thoughts!" She jumped at the sound of his voice. As she looked up at him, his brow furrowed. "Such deep, sad thoughts!"

"That song . . ." She waved her hand dismissively.

"What song?"

"*Jesse's Girl . . .*"

"Were you thinking of—him?"

"I was thinking of you and your lady friend, actually."

"Don't let my situation make you sad. It'll all work out, you'll see."

She needed to change the subject. His faith that everything would work out depressed her.

"Did you figure out what was wrong with the car?"

"Figured out and fixed."

"Really? I only expected you to tell what was wrong with it. Thank you so much, Zeus!"

"What would you do without me?" He grinned at her.

"What indeed?" She said sarcastically, and yet thought to herself that unfortunately she'd have to find out, sooner or later.

They ate supper as they chatted about each others day, including Jasmine's day with Christopher. The more Jasmine spoke of the small boy, the more Meg noticed something in Zeus' eyes. She watched him, as much as she could without being obvious. When she finally realized it was the look of recognition, she attempted to change his line of thoughts.

"What do I owe you for fixing my car?"

"You feed me—often."

"And you do things around here—often."

"Then I'd say we're even." She gave him one of those looks. "Okay, I'll think of something." There was something in his voice . . .

"I'm sure you will! Anyway, it's time to go to the butcher's for the meat we'll be grilling. Then I'll marinate it so it will be ready by Saturday."

"Did we even figure out how many people will be here?"

"I think we stopped somewhere around two hundred."

"Oh, man! Really?"

He sounded so much like a little boy that both Meg and Jasmine laughed.

"Maybe. If everyone brings someone, it might be close to what we figured."

"Were we serious?"

"Probably not, but there's still going to be a bus load."

"When do we go to the butcher's?"

"A few days after I place the order. Actually, we can go there tomorrow after work and pick out the meat ourselves. I think that will take less time than calling. Would you like to come along and help me pick out the pieces?"

"Sure. Will we need both cars to haul everything?"

"I've actually rented a truck."

"Really?"

"No. We should be able to get it in one car."

The next night after work they met at Mary's when Meg picked up Jasmine. Christopher ran to greet them, giving Zeus what appeared to be a secret smile and as he hugged Meg, he whispered in her ear.

"Soon."

It wasn't a question. It was a statement. She hugged him a little tighter just before putting him down. She wished she had his faith the courts would let her adopt him. As of yet, he had no idea she was trying to make him her own. She also wished she didn't have such a strong urge to take him home now. She was comforted by his self assurance, however.

At Dave's Meat Market, Meg was greeted by Dave himself. This being where she often bought her meat, they knew each other well. She told him about the barbeque, roughly how many people were expected, then between the three of them they settled on a large freezer pack. Instead of having it delivered, they decided to take it with them.

That night, and the following two nights, Meg and Zeus, sometimes with the help of Jasmine, prepared marinade and made their own barbeque sauce and meat rub. Both were amazed at the others knowledge of various seasonings for the different types of meat. The night before, they were preparing side dishes and setting up tables in the back yard. By the time they were finished, both were exhausted and sat on the deck relaxing with a glass of wine.

"How many people will really be here tomorrow?" Zeus asked.

"Between forty and fifty, I believe."

"In the morning I'll hang the lights and put the Tiki torches up."

"The—what?"

"I didn't tell you I bought those?" She shook her head. "More than likely people will be here after dark so I thought lights around the edges of the lawn and leading down to the lake, plus the torches around the deck, would be nice."

"When did you get all that?"

"At the same time I built the pit and deck."

"That sounds like a lot of work." He shrugged. "You may as well spend the night." He flashed her a smile making her believe that was his plan all along.

"Plan A?" She rolled her eyes at him.

"In your dreams!"

"Probably."

"Will your lady friend be here? I'd love to meet her." He simply smiled at her.

"More wine?"

"I'm good." She vividly remembered the last time she drank wine with him and didn't want a repeat of that night.

"No? We might as well go to bed, then." She shot him a look wondering if he was referring to Plan A. "Change your mind?"

"About you spending the night? I'm starting to."

He followed her into the house chuckling. As she handed him his blankets and a pillow, he commented about bringing some clothes to leave there.

"Are we going through this again?"

"I'm serious. I spend enough time here and a change of clothes would be handy. I just happen to have an extra set in the car."

"Why—? Never mind, I don't really want to know."

Their day started early. While Jasmine and Zeus strung the tiny white lights all around the parameter and down the steps leading to the lake, Meg placed the torches around the deck, filled them and trimmed the wicks. The grill was fired up around noon as people started arriving with whatever they had chosen to bring. By two-thirty, tables were laden with food of just about every description and the backyard and deck filled with adults and children.

Zeus, Michael, and Lance took turns manning the barbeque pit. Some children played in the yard while some, accompanied by adults, played on the beach and in the water. The only mishap occurred when a child, roughly the age of six, walked, unnoticed out into the lake up to her chest. Meg heard an odd screeching and a lake shadow flying her way and knew something was wrong. She took off for the lake, arriving to see several shadows pushing the child toward shore; the child was looking up as if she saw them. Meg waded into the water, taking the child's arm and pulling her onto dry land.

"What were you doing?"

"Do you see them? Do you see the shadows with white eyes? I was trying to reach them. Aren't they beautiful?"

"Yes, sweetheart, they are beautiful, but you never, ever go near the lake without a grownup." The child saw them. She asked the child through thought. "*Understand?*"

She nodded. Meg smiled as they walked back up the steps toward the backyard. Half a dozen steps to the top there was a commotion above them. People were calling for someone and hurrying around. As they came into view, a woman spied them and came running up to them, grabbing the girl in a hard hug.

"Brittany! Oh my God, you're okay! Where were you?" She pointed back toward the lake but didn't have a chance to say anything.

"Were you with her?" The mother asked Meg. Brittany finally spoke.

"She came to get me, Mommy."

"Oh my God! You were by yourself?" She looked at Meg. "Thank you—thank you for finding my little girl!"

Before she could say anything, the woman whisked Brittany toward the deck, exclaiming how wet she was, how happy she was the child was okay, and telling her to never go near the water without an adult.

Meg smiled to herself continuing toward the deck, stopping to get a cool drink as she went. She looked up when she heard her brother, Michael, speak in a slightly louder than usual voice.

"I bet she does!"

Strong arms wrapped around her middle. Instantly she started to stiffen. A deep whisper met her ear where a face rested on the side of her head.

"Your brother says you'll knock my block off if I do this."

Meg relaxed and took a sip of her drink. As much as she wanted to look in Michael's direction, she resisted, turning her face slightly toward Zeus and smiled.

"Normally he would be right. Luckily, for you, I refuse to give him the satisfaction."

She turned to face Zeus. His arms were snugly wrapped around her. They felt too good.

"Sibling rivalry can be a good thing." He reached past her for a drink, bringing his body very close to hers.

"Do the two of you always discuss me or was this simply a challenge?"

"Just a challenge, though we observed something about you at the same time."

"Really? And what did you observe?"

"We observed how that pretty yellow sundress you're wearing is rather revealing when it's wet. You're wearing the lingerie I got for you."

His arm encircled her waist propelling her toward the house.

"Oh, my . . . I didn't realize . . ."

"I figured as much." They mounted the steps to the deck. "Not that I didn't enjoy the view!"

Meg reddened considerably as he opened the sliding glass door. She hurried inside, quickly changing into a pair of shorts and a blouse. Anyone else who had noticed "the view" of her wet dress, didn't show it now. Luckily her mind was taken off the incident when Brittany and her mother approached her.

"I wanted to thank you again for rescuing my daughter. It seems she's always wandering off or staring at something no one else can see. This time it was shadows or something. What made you look at the lake?" She couldn't tell her about the shadows.

"Kids—water—you know." She shrugged. She hadn't even known Brittany had been missing. "I can talk with her if you'd like."

"Maybe you should. It seems each year it gets worse. She even has a couple of invisible friends!"

"Really?" She thought about Brittany's Spirit Guide and at least one Angel.

"Do you think something is wrong with her?"

"No, actually that's fairly normal. Get in touch with me the first part of next week and we'll set up a time to bring her by."

"If you think I should." She suddenly seemed unsure.

"No, if *you* think you should. One visit won't hurt and any more will probably be unnecessary."

This seemed to appease the mother. She took Brittany's hand, thanked her again and walked away. Her mother's mind would certainly be blown if she knew her daughter had seen shadows and they had been the ones to save her!

The rest of the barbeque was uneventful, as barbeques go anyway. The children and adults played games together. The children played in the sandbox, with various toys, and generally ran around tiring themselves out. After everyone had left, Meg's family and Zeus stayed to clean up. Jasmine was put to bed after Meg's family left, leaving her and Zeus to relax and unwind.

On the deck, the string of lights still on, the torches extinguished and the fire pit burning, Zeus and Meg heaved a sigh of relief. For several minutes they sat sipping lemonade and enjoying the quiet. Eventually Meg broke the silence.

"I think the day went very well. Except for Brittany, there were no mishaps."

"It went extremely well, but you look beat." She looked over at him.

"And you don't?" He smiled at her.

"It was fun though."

"Very, but not something I'd want to do more than twice a year."

"Can I be one of the grill masters next time, too?"

"Of course! What would a barbeque be without you manning the grill?"

"You just like seeing me sweat over a hot grill!" He laughed.

"That, too." She joined in his laughter.

The following weeks were very busy for Meg. Surprisingly she didn't have to go through the things to get Christopher as she had Jasmine. What was required was still trying and nerve wracking. She was investigated again—mainly checking to make sure of her work and financial status hadn't changed. They checked to make sure Jasmine was well taken care of by interviewing Jasmine's doctor and also Mary. And, they spoke with Jasmine herself.

Her first court date was preliminary. The second would be the determining factor where Mary and Christopher would be present. Meg was surprised to see the same judge she had with Jasmine's case.

"Miss Wolfe, we meet again. It hasn't been that long and nothing seems to have changed with your financial or personal situations. You're still unmarried and have acquired a house now. Can you tell me why you want to adopt—" he glanced at a paper in front of him, "Christopher Coulter?"

"I love him, Judge. He has become very attached to my daughter, Jasmine, and to myself, very quickly, as we have to him. I know I can give him a good home and proper upbringing."

"As am I. According to the foster mother, Mary Leeds, the child seemed to act as though he knows you and your daughter. Did you know him previously, Miss Wolfe?"

"No Judge, not in this lifetime."

Meg spoke without thinking. Once out of her mouth, she could have bitten her tongue off, especially when the judge raised an eyebrow at her words. The best she could do was to give him a weak smile.

"Okay, Miss Wolfe, everything looks good. I'll see you in two weeks . . ."

Meg's mind was so flooded with relief she didn't hear the rest of what he said until he gave her the next court date. As soon as she left the courtroom, Meg called Zeus and told him the news.

"Meg, that's fantastic!"

"Getting the same judge was a stroke of luck, too!"

"I don't think that has anything to do with it, Meg. I think we need to go out to celebrate."

"Let's wait until it's a done deal. Besides, I have to get to work. I have a back to back afternoon ahead of me."

Meg hadn't been kidding about having a busy afternoon ahead of her. With only a ten minute break between clients for paperwork, her afternoon went quickly. She was out of the door fifteen minutes later than usual. She arrived at Mary's twenty five minutes late. She spent a little time with Christopher before she and Jasmine left.

Instead of going home, they stopped for something to eat, then together they went to a furniture store where a bed and bureau set was purchased for Christopher and would be delivered the next week. From there they went to a department store for bedding, curtains, and a car seat, and also walked out with clothes and toys for him and for Jasmine.

Meg was surprised to not see Zeus at the house when she pulled in. She had become so used to his presence more often than not that she was somewhat disappointed. She reminded herself that she had to get used to it. Just like in their past life, she would raise his children basically alone.

With Jasmine's help she busied herself preparing Christopher's room. His new clothes were hung in the closet, toys left in the bags awaiting the bed and bureau, sheets on the closet shelf, and curtains hung.

Chapter Thirty Two

A car horn honking as it pulled into the driveway pulled Meg and Jasmine to the front of the house. As they stepped out onto the porch, Zeus was just rolling to a stop and jumping out, a broad smile on his face.

"Come see what I got!"

As both Meg and Jasmine approached the car they saw the back seat filled with bags When he opened the trunk, it was also nearly as full.

"Beware of Greeks bearing gifts?"

"I'm not Greek—I don't think."

"It's either that or you're a big ugly dog." She muttered quietly for his ears only.

"Be nice or you won't get your toys." Zeus warned with good humor.

Two trips from the car to the house, the living room floor covered with bags, the three of them sitting amongst them, Zeus opened one bag at a time extracting their contents. All except one bag had clothes, toys, and bedroom accessories—lamps, scatter rugs, pictures for the walls. Jasmine jumped onto his lap, her arms around his neck in a hard hug.

"Thank you! I love you, Daddy!"

As if he hadn't heard, or perhaps it hadn't registered yet, Zeus hugged her back.

"You're welcome sweetie."

Jasmine took off to bring her new things to her room. Zeus looked at Meg smiling.

"Your turn."

"You really got something for me? I thought you were joking."

"Come here." She scooted closer to him as he reached into the last bag, pulling out a T-shirt nightgown. Meg held it up and laughed.

On the front was a cartoon of a woman with curlers in her hair, bags under her eyes, a forlorn, exhausted expression on her face, and a pink baggy bathrobe with large pink bunny slippers on her feet. Above her was the word "Mommy."

"Thank you Zeus—I'm sure I'll look like this often!"

"That's what I was thinking. That's why I got you this, too."

He extracted a tortoise shell comb, brush, and mirror set. The array of colors were exquisite as she held them. She knew it cost him a pretty penny and was at a loss for words when she looked at him dumbstruck.

"Do you like it?"

"I—it's beautiful Zeus! Thank you!"

"Don't you think I deserve a little more than that?" She leaned over kissing his cheek. "Perhaps more like what I got from Jasmine?"

He scooped her onto his lap smiling down at her with an eyebrow raised expectantly, challengingly. She wrapped her arms around his neck in a hard hug as Jasmine had.

"Thank you!" He pulled back to look at her.

"I believe she said more than that."

Meg knit her brow as if trying to remember, then smiled.

"Thank you, Daddy!" Zeus let out a hearty laugh.

"Be careful—I might like that!"

"Speaking of which," she slid off his lap, "you handled that very well."

"I was too surprised to react—I think. A few seconds later—it felt—good—natural."

"Does that mean you've changed your mind about having kids?"

"It does. Amazing, huh?"

"Amazing and a huge step forward! Have the two of you discussed having kids?"

"Not yet, but I don't think she will object." He smiled to himself. "How about you—do you ever plan to have kids of your own?"

Meg opened her mouth, then closed it again. She had been about to say Jasmine and Christopher were *her* kids as well as *his.*

"It's a possibility—one day." He thought he knew why she had hesitated.

"I know Jasmine and Christopher *are* your children—I just meant . . ."

"I know. It's okay. My answer stands." Sadness passed through her like a shudder. She inhaled, brightening somewhat. "Have you eaten? I can whip something up for you."

"I grabbed something earlier. Thank you though." She smiled.

"We've got to stop. Between the two of us, we're spoiling these kids rotten. I bought out half the store earlier, then you bought out the other half!"

"They deserve to be happy. So do we."

"Obviously spoiling them makes us happy!" She had missed his meaning.

"Obviously." He reached for her brush. "Let me test this out."

Meg obliged by turning her back to him. He started brushing her hair, with his free hand following the path of the brush. He was mesmerized by the silkiness of her hair, the way the natural waves bounced back. She was mesmerized by the feel of both the brush going through her hair and his hand smoothing it down.

"Yippee!" Meg jumped at the sound of Clansey's voice.

"Clansey! Will you please announce yourself? I am much too young for a heart attack!"

"*Sorry.*"

"Hi, Clansey." Zeus greeted him. "I trust you've been staying out of trouble."

"*Why, what have you heard?*" Meg laughed relaying his question.

"I hear everything—eventually." He shivered as Clansey patted his shoulder.

"*Good luck catching me son!*" Zeus chuckled when he heard the answer.

"There has to be a way for you and Clansey to hear one another." Meg mused.

"*I'm working on that.*" Clansey announced. "*I see you're working on having that little boy and girl!*"

"According to the judge, Christopher will be mine next week."

"*Next week? Yes, of course. I'm going to check in with Jasmine. You two—carry on.*"

Meg told Zeus what Clansey had said. He handed her the brush, playing with her hair instead.

"If between the three of us we can figure out how I can hear Clansey I'm sure we'll have some quite interesting conversations!"

"I believe that will be a big drawback for me!"

Zeus ran his fingers through her hair, moving it away from her neck, watching it fall back into place. At one point he moved her hair enough to see a vein in her neck. He knew he'd feel her pulse if he lightly pressed his lips over it. He knew he'd feel her pulse quicken as her heart sped up from him doing that. He went so far as to tilt his head and move closer to that vein.

Meg was thoroughly enjoying Zeus playing with her hair. She sat, eyes closed, trying not to lean back against him. It felt so good, so relaxing. His warm breath on her neck—she tilted her head—his warm breath got closer—warmer.

"*I'm gone.*" Her eyes snapped open. "*I'll ring a bell or something next time.*" She sat up straight.

"Okay, Clansey. Behave."

"*I can't promise that, but I can promise not to get caught.*"

"Bye, Clansey." Zeus sounded ever so slightly annoyed. His voice softened. "Now, where were we?"

Meg started to respond but his cell phone ringing stopped whatever she might have said. She stood, collecting the brush set, letting Zeus talk as she took it to her bedroom. More than giving him privacy, she needed the distance. She was quite sure what would have happened if Clansey hadn't interrupted them and the phone call hadn't stopped it from starting up again.

She had been reveling in the feel of his warm breath on her neck, the anticipated feel of his lips, soft and warm, on her skin. She was quite sure she would have given in to the feeling, allowing much more to take place. Just thinking about it caused a warmth to quickly spread through her. She closed her eyes against it. At all cost she couldn't allow it to ever happen—or ever come close like that again. She couldn't trust herself to resist.

Hearing his phone snap shut and knowing he'd come looking for her, she quickly left the bedroom, meeting him back in the living room. He raised his phone toward her.

"Duty calls." He shoved the phone into a pocket. "I'll be back as soon as possible."

"You don't have to Zeus . . ." He walked up to her placing a hand on either side of her head, looking down into her eyes.

"I'll be back." He repeated.

He was going to kiss her. She needed a distraction.

"*Jasmine, Zeus is leaving.*" She thought in desperation.

The corners of his mouth twitched into a smile as Jasmine came flying out of her room. He stepped back, turning to catch her in mid-jump. She hugged him.

"Do you have to go?"

"Yes, work called."

Jasmine pouted. He kissed her cheek. Then to Meg's surprise, he turned to her and lightly kissed her lips. Then, handing Jasmine to her, he walked away. Jasmine was smiling while Meg stood watching him, her lips slightly parted. At the door, he turned back toward them, smiling.

"Be safe." Meg managed to get out.

He nodded, still smiling, opened the door, closing it behind him. The clicking as the door shut snapped her out of the confusion she had been in.

"Okay, bath time!" Meg told Jasmine.

Normalcy. That was what she needed. Every day activity would put things into prospective. What had just happened, hadn't really happened. It wasn't even a matter of her imagination. She was sure she could convince herself of that, eventually, and that she didn't want Zeus to return—as much as she did want him to. Normalcy seemed just out of reach.

Zeus didn't return that night, though he did call Meg in the morning as she was getting ready for work. He sounded drained and mentally exhausted.

"I'm sorry about last night." Vaguely she wondered if he meant what had almost happened or that he hadn't made it back.

"It's okay."

"This case—somehow I feel personally—I don't know. It's like I knew them but I don't. It hit me kinda hard."

"Would you like to talk about it?"

"If I can't shake it, yes. It may just be because a young mother and her two children died horribly."

"How did it happen? Car crash?"

"Fire." That was what she was afraid of. "They were trapped in the house."

Tears sprang to her eyes. The case was hitting him hard—he was taking it personally—because he was remembering.

"Zeus . . ." She stopped. She was about to tell him something she never wanted him to find out—about their past lives, "keep your prospective."

"I'm trying. It just feels so . . . familiar. I guess . . . like they were people I . . . loved. I don't know—that's the only way I can describe it."

"Center yourself. Be objective."

"I'll try to or I'll have to remove myself from the case."

"Let me know if you want to talk about it. I'll make the time for you."

"I appreciate that Meg. I'll let you go now so you can get to work."

Meg's day was peppered with thoughts of Zeus remembering how their past lives had ended. She really didn't know how she would handle that. How would that effect their lives? How would it effect his life? His relationship with—what *was* her name?

She barely heard from Zeus except for an occasional phone call or a couple mental calls just to let her know he was busier than usual with the case. He was, however, slowly coming to terms with how it effected him.

The following week went by about the same. Jasmine was really feeling Zeus' absence as he had only spoken to her on the phone. Meg wondered if this was how they'd separate from one another and how long it would take for them to adjust to it.

With the final court date approaching, Meg had something else to occupy her mind. Mary's assurance and even the judge's words did nothing to ease her worrying about the outcome. Until Christopher was legally hers, she couldn't help thinking it would all be taken away for any number of imagined reasons.

Wednesday morning. Eight o'clock. Meg sat in court again. This time Jasmine sat with her. One felt nervous, the other excited. As Mary entered with Christopher, he ran to Meg, hugging her.

"Today I'm your Topher again." He stated.

"I hope so. We'll have to wait and see what the judge says."

"All rise."

Meg stood trying to get Christopher to go back with Mary, but he clung to her neck, refusing to be put down. Jasmine stood with her arm around Meg's waist. Someone entered the courtroom through the door in the back; only the judge looked at who entered.

"Please be seated."

Meg sat with Christopher in her lap, Jasmine close beside her. Someone sat behind her. She presumed it was whoever had come in moments earlier. Christopher emanated excitement as he reached behind her toward that person.

"Hi, Little Man." Meg turned her head enough to see Zeus gesturing for him to be quiet. Her eyes widened. He winked at her.

"Again, Miss Wolfe, I see you have your hands full."

"Yes, Sir, I'm sorry . . ."

"Don't be. It's obvious how he feels about you." He turned his attention to Christopher.

"Young man—Christopher, how are you this morning?"

"In a hurry." The judge chuckled.

"Why?"

"I want to go home."

"Where is home?"

"With Meg and Jasmine."

"I see." The judge picked up a pen.

"Mr. Judge," Christoper asked, and the judge looked up at Christopher, "can anyone live there if you say so?"

"I suppose. Who else do you want to live there?"

"My—Mr. Garrett." He pointed to Zeus behind him.

Meg blushed. The judge laughed. Zeus cleared his throat. Meg knew, without turning around, he was smiling.

Chapter Thirty Three

"Miss Wolfe, you're outnumbered. As I remember, first your daughter," he signed the paper in on his desk, "and now your son wants Mr. Garrett as part of the household!"

Meg reddened considerably.

"They are quite attached to him, too."

"What are you going to do about that?" Zeus stood.

"We'll figure something out, Your Honor."

By the smile that appeared on the judge's face, Meg knew Zeus was smiling, too. She wanted to melt under the floorboards and disappear.

"Good luck with that!" His eyes returned to Christopher. "To answer your question young man, I can only say where a child can live, not a grown up."

"Oh." Christopher was clearly disappointed.

"Fear not young man, the tenacity of you and your sister will surely prevail!"

Christopher didn't understand a word the judge had said, but Meg and Zeus did. One looked at the floor in front of her, the other laughed out loud.

"As before," the judge continued, "Christopher, Meg is now your mommy forever and ever."

Once the judge left the room, Meg, with Jasmine at her side and Christopher still in her arms, stepped into the aisle. Zeus joined them casually placing an arm around Meg's shoulders. She elbowed him in his ribs causing him to chuckle softly, removing his arm.

"They have spoken, Meg. So be it!"

In the hallway, she turned to him wanting to smile but not allowing herself to.

"If we weren't in a courthouse, I swear . . ."

"Now, now Dear, not in front of the k-i-d-s."

His smile was infectious. She turned toward Mary as she stepped into the hall just before the corners of her mouth turned up.

"I suppose you have Christopher's things in your car?"

"I certainly do!" Together they walked toward the exit. Christopher still in her arms while Jasmine was scooped up in Zeus'.

The transference of Christopher's belongings from Mary's car to Meg's didn't take long as he owned pathetically few things.

"Meg," Mary started, "I must inform you that from now on, any child you adopt while in my care will require a finder's fee."

"Of which I will gladly give you!" Meg laughed.

As Mary pulled away, Zeus put first Jasmine, then Christopher, in their car seats before turning to Meg.

"Lunch? I'm sure you and the kids barely ate, if at all!" The sounds coming from Meg's back seat meant the children agreed.

"Apparently, yes. I'm starving anyway."

"Mommy?" Christopher's voice came from the car.

"Yes, Topher?" Meg bent down to see him on the further side of the car.

"I love you!" His words warmed her heart.

"I love you more!"

With eyes misting, she stood facing Zeus. She recognized his expression. He was remembering. That had always been her answer to any of them in their past lives. She drew his mind away.

"Where are we going for lunch?"

"I have the perfect place in mind and we're all dressed for it. Follow me."

As instructed, Meg followed Zeus. When he stopped, they were outside of Kendon's, an upscale restaurant. Meg wondered how far back financially that eating at this restaurant would set Zeus. With her income, she could afford it better but it wasn't a place she would or had frequented.

"Zeus?" She spoke as they exited their cars and started unbuckling the kids.

"I think you'll love this place." He hoisted Christopher into his arms. "The food is wonderful!"

With Jasmine holding Meg's hand on one side, Zeus on her other side, one hand on the small of her back, and Christopher encircled by his other arm, they entered the restaurant. They were greeted warmly and seated immediately.

"Detective!" An elderly man approached them. "So nice to see you again—and you brought your family! Are you celebrating?"

"Hello, Carlyle. Yes, we are. We're celebrating being a family."

"Splendid! I'll leave you to look over the menu." He looked at Meg. "Pleasure to meet you Mrs. Garrett!"

Meg's mouth fell open as Carlyle retreated. Looking around the table she saw three grinning faces. She closed her mouth, almost used to being greeted as a family, but not as Zeus' wife.

"Have you ever eaten here—*Dear*?"

"No *Darling,* it's a little beyond my means."

"Then you're in for a treat!" He looked at Jasmine and Christopher. "What would you two like to eat? If they don't have it, they'll get it for you!"

"Anything?" They asked together.

"Anything." Zeus confirmed as Meg heard the things going through the kids minds.

"Um, let's keep it to lunch food, kids."

"Later?" Jasmine's question received a nod from Meg.

Zeus had been one hundred percent correct—the food was beyond compare. The meat melted in your mouth with an assortment of flavors blended delicately together. The rest of the meal was no less spectacular. Even Jasmine's hamburger and Christopher's breaded chicken pieces, both with fries, looked extra special and flavorful.

By the time they finished their meal, everyone was full. Zeus instructed Meg to take the kids home and he'd be along shortly. She was more than willing to do that. After having not slept well the night before, the mental strain of court, and the excellent meat at Kendon's, home sounded good.

Taking Christopher's meager belongings into the house, they showed him his new room. His bed had been delivered, assembled, and made. The curtains had been hung, as well as most of his clothes. What was left went into the bureau. Toys were put in the toy box and pictures hung on the wall. He and Jasmine ran around excitedly looking at everything while Meg put his things from Mary's away.

From there they went outside. After Jasmine took him all over the backyard showing him everything there, Meg pushed them both on the swings. She helped him up the ladder to the slide, Jasmine helped him onto the jungle gym and eventually into the sandbox. When Zeus arrived, going first to the kitchen, he joined Meg and the kids outside. Christopher was pushing a large dump truck around the yard, complete with the appropriate noises, and Jasmine was pushing a toy stroller with her doll in it. Zeus handed Meg a cool drink nodding toward Christopher.

"How long has he been here—his whole life?"

"I believe so."

Christopher had pushed his truck to the sandbox where he and Jasmine were filling it and dumping sand into piles and giggling about something.

"Did he like his new things?"

"Definitely! You should have heard the excited sounds he made. He looked at and touched everything at least once!"

"Good, I'm glad." He watched the kids for a minute before suddenly standing. "I've got to join them!"

He stepped off the deck without using the steps. Within seconds he was lifting each child in turn, flying them around the yard like airplanes, twirling them around and watching them stumble around on the ground. Horseback rides and chase followed and finally both Jasmine and Christopher tackled Zeus to the ground, tickling him unmercifully. When all three had had enough, racing each other to the deck where they found sandwiches and milk waiting for them.

To top off the meal, Zeus disappeared into the house, reappearing with banana splits for everyone. He spared no toppings, giving everyone plenty of ice cream, syrup, whipped cream, nuts, and cherries on top. It surprised Meg no one went into hyperglycemia.

By the time the sugar high kicked in, they were on the beach. Jasmine and Christopher chased each other around while Meg and Zeus walked leisurely behind them, each smiling at the squeals and giggles coming from the children.

Zeus taught them how to skip stones, which eventually turned into splashing each other. Meg sat a short distance away watching them, a distant smile on her face. She saw a distant time of Darius playing with Darlene and Topher—her heart full of love for all three.

Darius left the children at play to squat down in front of her. She looked at him with love and adoration, which was mirrored in his eyes.

"What are you thinking?"

She placed her hands, one on either side of his face, smiling.

"Of my deep, deep love for . . ." He brushed a strand of hair out of her face bringing her back to Zeus, Jasmine, and Christopher. She dropped her hands into her lap as casually as she could. "my family."

"Am I part of that family?"

"Of course." Too late she realized what he meant. "Jasmine and Christoper are very attached to you—that makes you family."

He moved to sit beside her patting her leg just above the knee.

"That'll do, for now."

An argument broke out between Jasmine and Christopher. Soon both stood in front of Meg, pleading their case, one just as adamant as the other.

"Tell him, Mommy!"

"Tell him what?"

"Tell him we're going to have a brother!" While Meg's mind sorted out the meaning of Jasmine's words, Christopher added his version.

"We're going to get a sister, right Mommy?"

"We—you," She looked first from Christopher then to Jasmine, "have a sister and you have a brother."

"But we're going to get *another* brother." Jasmine clarified.

"No, another sister!"

"For right now the two of you are enough."

Both children looked at Zeus who held up his hands in a defensive gesture.

"I agree with your mother on this one guys. The two of you keep us busy enough!"

Jasmine and Christopher looked at Meg and Zeus as if they were hopeless and scampered off toward the lake.

"They aren't—you haven't—Is Mary about to lose another child?"

"Not that I'm aware of." She watched the kids splashing one another, apparently the argument forgotten. "Maybe they're confused about being brother and sister now."

After letting them play for another hour, Meg called to them, telling them it was time to take a bath. As she and Zeus stood, both children raced each other to the steps, bounding up them. Meg and Zeus followed at a slower pace.

By the time they entered the house, both children had stripped out of their clothes and were running around naked, clothes scattered around the living room. Meg looked at Zeus who shrugged with a slight smile and looked at the ceiling.

"Hey guys, we don't run around without clothes on."

Both stopped, looking at her, clearly neither saw anything wrong with it.

"Okay," Zeus broke in, "I'll take Mr. Butt Cheeks, you take Miss Button Nose there and hopefully the next time we see each other everyone will have pajamas on."

"Divide and conquer!"

Zeus gave Christopher a bath in the main bathroom while Meg took Jasmine to the master bathroom. With Jasmine dressed for bed they went to the living room where Zeus and Christopher sat waiting for them. A movie was put on for them to watch and Zeus motioned for Meg to follow him to the kitchen. There he stood very close to her, whispering in her ear.

"I'm dying here! I didn't react so he wouldn't think he's asked something stupid, but I'm really dying keeping it in!"

"What happened?"

"I had a talk with him—probably his first sex talk."

"What? Why?" Meg couldn't imagine a three year old needing a sex talk.

"He confided in me, while they were running around naked, he noticed she was broken and wanted to know if she'd grow another one."

Meg's mind quickly went through the scene they had seen when they entered the house. His words followed. She started to giggle, then laugh, joined by Zeus.

"Apparently girls are very careless if they go around breaking off their . . ."

Another fit of laughter engulfed them before Meg could finish the sentence.

"There are a dozen or so comments I could . . ." He stopped, looking up at the same time as Meg who had just heard a bell ring.

"Hello, Clansey."

"*He heard it!*" Meg looked at Zeus.

"Did you hear something?"

"I swear I faintly heard a bell."

"That was Clansey—that's how he lets me know he's here!"

"*Tell him to concentrate—listen.*" She did. "*Zeus, I'm standing right in front of you. Look at me.*"

Nothing. Zeus closed his eyes, his brow slightly knit.

"*I'm talking to you boy!*"

Nothing.

"*Damn it!*"

Zeus' eyes opened. He looked at Clansey without seeing him.

"Cursing? Really?" Clansey did a jig.

"*He heard me! I found his wavelength!*"

"Wavelength?"

"*You'll get it eventually. You're not as dumb as you look.*" Clansey chuckled.

"Old man . . ." Zeus chuckled back.

"*Okay, son, look straight ahead, concentrate—now see me.*"

A long minute passed before Zeus relaxed his body and shook his head.

"*Nothing?*" Clansey was clearly disappointed.

"All I see is an old woman with a mustache and a ponytail, a scruffy few days growth of whiskers . . ."

"*An old woman! You insolent whelp!*"

"You're not solid. I can see through you."

"*You'll get stronger.*" Clansey rubbed his palms together in excitement. "*You'll also be able to hear me clearer.*"

Meg had leaned back against the counter watching and listening to them with a wide smile on her face.

"*Now you've had it Missy—we can talk!*"

"Mm," the smile never left her face, "I know."

"*I hate to force your mind open and leave but I have something to do. We'll talk later Zeus. I'm gone.*"

"I can't believe I heard and saw him!"

"There really must be something to that wavelength thing."

"Will I be able to hear—all of them now?"

"Interesting thought. If he's opened a link like that I'll help you control it."

"Isn't hearing voices no one else can hear a sign of schizophrenia?" Meg laughed.

"Welcome to my world!"

Chapter Thirty Four

They talked about Zeus' new development until it was time for Jasmine and Christopher to go to bed. Once both kids were tucked in and a story read, Meg and Zeus retreated to the living room. Zeus only stayed another hour, and yet in that time, their conversation turned more personal. The latter of which left Meg hopeful and confused.

"Does Jasmine and Christopher's earlier argument mean you'll be having two more children?"

"I'm not sure what was behind all of that."

He shifted closer to her taking a lock of her hair between two fingers, concentrating as he played with it.

"So," he looked at her, "if you do, will I be part of their lives, too?"

He had locked eyes with her. She couldn't look away—she couldn't think straight and had no idea what to say to him. He released her hair and stood.

"Think about it." He glanced at his watch, then leaned down kissing her forehead. "I'll see you tomorrow."

She sat, her body frozen, her mind spinning as she watched him approach the front door, turn, wink at her and leave. Still she didn't move as she stared at the closed door. With her thoughts whirling, she could only think in fragments.

"Two . . . part of their lives . . . a boy and a girl . . . theirs?"

Feelings. No, she couldn't—shouldn't have these feelings. He loved someone else. In her mind he was taken and may as well be married. But there were times . . . So what was it? She must be giving off signals, signals so strong and so constant, mixed with his lack of physical progress with his lady love . . . what? He couldn't resist? Is he settling for Miss Right Now while waiting for the real Miss Right to come around?

Well, she refused to have a one-night, perhaps extended one-night, stand. She had to figure out how to be around him and be neutral—no signals. Seeing less of him would certainly help. She'd encourage him to spend time with . . . *her*.

Trying to cement this plan in her mind, she answered her cell phone without looking to see who the caller was. The voice that met her ears sounded familiar, yet strange.

"Zeus?"

"It's either me or the Easter Bunny."

"Your voice is different." Sexy is what it was. "You must be thinking about your lady love. What *is* her name anyway?"

She had to make it more personal, to use her name. To her surprise, he chuckled. That sounded sexy, too.

"Open the door and I'll tell you."

"Open the . . ."

As she spoke, she went to the door and opened it. There stood Zeus, shutting his cell phone, eyes locked with hers. She stepped back, not so much to let him enter as to remove herself from his closeness and intense stare. He closed the distance between them while giving the door a shove to close it. Her emotions were flying in all directions.

"What . . . what brings you by?"

"You asked a question, didn't you?"

"I did?" Her mind raced. "Oh, yes—what is her name?"

"Are you referring to my lady love?"

Confusion. Was she? Yes, she was.

"Yes, that would be her."

She turned walking away, distancing herself from him physically, hoping for the same effect emotionally. A little control seeped into her, enough so she trusted herself to face him. He had moved with her. Facing him, he was only inches away. What little control she'd had suddenly evaporated like mist in sunlight.

"You told me once you're not psychic about yourself. I've found that to be very, very true."

Her thoughts tumbled, not settling on any one thing. His closeness. His smell. His body heat. She couldn't think. Her legs went squishy. Her lower lip trembled. She couldn't look him in the eye. Instead, she concentrated on a spot on his chest—a button. A crooked finger under her chin and slight pressure brought her eyes to his.

"S—so what's her name?"

He smiled down at her, bent his head and kissed her. She thought about resisting as she melted against him, returning his kiss. Thankfully, somewhere along the way his arms had encircled her waist. If they hadn't, when he lifted his head, his lips a breath away from hers, she would have crumbled to the floor in a heap. His voice was barely above a whisper.

"Her name is Abby, but everyone calls her Meg."

"Abby . . . ?" She was trying to wrap her mind around what he had said.

"I think you know her."

He pulled her tighter against him, kissing her with tender passion. Somehow this cleared her mind.

"All this time . . ."

"wasted." He finished for her.

"What made you come back?"

"I never left. Clansey was waiting for me outside. We talked for a long time in the car. He explained a lot of things to me about you—us—the kids."

"Like what?"

"Our past lives together—all four of us."

"He knows?!"

"Yes, and now so do I. It explains a lot of things—like how I knew the second I met you that I was in love with you—how I instantly felt attached to Jasmine and

Christopher—why I felt so personally involved with the case of the mother and her two children. As you told me, I lost the love of my life and my children in a fire—not my wife, as I presumed. I lost you and the kids—killed by my wife. I swore we'd be together again just before I committed suicide. That stuck. All of my relationship issues were because they weren't you. I went through several relationships before I found you."

"Where does Clansey fit into all this?" They both heard a bell ring.

"Let's go ask him."

Clansey stood in a corner of the kitchen, on the far side of the room. Meg knew where to go. Clansey was waiting for them as they entered. Meg walked toward him, but he held up a hand to stop her, his face averted.

"Clansey?" He had never acted like that

"You may not want to get any closer."

"Why not? Clansey, what's wrong with you?"

"You know you bore Darius' two children. You know he was married. You know she found out. You know the three of you died trapped in your burning cottage. But do you know who started the fire?"

"My wife?" Clansey shook his head.

"Oh no . . ." Meg was starting to understand.

"It was me. She had me set the fire to the cottage." Clansey looked at them, his eyes pleading for understanding. *"I swear I didn't know you were in there. It was suppose to be empty. Please believe me—I didn't know!"*

Clansey sobbed heart wrenching sobs. His body heaved with the effort. Tears rolled down his face—tears that landed on the floor, pooling there. Meg watched the puddle of tears in astonishment, then looked at Clansey.

"Why?' Zeus' voice was both demanding and unforgiving. "Why Clansey? We were friends!"

"*She—your wife—Adelle, told me you wanted it burned—that you intended to build a better structure. I didn't think she knew—I did—I knew about your true family and your love for them. I understood you wanting to make them a better home. I'm so sorry. If I had known—if I had heard you inside—no sound came from within, I swear it.*"

"We didn't make any." Meg sadly told him. "We were staying there until Darius returned and the house seem to blow up before we could run. It burned very quickly. Even if we had screamed, there was nothing you could have done to save us."

"*I'll never forgive myself.*"

"You have to Clansey or you'll never cross over. I forgive you."

She looked at Zeus. For a long minute, he glared at Clansey. Finally, he nodded.

"I also forgive you. You thought you were doing something good for me—us."

"*But I killed your family and though it was done by your own hand, I killed you, too.*"

"Trust me, from what I can sense from that life, that was preferable to spending the rest of my life with Adelle. And now we are all together again and I'm free to marry the mother of my children. I never could have then. All we had were stolen moments, and not nearly enough of those. It all worked out right."

"Clansey, I'll miss you terribly but it's time for you to cross over." Her eyes teared. "I wish I could hug you."

"*I can hug you.*" He crossed the room. Standing close to her, he put his arms around her. She felt the chill of him and cried.

"Old man," Zeus spoke when Clansey stepped back, "it was an honor to call you my friend, then, and it's an honor to call you my friend, now."

Clansey put a hand on Zeus' shoulders, squeezing lightly.

"Until we meet again my friend." He turned, walking through the wall and was gone.

Silence followed, each in their own thoughts. Shortly Zeus went to Meg, holding her close. Words weren't necessary, their closeness and sharing their grief and sadness was enough. The moment was broken when Meg's phone rang. She clung to him for the count of three rings before finally answering it.

"Meg," her mother's voice reached her ears, "your father has decided he wants to barbeque . . . he's out there now, grilling everything he can get his hands on. Why don't you, Zeus, and the kids come over?"

"A barbeque? Now?" She looked at Zeus, who appeared excited about the idea. "Okay, we'll be there shortly." After hanging up, she turned to Zeus. "Are you sure you want to go?"

"Definitely!"

Meg didn't understand his excitement. They gathered the children and headed to her parent's house. As usual her siblings and grandparents were there. As usual, there was a lot of talking, joking, and eating, Sufficiently full, everyone sat back on the deck content with bellies full. Zeus left the group, returning in a few minutes.

"Meg," she looked up at him as he knelt in front of her, "will you marry me so we can finally be a united family and so I can show the love I have for you to everyone, every day?"

Meg looked at him, stunned. She definitely hadn't expected him to propose. She heard her brother's unspoken words, *"An answer is required, Sis."* Worry was just starting to show in Zeus' eyes when she flung her arms around his neck.

"Yes!" Zeus slid the ring onto her finger.

Amongst all of the hooping, hollering, and congratulations, Zeus' cell rang. He let it ring a few times before answering it. The conversation was short. He slid the phone back into his pocket, then looked at Meg.

"I've got to go. There's another case . . ." He trailed off, wishing he could stay. "I'm sorry."

Meg tried to control her voice. Though she was disappointed, she didn't want him to feel guilty. Her words came out unintentionally a little cool with the effort.

"Nonsense, I understand, Zeus."

Zeus took her and the children back to Meg's house. As they got out of the car, he took her hand, stopping her.

"I'm sorry, Meg."

"It's okay. I'll be here when you're finished."

He kissed her lightly, then was gone.

Chapter Thirty Five

Whatever the case was, it kept him busy enough so he didn't call, or even stop by that afternoon, or the next day. Meg presumed he was staying at his apartment. Though her feelings were hurt, she tried to understand. When he did finally call, he sounded exhausted. When she mentioned that to him, he told her that he hadn't slept since she had last seen him—more than thirty six hours before. She told him to be careful and to get some sleep. He said he would, told her he loved her, and hung up.

For the next week, Zeus called her every other day or so. He always sounded as though he were about to fall asleep. In truth, he was. He continued to work thirty-six hour shifts, calling her when he was finally headed to his apartment to sleep. It was the best he could do. Still, though she tried to hide it, he heard disappointment in her voice. He worried his best wasn't good enough.

It was two weeks before there was a break in the case. An anonymous tip led Zeus and his team to the possible killer. The suspect was brought in for questioning while a search warrant was acquired and his apartment searched. Finding all the evidence needed, he was arrested shortly afterward. Zeus called Meg.

"It's done." He stifled a yawn. "I'm coming home to you."

"When was the last time you slept?" She was concerned about his lack of sleep and the long drive there. "Shouldn't you just go to the apartment and sleep?"

"I can do that." There was a long pause. "I'll talk with you later, then."

As Zeus hung up, he feared his worries were a reality. Meg would rather he stay at the apartment instead of being with her. This was his job. Granted it wasn't always like this. In fact, it was rare he was called away for so long, but were these times something Meg couldn't deal with? Was his job going to come between them? With a heavy heart, Zeus headed for his apartment. He showered and laid on the bed, his mind reeling with thoughts of Meg. He dozed and slept in fitful snatches. Now that he had found her, now that he was ready to commit to her, would she . . . could she?

It was late that night when he finally gave up on getting any decent sleep. He prowled around the apartment for a while, then decided he'd walk around the neighborhood. By the time he had made it back to the apartment building, he had made up his mind. He got into his car and drove toward Meg's house. He hoped it was his house, too. Zeus caught himself falling asleep twice as he neared his destination. He thought about accidents happening just a few short miles from home. He thought about all of the accident scenes he had been to . . . the mangled vehicles . . . the dead bodies. These thoughts snapped him to attention. They kept him awake and alert.

Meg hadn't slept well herself. She was awake when she heard Zeus pull into the driveway. It was barely dawn as she opened the door to see him exit his car, looking beyond exhausted. Neither said anything as they neared each other. They simply hugged in silence for several minutes before stepping inside.

"Zeus, you look absolutely horrible!"

"Thanks, Sweetheart, you look a little rough around the edges yourself."

"Sweet talk will get you everywhere. Now go to bed and get some decent sleep."

"That sounds like a good idea." He stopped. "Are you coming?"

They both crawled into bed, snuggled together. He tucked her head under his chin and held her a little closer.

"We need to talk, Meg."

"Whatever it is, can wait . . ." she drew back to look into his face. He was sound asleep. "Sleep first," she finished to herself, resting her head against his chest and falling asleep, too.

Later Meg was up getting the kids ready to go to Mary's. She had already decided she wasn't going in to work, and had called them. Even if she had to hog-tie Zeus, he wasn't going to work either. He had mentioned before falling asleep that they needed to talk, but first she was going to let him sleep as long as he needed to. She dropped the kids off and headed back to the house. She checked on Zeus—he hadn't moved. She thought about crawling in beside him, but she didn't want to wake him.

By mid-afternoon, when she checked on him again, he was just starting to stir. Meg started cooking a late breakfast. By the time she was finished, he was awake, making his way to the kitchen. She handed him a plate of scrambled eggs, sausage, and fried potatoes.

"You look much better. How do you feel?"

"Like a new man." He scarfed down a few bites. He ate while she talked.

"I took the kids to Mary's."

"And what about work?"

"I called in using one of my sick days." He finished eating, sitting back, looking at her.

"Why didn't you come back to bed?"

"I didn't want to wake you." Meg took his dishes, placing them in the sink.

"Have you eaten?"

"Yes, I ate when I got back." He picked up his coffee cup, walking toward her. Standing snugly against her back as he

Lake of Shadows

placed it in the sink. Placing his arms around her waist, he kissed her neck, sending electric shocks through her body.

"Why don't you come into the bedroom and make good use of that sick day?" She turned in his arms, sliding her arms around his neck. The clock caught her eye.

"I'd love to Zeus . . . however, I have to pick the kids up."

He placed his face against her neck, groaning, which vibrated through her neck and into her brain, in turn making her whole body tingle.

"I slept well, but you look like forty miles of bad road."

"You say the sweetest things!" She giggled.

"I'll get the kids, take them to a park or something so you get some sleep."

But I can't sleep now—I'll be up all night."

"I know." He grinned at her. "And, you *will* sleep, trust me."

He pulled her into him, giving her a hungry kiss that promised what he had alluded to, and much more, leaving her legs weak and her body trembling.

"Go on now." He coaxed in a deep, husky voice as he gently pushed her toward her room. "Sweet dreams."

Zeus left the house as Meg was getting into bed. Sleep? Now? After that kiss? Right! Surprisingly she feel asleep quickly. The thoughts she had about that kiss were manifested into a dream. Meg dreamed Zeus was there beside her. She knew it was him because she could smell the unique smell of him. He was softly playing with her nipples until they were erect. She groaned, arcing her back slightly. He slowly rolled them between his thumb and forefinger, gently pulling on them. They hardened, she groaned louder.

Slowly wakening, but still dreaming, she reached for him as she felt his lips on, first one nipple, then the other, his tongues teasing. Her nipples ached with their stiffness, though not an unpleasant feeling. Her back arced more. It felt so real. Was she dreaming? She felt his hand slide between

295

her thighs, his fingers spreading and playing with her hot, wet, sexual pleasure spots. She groaned his name as, first one, then two, fingers entered her. She wasn't dreaming—she couldn't be. Her eyes flew open. She found herself looking into Zeus' smoldering, hungry eyes as he watched her react to his touch.

"Zeus . . ." She groaned his name again as she pulled him to her.

Zeus complied, rolling on top of her, spreading her legs further apart with his own, and sliding slowly, deeply inside her. Their groans mingling at the sensations of filling, and being filled. Her hips met each of his deep thrusts, her legs wrapped around him, pulling him deeper into her, urging him to go faster. He didn't need to be urged. He was quickly losing control, as she was. Their bodies slammed together over and over until there was one last, body jarring thrust. Suspended together, their groans were deep and feral as he became empty to fill her. They clung to each other, their breathing jagged, their bodies wet, fully sated. When, for the most part, their breathing was controlled, Zeus started to roll off of her. She tightened her arms and legs that were still around him, holding him in place.

"Stay." Meg whispered.

Zeus settled back onto her, resting the bulk of his weight on his forearms. He softly kissed her lips and each closed eyelid.

"Are you okay?"

"If I was any more okay, I would be on the Other Side." She smiled as she opened her eyes. "I am more than okay!" Suddenly she stiffened underneath him. "Oh no! Where are the kids?"

"At your mom's until Sunday evening. We have what's left of today and the weekend to ourselves, though I can't imagine what we'll do all alone for that long."

"Neither can I!" She pulled his head down kissing him. "But, we'll think of something."

"I suggest . . ." he kissed her jaw, her earlobe, her neck "we get something to fuel our bodies before round two." He kissed her lips. "I am not seventeen any more. I don't bounce back like I used to."

Naked, they went to the kitchen. To Meg's surprise, Zeus had gotten the ingredients for Hoagies. They each made their own sandwich, wrapped themselves in a blanket, turned on the TV, and sat on the couch, snuggled against one another while eating. They never finished the meal. Instead they made love again on the couch, then fell asleep with their arms wrapped around each other. They woke chilly. Their bodies were wet and the blanket nowhere to be found. In the bedroom once again, they fell into a happily exhausted sleep. Mid-morning arrived and they started cooking a late breakfast. Neither had bothered to get dressed, or even put a robe on. Before the meal was finished cooking, they were back in the bedroom, making love. By mid-afternoon, sated, rested, and snuggling in bed, Zeus nudged her.

"Get dressed, we're going out to eat. I'm afraid we'll starve to death if we don't!"

"I don't want to." Meg made herself sound like a petulant child.

"You have to." Zeus demanded.

"Okay, but don't think for a minute that I won't start something in the restaurant!"

"You'd better not!" Meg smiled at him and got out of bed. "Meg, you wouldn't, would you?"

She gave him a grin and a wink as she got into the shower. He wasn't far behind.

After finally eating a complete meal, a glass of after-dinner wine, and a walk through the park, they headed home. Full and content, Zeus and Meg watched a movie, then sat on the couch, snuggling.

"I meant what I said to Clansey." Zeus announced. She searched his face not sure what he was talking about.

"About what?"

"I'm free to marry the mother of my children."

"If you're proposing, you suck at it." He moved his head back a little "Besides, you're too late. I have already been proposed to, and have accepted.

"Let me see if I can change your mind."

Their love making was much slower this time, though no less intense. Basking in the afterglow, they laid in each others arms, pleasantly tired, completely sated, content with their world.

"So?" Zeus asked. "Have I changed your mind?"

"Do you mean about marrying . . . what was his name?" She shrugged.

"Have I?" He rolled, pinning her down with his chest.

"I'll get back to you with that answer."

Sunday, their last day alone together, was spent relaxing on the deck, swimming in the lake, and going for a walk along the beach. By late morning, they went to Meg's parent's to spend some time with them and to pick up Jasmine and Christopher. Sunday was also the day they got together to eat as a family, so Meg's brother and sisters were also there. After the meal, while relaxing on the patio, the family brought up Zeus and Meg's wedding. Soon it turned to wedding plans. They wanted to know what Meg and Zeus had come up with for a date, the dress, where they wanted to get married . . . the questions went on and on.

Meg hadn't really thought about any of it since Zeus' proposal. She told them as much, which they understood, as they all knew Zeus had been called away to work on a case. This was cause for the women to start making plans, throwing around suggestions and ideas. The wedding plans were in full motion, almost taking on a life of their own.

A month later, Meg was frazzled from all of the activity. Between work and dress selection and fittings, consultations with her sisters, mother, and grandmother, plus a flurry of other people they had set up meetings with, she was seriously thinking about eloping. The only thing stopping her was the knowledge her family would hunt her down. It was all worth it, however. The wedding was to be at her parent's house, which had been decorated, inside and out. A gazebo had been erected and decorated with yellow roses, the lawn manicured, a stone walkway to the gazebo laid. She knew next to nothing about the food to be served as her mother and sisters prepared that themselves. All she knew was that her nerves had had enough and she couldn't wait for life to return to normal. Zeus, however, seemed to take it all in stride.

The night before the wedding, after Jasmine and Christopher had been put to bed, Zeus and Meg laid in bed talking about the next day. He was anxious for it to arrive. She was anxious for it to be over.

"Hey," he said, jiggling her, "you never did answer me."

"What was the question?"

"Are you going to marry me, or whats-his-name?"

Meg smiled. She had forgotten about that conversation and telling him she would get back to him. She turned her head to look up at him. Something changed. She was no longer looking at him, as much as looking in his direction, but seemed withdrawn into herself. She felt something deep inside her. It wasn't a twinge. It wasn't a bump. It wasn't a bubble. Yet it was all of that and more. Suddenly she knew exactly what it was.

"Meg?" She refocused on Zeus' face. "The question was, will you marry me?"

"I guess I have to now." She started to smile.

"If that was accepting my proposal, you suck at it." He looked at her closer. Something was different. "What do you mean you *have* to now?"

She just smiled at him. Suddenly, it sank in. Why does a man *have* to marry a woman?

"A brother *and* a sister, as Jasmine and Christopher said!" She exclaimed.

Printed in the United States
By Bookmasters